PIES BEFORE
GUYS

Also by Kirsten Weiss

Pie Hard

Bleeding Tarts

The Quiche and the Dead

PIES BEFORE GUYS

Kirsten Weiss

KENSINGTON BOOKS
www.kensingtonbooks.com

KENSINGTON BOOKS are published by

Kensington Publishing Corp.
119 West 40th Street
New York, NY 10018

All Kensington titles, imprints, and distributed lines are available at special quantity discounts for bulk purchases for sales promotion, premiums, fund-raising, educational, or institutional use.

Special book excerpts or customized printings can also be created to fit specific needs. For details, write or phone the office of the Kensington Sales Manager: Kensington Publishing Corp., 119 West 40th Street, New York, NY 10018. Attn. Sales Department. Phone: 1-800-221-2647.

Kensington and the K logo Reg. U.S. Pat. & TM Off.

ISBN-13: 978-1-4967-2354-3 (ebook)
ISBN-10: 1-4967-2354-6 (ebook)
Kensington Electronic Edition: March 2020

ISBN-13: 978-1-4967-2353-6
ISBN-10: 1-4967-2353-8
First Kensington Trade Paperback Printing: March 2020

10 9 8 7 6 5 4 3 2 1

Printed in the United States of America

CHAPTER 1

A poet was threatening to skewer my freshly painted ceiling, and I had no one to blame but myself.

"Die!" Professor Starke tossed his head, blond locks gleaming beneath Pie Town's metal overhead lights. Again, he thrust his saber upward, and I tried not to cringe. "Die—"

Plink!

This time I did flinch, and I twisted in my seat to glare.

In a pink corner booth, my seventysomething piecrust maker, Charlene, held a screwdriver in her fist. She raised it over an upturned pie tin.

The darkening sky made a black mirror of the window behind her and reflected her snowy curls. Her white cat, Frederick, lay draped over her shoulders. The two were inseparable, largely because Frederick was too lazy to perambulate on his own four paws.

Charlene punched the screwdriver into the center of the tin, making a hole. With a metallic squeak, she pulled it free and caught my eye.

"Sorry," she mouthed, looking less than contrite. Charlene

slipped the screwdriver into the pocket of her green knit tunic and folded her hands on the Formica table.

I narrowed my eyes at her and got caught in the intent stare of another of the visiting professors. Professor Jezek sat in the row of chairs between Charlene and me. His sunken, near-black eyes and lank gray hair and mustache gave him a Rasputin look. Beads of sweat dampened his domed forehead. His lips moved, soundless. He could have been spellcasting, praying, or reviewing his shopping list. Anything was possible with this crew.

I smiled weakly.

Jezek's head twitched, and I realized he was looking past me, at the reader.

Grimacing, I returned to facing forward. I'd thought holding a poetry slam in Pie Town might be fun. Chalk that up to the had-I-but-known category.

The reader, Michael Starke, glared at us both. "Die," he finished, and jerked his saber for what I hoped was one last time toward Pie Town's ceiling.

But in spite of the flourish, his poem had ended with a whimper, rather than a bang. Not that I'd paid much attention to its beginning or middle. At some point, I'd gotten lost in the poetry professor's tangles of metaphors.

My employee Abril leaped to her feet and applauded, cheeks glowing. A lock of long, glossy black hair escaped the young woman's bun. She wore a Pie Town t-shirt, and I beamed with pride. After all, this was Abril's show. The budding poet worked part-time in the Pie Town kitchen and studied English at the local community college.

Another college-aged, olive-skinned woman rose and clapped as well.

Others joined in. Belatedly, I followed along with the small audience's less-than-enthusiastic applause.

Professor Starke nodded and cleared his throat. Even in

his tweed blazer, he looked more like a beach bum than an authority figure.

I smiled. The poetry reading might not have been a smashing success, but Pie Town was a hit. My insides warmed at the sight of the black-and-white floor, the glass display case (near empty at this time of night), and the neon logo behind the counter. Its big pink smile was irresistible above our motto: *Turn Your Frown Upside Down at Pie Town!*

"The hole should be round," Charlene muttered behind me, and I shook my head. I had no idea why my friend was defacing pie tins. As far as I was concerned, ignorance was bliss.

"'Death in a Parking Lot,'" Starke began.

I braced my elbow on the table and tried to look interested.

The bell over the front door jingled, and I straightened, looking toward the door. A stranger walked in and took a seat.

I slumped in my chair. My brother, Doran, was late. What had happened to him?

Since I wouldn't get any answers listening to bad poetry, I stood and wove through the tables to the kitchen. Baking long over, it smelled of cleaning supplies. The floor-to-ceiling pie oven, industrial refrigerators, and metal countertops gleamed.

Leaning one hip against a counter, I blew out my breath. Why was I so disappointed Doran hadn't made it? Oh yeah, because he was my only living relative who wasn't a criminal.

The door swung open, and Charlene breezed into the kitchen. "What a snooze." She set her damaged pie tin on the pie safe.

I eyed the elderly woman, who still wore Frederick like a stole. She knew the cat wasn't allowed inside the kitchen, but she had stopped beside our antique pie safe. It was just outside the work area, and she'd declared it a safe zone, pun intended.

"We did sell some pies," I said. "And the event's important to Abril." I wanted to support Abril and the college, even if the school wasn't strictly in San Nicholas.

"I thought that brother of yours was coming tonight."

I grabbed a cloth and wiped a counter that was already clean. "He said he might not be able to make it."

"There's still a lot you don't know about him," she said cautiously.

"Which is why I'm glad he moved to San Nicholas." We hadn't known the other had existed until recently. The discovery that I had a half brother had been a shock, but a good one.

"I thought he came here for work."

"Mostly for work." But partly because of me. He'd moved to San Nicholas to try his luck as a graphic designer in nearby Silicon Valley. I hoped it worked out for him. Having a family again had filled a hole in my life I'd been refusing to recognize.

The kitchen door edged open, and Abril stuck her head inside. Her brown eyes crinkled with concern. "Val, we need help."

"What's wrong?" I straightened off the counter. I didn't smell smoke, so it couldn't be too awful.

She fingered the tiny gold cross at the base of her neck. "The reading is over, and people are leaving. But then Professor Starke and Professor McClary began arguing." Abril edged farther inside the kitchen. "It's getting kind of heated."

Charlene grabbed a rubber spatula from a ceramic holder. "A fight in Pie Town? I'll take care of that." She bustled out the door.

Ice chilled my midsection. When Charlene decided to

"take care of" things, all sorts of bad things happened. Big-foot hunts. Belly dancers. Boxing matches . . .

"Uh-oh." I hurried past Abril and into the dining area.

On the opposite side of Pie Town's counter, the two pro-fessors faced off. They wore similar tweed blazers, right down to their elbow patches. But otherwise, they were a study in contrasts. Professor McClary was dark-haired, with soulful, deep-set eyes that hinted at both dreaminess and passion, if that was possible. But tonight, his striking, pale face was mottled with fury.

Starke was more solid. Blond. Tanned. Clear blue eyes. He could have been any of the surfers who ambled into Pie Town after an afternoon riding waves.

Slightly off to the side, Charlene's white curls quivered, and she scowled at the combatants. Frederick yawned and rested his head on her shoulder.

Professor McClary's ivory hands fisted, his words flow-ing in an Irish lilt. "That was derivative at best and plagia-rism at worst!"

Professor Starke's lip curled, his blue eyes blazing. I was suddenly glad he'd left his sword at the podium.

"It's not your *story* at all." He glanced over his shoulder. McClary's elegant nostrils flared. "Eff off."

"Hack."

Charlene's hand snaked out. She whacked Starke in the ear with the rubber spatula.

He jumped and rubbed his ear. "Ow!"

"I'll have none of that language." She shook her spatula at him. "Pie Town's a family restaurant."

"What language?" he asked. "I called him a hack."

"Hack?" She rubbed her chin with the tip of the spatula. "I thought you said something else."

The Irishman stiffened. "Your blasted poem—"

Charlene raised her spatula. "Watch it, Riverdance."

McClary edged backward and eyed her warily, his lips twitching. "Never mind."

"Academics," Charlene growled.

Professor McClary turned to me with a smile and bowed shortly. "I'm mortified by my bad manners. Thank you, Ms. Harris, for hosting us tonight."

Call me weak, but it's hard to stay annoyed at a man with an Irish accent.

"I don't think the dean would have come without the lure of pie," Professor Starke said in a low voice. He nodded toward a gray-haired man of Santa Claus proportions and wearing the inevitable tweed.

Through his glasses, the dean studied the remaining treats—individual servings of pie in mason jars—on the glass counter. He scratched his neatly trimmed beard.

"You're welcome," I said. "But it was all due to Abril. The poetry reading was her idea."

Abril edged from the kitchen and into the dining area. Pretending not to hear us, she scuttled to the podium she'd set up in front of the booths.

Professor Starke smiled, his oceanic eyes gleaming. "I'll be sure to thank her. She's one of my best students."

"I've no doubt," I said, watching Abril blush. "She's an amazing poet. And she's right over there." I pointed toward the podium on the opposite side of the room. Abril had brought it from the college for the occasion.

The bell jangled over the front door, signaling the audience's slow departure. A black-clad figure struggled against the flow and made his way inside the restaurant. My heart lifted. *Doran.*

Although his mother was Japanese, Doran and I looked a lot alike. Same oval-shaped face. Same blue eyes. His thick black hair, however, tended to fall into his face, hiding them. My long, brown hair was almost always pulled into a bun, as it was tonight. It's a food-service thing.

My brother sketched a casual wave, the shoulders of his black motorcycle jacket lifting. "Hey, Val," he called. "Sorry I'm late." He smiled at Abril. "I'll help with the cleanup."

Hawklike, Charlene watched the two professors, who'd begun arguing again. She slowly raised the spatula.

"Um, Charlene?" I asked, glancing Doran's way. "Would you mind helping me with something in the kitchen?" As much as I wanted to chat with my brother, the only way to guarantee no more spatula assaults was to get her away from the two professors.

Charlene folded her arms over her green tunic. "I'm piecrusts only, remember? I don't do cleanup."

"This is about the piecrusts."

"What about them?"

"I'm thinking of changing the recipe," I said, feeling desperate. If she hit one of the professors again, she might get charged with assault.

"What?" Her eyes widened. Our piecrusts were her own not-so-secret recipe. "You don't mess with perfection!"

Behind the counter, I backed out of spatula-striking distance. "Still, our other changes have been successful." I nodded to the top of the display case, and the pies in mason jars. There were only a handful of the jars left—they'd been an audience favorite.

She charged through the Dutch door and into striking range. "Change the crust! You can't do it."

I fled into the kitchen, Charlene close behind me.

She teetered to a halt on the tips of her hi-tops just inside the door and adjusted the cat on her shoulders. "Adding chocolate to the mix for your holiday pies is one thing," she said. "But a recipe change? I'll quit!"

I raised my hands in a defensive gesture. "Your crusts are perfection, and I'm not going to change a thing. I just needed to talk to you privately."

She dropped the spatula, and it clattered on the metal counter. "So talk."

My mind hamster-wheeled. I couldn't exactly tell her this had been a ruse to keep her from assaulting more visiting professors. "Any cases for the Baker Street Bakers on the horizon?" I asked, grasping at straws. The Baker Street Bakers was our not-so-armchair crime-solving club. It had only two regular members—Charlene and myself. But we had allowed in the occasional associate, like my boyfriend, Detective Gordon Carmichael.

She slumped against the counter. "Not since the mystery of Gil Diefenderfer's missing surfboard."

And that hadn't been much of a mystery. His wife had "lost" it at a church sale in a vain attempt to free up his time for more household chores.

"What's with the pie tin?" I asked.

"Oh, this?" She picked up the tin and held it in front of her face. I guessed she was staring through the hole she'd punched in its center, but it was too small for me to really tell. "It's our newest promotion."

I eyed it askance. "Pie tins with holes?" We'd already added pie-baking classes, and sampler plates, and pies in a jar. I loved all the fun ideas, but I was starting to feel overwhelmed.

"It's the famous McMinnville UFO hoax of 1950!"

I stared, uncomprehending.

"Oh, come on. Even *you've* seen those UFO photos. They were reprinted in *Life* magazine! The so-called UFO was obviously a pie tin hung on a wire. It was also just as obviously a false-flag operation."

"False flag?" I asked.

"Designed to divert attention from our country's real UFO problem," she said darkly.

Moving along. "And this has to do with promoting Pie Town because . . . ?"

"Because we make pies, and I have the hottest paranormal Twitter feed this side of Northern California."

Okay, the scheme was probably harmless, even if I did lose some perfectly good pie tins in the process. "Excellent idea. I'm in."

"You are? Good. Because I know you're still a bit iffy about UFOs, even if you were never abducted by one." Charlene managed to sound disappointed by that fact. She brightened. "Now I've got an old fishing rod we can use—"

"Whatever you need." Anything beat clambering on the nearby cliffs hunting Bigfoot or chasing mythical fairies in the dog park. And yes, Charlene had dragged me into those adventures and more. I'd gotten the poison oak to prove it.

Charlene sat on the stool beside our old-fashioned pie safe and made a list, while Frederick snoozed. I cleaned and loaded dishes into the industrial washer.

Abril and Doran set the dining area in order and lugged plastic bins of dirty plates into the kitchen. I presumed Doran was helping because he felt guilty about being late. Whatever the reason, I'd take it.

The kitchen door swung open, and my boyfriend, Gordon, strode into the kitchen in his favorite navy suit.

My heart jumped at the sight of the tall, dark, and handsome detective. He'd had to work tonight and hadn't been able to make the poetry reading, but he'd come.

Charlene looked up from her notepad. "You missed—"

He hauled me roughly against him, wrapping his muscular arms around my midriff and pulling me into a bone-melting kiss.

My knees wobbled. I gasped coming up for air.

From the corner, Charlene whistled. "Detective Carmichael! Unhand that young woman."

Gordon ignored her, his jade eyes boring intently into mine. "Val, there's something I need to ask you."

My heart pounded faster. We hadn't been dating long. I

hadn't even met his parents. Did he want me to meet his parents? Or . . . something more serious? Surely not. He knew I'd had a disastrous broken engagement. I wanted to be absolutely certain before jumping into anything permanent.

"Sure." I gulped.

His head bent closer, and his voice dropped to a rumble. "Where were you between the hours of eight and nine o'clock tonight?"

CHAPTER 2

The kitchen door drifted back and forth, its motions slowing creakily.

I gaped at my boyfriend. *Uh, what?* "Why, Detective Carmichael," I joked, pressing a hand to my heart and laughing uneasily, "this is so sudden."

He released me, stepping away. "I'm serious."

Charlene rose from her stool by the door, her joints cracking. It was getting late in the evening. She must be exhausted. On her shoulders, Frederick yawned.

"Oh." I gnawed my bottom lip. Well then, why the heck had he given me that Rhett Butler kiss? And hang on. Serious? Serious about my whereabouts? I looked about the sparkling kitchen for answers and found none.

"So were you here?" he asked.

"Sorry," I said, all business. "Yeah, I was here, with Charlene." Baffled, I stared at his chiseled face. Did I need an alibi? What was going on?

In the dining area, a chair scraped across the floor.

"And I guess Abril and Doran are still here." A wash of heat flushed through me, as if I'd been standing too close to the pie oven. Doran would have said goodbye before leaving, wouldn't he? "But you would already know if they were because you came through the dining area. What's going on?"

He pulled his cell phone from his blazer's inside pocket and handed it to me. Professor Starke's tanned face stared blankly from the screen, his blond hair mussed. Blood trickled from one corner of his mouth.

I gasped. "That's— Is that . . . ?" I took an involuntary step back and bumped into the metal counter.

"What?" Charlene asked. Her white cat's ear flicked, his tail coiling around her neck. "What's happened?"

"Do you recognize that man?" Gordon asked me.

I nodded, swallowing. "That's Michael Starke—Professor Starke. He was here thirty minutes ago." And he'd been alive. It didn't seem possible that he wasn't anymore.

I scrubbed a hand over my face, heaviness dulling my chest. What had happened? A car accident? And poor Abril— did she know yet?

Gordon reached into another pocket and pulled out a folded sheet of goldenrod paper. He opened it. "He was the star of your poetry reading, right?"

"Not *my* poetry reading," I bleated. "I mean, yeah. I guess." Why was I so defensive? This was awful, but it had nothing to do with Pie Town.

"Who? What?" Charlene grabbed his phone from my hand and sucked in her breath. "Great googly moogly, that's the blowhard blond professor. Who killed him?"

"That's what we're trying to determine," Gordon said. "You said he left thirty minutes ago. Are you sure?"

I looked to Charlene, and she shook her head.

"I don't know," I admitted. This was awful. How could this have happened? I reached to scrape my hand through my hair, then remembered it was in a bun. "The reading ended around eight, and then I was back here loading the dishwasher for the most part. I didn't see him go. Abril and Doran may know exactly when he left."

"When's the last time you did see Professor Starke?"

I shot a wary glance at Charlene. "Um, he was the last person to read. Abril came into the kitchen to warn me that he and another professor, Professor McClary, were arguing. So I went to see what was going on. Fortunately, Charlene calmed them down, and Charlene and I returned to the kitchen. I didn't see anything after that. Did you, Charlene?"

She shook her head. "Has Starke got a small red mark on his right ear?" she asked.

Gordon nodded.

"Tell your coroner not to worry about it," she said. "That was me. Whacked him with a spatula. It's got nothing to do with the murder. How was he killed?"

I smothered a groan.

Gordon's expression didn't change. "You hit him with a spatula?"

"Well, he deserved it," she said. "He and that Aidan fellow—"

"Aidan?" Gordon asked.

"The whole English department must have been here," she said. "Dean Prophet; that guy who looked like a Russian hippie, Jezek; and Aidan McClary. One of those arty-farty Irish poets. If you ask me, his parents must have been hippies. Anyway, things were getting heated, so I decided to cool things down."

"By hitting Mr. Starke with a spatula." Gordon's tone was flat.

"It was only a rubber spatula," she said. "I wouldn't have used a metal one. Not on an ear."

"The point is," I said quickly, "we didn't see him leave." And *not* that Charlene had assaulted a future murder victim. I forced a smile.

"Don't look at me that way." Charlene folded her arms over her green knit tunic and jerked her chin at me. "I've got an alibi."

Gordon rubbed the back of one thumb across his brow. "All right. I'll have a word with Abril and Doran." He strode toward the swinging door.

I hurried after him and touched his jacket sleeve.

"Did you remember something else?" he asked, turning.

"So what was that big kiss all about?" I asked. "Not that I minded or anything, but under the circumstances . . ."

He grinned. "Potential conflict of interest diverted."

I gave him a questioning look.

"Just in case you were a material witness in the murder and got me knocked off the case. Again. I wanted to get that kiss in first. The chief is starting to wonder about all the Pie Town–related murders this town has been having."

"Pie Town–related? That's not true." Just because I'd found a body or two in the past, and . . .

Oh. They kind of all *had* been indirectly linked to Pie Town. "Did Chief Shaw really say that?" I asked, anxious.

"Don't worry about it." He pulled me into another quick embrace. "I may have more questions for you later."

He vanished through the swinging kitchen door.

"Don't worry about it?" I sputtered. How could I *not* worry about it?

Charlene stared at the door, her eyes narrowing.

"He had to be joking, right?" I asked her. "Chief Shaw can't really believe Pie Town is at the center of some sort of . . . criminal conspiracy!"

"Well . . ." She adjusted Frederick around her neck.

"Well what? Don't tell me the town thinks Pie Town is a murder vortex."

"No, of course not. But you know how Shaw is. Er, how much does he know about your father?"

My father. My stomach hit the kitchen's black fatigue

mat. Shaking myself, I returned to loading the dishwasher. "I don't know what happened to Professor Starke, but this had nothing to do with Pie Town or my father."

I took my time setting the dishes and coffee cups in their racks and tried not to think of the man who'd given me his genetic code. I wasn't like my dad. Everyone had to know that. Besides, my father was a lot of things, but he was no killer. Just a weird sort of enforcer for the mob.

Totally different.

I added soap to the dishwasher and turned it on. Spraying a cloth with cleaning fluid, I wiped down a lot of things that didn't need cleaning.

"You know what this means," Charlene finally said, "don't you?"

"Gordon really doesn't like it when he gets tossed off murder cases?" But everybody knew that.

Doran jogged into the kitchen, his dark brows slashing downward. "Abril's professor was murdered?"

"We don't know what happened," I said. "Not for sure. Gordon finished interviewing you already?"

"I told him I didn't know anything or anyone and got here late. Your boyfriend let me go." He paced between the counters. "This is bad timing," he muttered.

"Bad timing?" I tugged at the hem of my Pie Town tee. "What do you mean? You didn't know Professor Starke, did you?"

"No," he said, "of course not."

"Then what?" I asked.

Charlene's mouth pursed.

"The thing is," he said, "I can't stay."

"Don't worry about it," I said. "We're ready to close."

"No. I mean . . ." He stared at the floor's rubbery mat, a shock of his raven-black hair falling across one eye. "I'm moving back to Southern California."

My heart caved in on itself. For a moment I couldn't

breathe, couldn't speak. "Oh," I finally managed. And then, "Oh." Reaching behind me, I gripped the edges of the counter.

"It's just too expensive here," he said rapidly. "The rent, the commute, the taxes, everything. There are plenty of gigs, but I can't figure out how to make the finances work."

"I get it," I said. "When I first started Pie Town, I was sleeping in the back room. But don't tell anyone. It was probably some code violation . . ." *Code violations*. I trailed off, thinking of our father, who was so far on the wrong side of the law both his ex-wives had disowned him.

Doran's forehead crinkled.

"Anyway," I said, mouth dry, "I'm just glad you were here for as long as you were. It's been really great getting to know you."

At least he regretted leaving. That meant he cared, right? Maybe we'd developed the beginnings of a real relationship.

"Yeah, but . . ." He frowned. "I'm going to get back out there. I'm worried about Abril." He pushed through the swinging door into the dining area.

Charlene and I didn't speak for what seemed like an eternity.

"We were among the last to see Starke alive," she finally said. "We've got a case."

I shook myself out of my malaise. "No. No! You heard Gordon."

"I heard him tell you Shaw thinks every crime in San Nicholas is Pie Town–related."

Crumb. "He didn't exactly say that." But if he was drawing connections between murder and Pie Town, would others?

"Gordon also said there was no conflict of interest. That means we can investigate."

"No conflict of interest *yet*." My voice rose. But truth be told, I was almost enjoying the argument. It beat thinking about my brother. "If we poke our nose into another murder, he's going to go ballistic."

Her blue eyes narrowed. "Are you going to let a man's opinion run your life? I thought better of you, Val."

Frederick raised his head from her shoulder and glared at me. I'm 99 percent certain the look was because I'd woken him up, and not because he agreed with Charlene.

"Well," I said, "no, but it *is* his job." Gordon had been pretty even-keeled about Charlene and me investigating in the past. But I didn't want to push it. Not that I was worried about our new relationship or anything, but I respected him. Gordon was a good cop. He knew what he was doing, and this was his case. "Gordon's a real detective."

"We're real detectives! That man died leaving Pie Town, our shop—"

"My shop."

"And he must have died nearby," she said.

"We actually don't know where he died."

We stared at each other, because it hadn't taken Gordon long to get to Pie Town. Charlene was right. Whatever had happened to Professor Starke, it had been close.

I grabbed my hoodie off its hook near the door. As one, Charlene and I raced through the swinging door. We bumped shoulders and pinballed into the dining area.

Gordon had already gone, leaving Abril slumped in one of the pink booths, a dazed expression on her face. Doran sat across from her. Speaking in a low voice, he held one of her hands.

"Abril," I said. "I'm so sorry about your professor."

Blankly, she looked up at us. Doran's leather jacket was slung over her slim shoulders. "I can't believe it. Professor Starke was just here. He was alive."

Charlene sighed. "By the look of things, Starke had a good run. That's the best we can hope for."

"But . . ." Abril shook her head. "He was so young."

Doran's forehead wrinkled. To him, everyone over thirty was ancient. *I* was closing in on that number. What did he think of me?

"Don't worry, Abril," Charlene said. "We'll figure out who killed him."

She blinked. "You will?"

We would. Of course, his murder had nothing to do with Pie Town. Not a thing. Nada. But there was nothing wrong with making absolutely, positively sure.

"We're on our way to the crime scene now," Charlene said.

Doran looked up at us, his brows drawing into the familiar slash that signaled his annoyance. "You are?"

"Um . . ." In for a penny, in for a pound. Gordon was going to flip his lid.

Judging from Doran's glare, he felt the same way.

"Not if you don't want us to," I finished. I mean, what would we really learn? I was probably panicking over nothing.

Charlene whacked my upper arm, and I winced.

"No," Abril said, and I slumped with a mixture of relief and disappointment.

That was that, then. No Baker Street Bakers. I'd just . . . let Gordon take care of things. There was no reason to get involved. None at all. Except for the fibers twitching in my gut warning me that Pie Town was once again in jeopardy. Maybe pie would settle my stomach.

"You should investigate," Abril said. "I'll feel better if you do. Professor Starke deserves justice."

"What?" I asked. "Are you sure? I mean, of course he does, but—"

"I think Abril knows what she wants," Doran said coolly. "And you've done this before."

"No time to waste." Charlene grabbed my arm. "Let's go."

I let Charlene lead me onto the sidewalk. Doran was down with my detecting? He'd seen Charlene and me do our thing before, but he'd kind of made fun of it. And in this case, I wasn't even sure *I* was down with it. Because if Professor Starke's death had nothing to do with Pie Town, sticking our noses into it was a sure way to make that connection.

The restaurant across the street was dark. But light and the clank of weights poured from Heidi's twenty-four-hour gym next door. Two blocks down, red and blue lights flashed faintly.

"That way," Charlene said, pointing.

We hurried down the empty sidewalk. The iron street lamps glowed amber. Mossy baskets filled with pink and orange impatiens hung from the base of the lights. It was one of those balmy September nights the Northern California coast was frequently blessed with. Fog hung off the coast, bringing the promise of nature's air-conditioning, while stars gleamed faintly above.

Running footsteps pattered behind us. I spun, hands fisting.

Abril and Doran panted to a halt on the sidewalk.

"We're coming too," Abril said. Beneath Doran's motorcycle jacket, she tugged down the hem of her *Pies Before Guys* t-shirt.

Doran gave her a fierce look. "We're involved. We're helping."

My heart lifted. My brother wanted in on the Baker Street Bakers! And it immediately dropped. But what was this "we're involved" stuff? Doran wasn't involved. At least, I hoped he wasn't, because that might make him a suspect.

Nah. He totally couldn't be a suspect.

"This is no place for amateurs," Charlene said loftily.

Doran quirked a skeptical brow, and my cheeks warmed. We weren't licensed PIs. No matter what Charlene said about our experience, we were *all* amateurs.

"Okay," I said, not meeting Doran's gaze, "we're wasting time. Let's go."

We reached the corner by a brick, Italian restaurant. The blue and red lights flashed brighter. A block away, police cars and other emergency vehicles clustered on the side street. Their lights cascaded, dizzying, across the faces of low adobe buildings and flat-roofed bungalows. Police officers milled in the street.

"There's no way they'll let us get close to the crime scene," I said.

Charlene smiled. "Oh, we'll get close." She pointed to a purple stucco one-story on the other side of the action. "Come on."

We circled the block and approached the crime scene from the opposite side.

One hand raised, a uniformed officer strode toward us. "You can't walk through this way."

My stomach wriggled. We'd been caught.

"We're not trying to go through," Charlene said. "We're having drinks at our friend's house." She canted her head toward the purple stucco.

The young officer hesitated. "All right," he said. "Go on through."

I could feel his eyes burning holes in the back of my Pie Town hoodie as we sped up the concrete walk to the little purple house.

"Charlene," I muttered, "what are we doing?" The cop would figure out soon enough we didn't know anyone here.

"Take it easy." Charlene thumped on the arched front door.

After a minute or two, a rusty male voice shouted, "What?"

I started. I *knew* that voice.

"It's me," Charlene said. "Let us in."

"Charlene?" The door opened, and an impossibly tall, elderly man peered out. He rubbed his drink-reddened nose. "I suppose you want my roof."

"What else?" she said. "We've got a cooling corpse on the street."

Looking at me, he said, "Hi, Val."

"Hey, Wally." I glanced anxiously over my shoulder as if the young cop might change his mind and arrest us.

He chuckled. "You don't miss a trick. Come on then." Wally, a.k.a. Tally Wally, opened the door wider. Stoop-shouldered, he led us through a neat house decorated with World War II memorabilia and to a small backyard. We followed him up a creaking exterior staircase to the roof.

"Had this built for the wife back in the seventies," he wheezed. "She read some article about Morocco and rooftop patios."

"I remember," Charlene said. Frederick snuggled his head against her neck. "Amy was a good woman. We had some nice parties up here."

"A lot of fun, she was," he said wistfully, clambering over a ledge and onto the roof. "Amy mixed a mean margarita."

He helped Charlene and me over the ledge, and then Doran followed us and gallantly assisted Abril.

Hm. Doran had never so much as opened a door for me.

We walked to the front of the roof.

"Damn it," Wally said. "I forgot the binoculars."

"No worries." Charlene pulled a set of mini binoculars from the pocket of her green tunic. "I've got it covered."

"Why do you—?" I shook my head. *Forget it*.

She stared through the binoculars. "There's a whole lot of blood around the victim's right armpit." She frowned. "Wait. No. That's my right, his left. And there's a sword lying next to the body—must be the murder weapon."

"Or the professor might have dropped the sword when he was attacked," I said. "Remember? I never really understood why he brought it in the first place."

"For 'Charge of the Global Warming Brigade,' " Abril said. "Remember?"

"Oh, right." Was global warming what the poem had been about? I'd thought it was about zombies. I really should have paid more attention. "What can you tell us about Professor Starke?"

"Oh, he was wonderful," she said, her brown eyes glowing.

"About who'd want him dead," Charlene elaborated.

"No one." Abril hugged her arms beneath the cape of Doran's jacket. "Professor Starke got along with everyone."

I raised an eyebrow. He hadn't been getting along with his colleagues at the reading.

"I mean," Abril continued, "his ex-wife is an English teacher, and she runs the drama department. It was so great the way they still stayed friends."

Charlene snorted. "The spouse is always the most likely suspect. Here." She handed me the tiny binoculars. "What do you see?"

I adjusted the focus. Michael Starke lay beside a blue Prius. The discarded sword or saber lay on the pavement beside him. I focused on the blade. It was hard to tell in the dim light, but the tip looked bloody. I shuddered. "I think you're right about the weapon." It looked like Starke's sword from the reading. How had the killer gotten hold of it? Maybe if Starke had put it down or on the Prius's roof while he'd unlocked the car . . .

I trained my gaze on the Prius. It would have one of those auto door unlocks. But still, he might have fumbled with the key fob. I frowned. The car tilted catawampus, sinking low on its far side.

"What?" Charlene asked. "What do you see?"

"Is there something weird about that car?"

"Gimme." Charlene snatched the binoculars from my eyes and looked through them. "It's at an angle. That's funny."

"Maybe he has a flat?" I asked.

"I think you're right," she said. "Suspicious."

"You think someone flattened the professor's tire to delay him?" Doran asked.

I pursed my lips. "It's possible. Or someone damaged his tire for a different reason. Or it's just an ordinary flat. Or it's not a flat at all, because we can't actually see the other side of the car."

He gave me a look I was coming to recognize as his "Seriously?" expression.

"What I'm getting at is we shouldn't jump to conclusions," I said. "We need more facts."

"So how are we going to get them?" he asked.

"We—" I'd been about to say, *We* aren't." But it was the first time Doran had suggested doing something together aside from eat. Maybe he wasn't so eager to leave San Nicholas after all. "We'll ask questions, like we have before."

Charlene nudged me with the binoculars. "Check it out."

I peered through the glasses.

An annoyed Gordon Carmichael stared back, fists on his hips.

I jerked the lenses away from my face. "Uh, Gordon saw us."

"Time to go." Charlene scuttled across the roof. "Downstairs! We've been compromised."

We chased her down the stairs. She stumbled on the last step, and I grabbed her before she could fall.

"Are you okay?" I asked, my chest squeezing. In spite of the age she'd put on her job application (forty-two), Charlene was no spring chicken.

She straightened, panting. "I'm not feeling so well. Maybe I should go home."

Powerhouse Charlene calling an early evening? "I'll take

you," I said quickly. That way I could keep an eye on her in case things got worse.

Fear sparked through my veins. *Don't get worse. Don't get worse.* I still hadn't gotten over the loss of my mother. I couldn't lose Charlene.

CHAPTER 3

One hand beneath Charlene's elbow, I piloted her up her porch steps, past ferns and dusty wicker chairs. The first tentacles of fog stretched across Charlene's house, blotting out the stars in its path. Her hands trembled as she unlocked her front door, and my chest pinched.

"Maybe we should go to an emergency room." I'd wanted to take her there directly from Tally Wally's, but she'd insisted on coming home. I lifted Frederick off Charlene's shoulders. The white cat dangled limply and weighed roughly a ton.

She wheezed and opened the door. "I just need to rest." Charlene tottered inside.

I flipped on the light, illuminating the yellowish, floral-print couch, wall photos of Charlene and her family on various adventures, and doily-covered end tables. It was the sort of mismatched mishmash a home acquires after decades of living.

Frederick flinched, his head turning away from the overhead lamp.

"Faker," I muttered. He wasn't sleeping at all.

"What was that?" Charlene asked.

"Nothing," I said. Charlene loved that stupid cat, and my heart twisted again. I couldn't imagine Pie Town without Charlene. I couldn't imagine San Nicholas without Charlene. She'd been my first real friend here. "Charlene—"

She made her way to the couch and plopped onto a cushion. "Oof. I think a glass of my special root beer is in order."

"You know, heart attacks in women manifest completely differently than heart attacks in men. Cold sweats, light-headedness, nausea—"

"I'll get the drinks." She leaned forward and grunted.

"No, no. I've got it." Setting Frederick on the faded cushion beside her, I hurried to the kitchen and poured a tall glass of root beer with a shot of Kahlúa.

I whizzed into the living room and set it on a doily atop the end table. "Okay, what exactly are you feeling?"

"My legs hurt." She shifted on the couch and reached to rub her thigh, wincing. "Will you help me . . . ?"

Legs? I hadn't heard of that as a heart attack symptom. "Nothing in your upper body?" I propped her feet on the low, wooden coffee table.

"Not with the shoes on! They're dirty."

I grimaced. "Right." I helped her with her tennis shoes and set her feet on the table. "What about an aspirin?" An aspirin couldn't hurt, could it? But if I seriously thought she needed an aspirin for a heart attack, I needed to call 911. She might not like it, but this was no joke.

Charlene made a face. "The edge of the table hurts my ankles."

I grabbed a faded pillow off the couch and set it beneath her feet. "Charlene, what exactly are you feeling?"

She blinked up at me, her blue eyes innocent. "I feel fine. What's the problem?"

What? "You said you weren't feeling well. You tripped on the stairs."

"Anyone can trip. I just wanted an excuse to get away from the noobs."

"The . . . You mean you weren't feeling ill at all?" I asked, outraged.

"Nope. I always was a good actress, even if Marla Van Helsing beat me out for the role of Elaine in *Arsenic and Old Lace*. But I stole the show as Aunt Abby."

I sputtered. "You—"

"Of course, I never heard the end about how old I looked. Now about this murder—"

"I was really worried!"

"And I'm worried about you."

I pressed one hand to my chest. "Me?" Now she was just blame-shifting.

"You were flip-flopping on whether to investigate. It's not natural. What's really going on in that head of yours?"

I leaned one hip against the floral-print couch. "Well, we are getting pretty good at solving crimes."

"Even if it's bound to infuriate your hot detective?"

"And Gordon said Chief Shaw is starting to connect Pie Town with murder."

She raised a snowy brow. "And your brother's got nothing to do with it?"

"Doran?" Guiltily, I crossed my arms over my chest, rumpling my Pie Town hoodie. "No. What do you mean?"

"He seemed awfully hot on this investigation."

"I wouldn't say *hot*."

"Your brother's a damned Vulcan. For Doran, that was jumping up and down with excitement. What gives?"

"Nothing!" But yeah, his interest had surprised me. Doran didn't know any of these people. Why did he care?

"And you letting him come along tonight has nothing to do with him leaving San Nicholas?"

I dropped onto the wing chair across from her. "I forgot you'd heard that."

"It's obvious he's been frustrated. And you two haven't spent much time together, have you? He didn't even make it to the poetry reading."

"In fairness, poetry's not really his thing," I said.

"You sure about that?"

"No." I sighed. My shoulders curled inward, my hands dangling between my knees. "How do you make up for over two decades of separation? I know more about Doran now than I did—"

"You didn't know he existed two months ago."

"Exactly. He's been too busy trying to scare up graphic-design jobs to spend much time with family bonding. But I can tell he's a great guy. He's also been through the same garbage with my father that I have."

Charlene snorted. "Not exactly. He's lucky he didn't go through everything you did."

"I guess I want more. And I'm afraid if Doran goes back to SoCal now, we'll never build a real relationship."

"Hmph. All right. Then we'll think of something to keep him here." Her eyes narrowed with cunning.

"We will?" I fiddled with the zipper on my hoodie. I wasn't sure I wanted Charlene cooking up some scheme when it came to my brother. "I don't think—"

"Now that that's out of the way, let's talk murder. First step?"

Or maybe she'd forget the entire idea. "I'm not sure. I'm having a hard time getting past Chief Shaw thinking Pie Town is the town's murder epicenter."

"And since Professor Starke was killed leaving Pie Town . . ."

"Shaw's going to be even more sure of it."

"So?"

How was I going to break this to Gordon? "All right," I said. "We start by making a list of suspects. Assuming some-one followed Professor Starke from Pie Town"—an assumption I hated—"who was at tonight's reading from the college?"

She unfolded one of Abril's goldenrod flyers and slapped it on the coffee table. "The poets."

I scanned the list. "Professor Aidan McClary, Professor Piotr Jezek, Abril Rivas—Abril was great, wasn't she?"

"I'll say. That was some hot stuff!" Charlene frowned. "I'm just not sure if she knew it. That girl's a little repressed, if you ask me."

We pondered that. The house creaked uneasily on its foundation. From the nearby kitchen, the refrigerator hummed. Frederick yawned and rolled onto his back.

"And, of course," I said, "the victim, Michael Starke. What was the name of the other guy from the English department? The one who bought the extra helpings of pie?"

"Rudolph Prophet," she said, patting her stomach significantly. "He's a dean or some such."

I choked back a laugh. "Rudolph? Are you kidding me?"

"What?"

"He looks like Santa Claus, and his name is Rudolph Prophet? Was he born on Christmas?"

"I don't see what you're getting at," she said sniffily.

"Whatever," I said. "We know Professor McClary had a beef with Starke. He said something about plagiarism, didn't he?"

"Writers can get crazy about that sort of stuff. Plagiarism is definitely a motive for murder."

"So we've got three suspects to begin with," I said. "And didn't Abril say something about an ex-wife? She may not have been at the reading, but we can't ignore the ex."

Charlene nodded. "And there's someone else we should consider. Marla was at the reading."

I gave her a look. "Is there any reason to think your best frenemy killed Professor Starke?" Drama Queen Charlene and Marla Van Helsing had been competitors since their girlhood back in the Mesozoic era. I wanted to believe they'd gotten past it, but old habits were hard to break.

"She was at the reading, isn't that enough?"

"Not really. What motive would she have to kill Professor Starke?"

"She's Marla!"

On his cushion, Frederick coiled into a tight ball, nose toward the ceiling. His whiskers twitched.

"Hold that thought." Charlene leapt from the couch and strode into the kitchen.

The muscles between my shoulders relaxed. She really had been faking her earlier feebleness.

Charlene returned with her laptop, and we set it on the coffee table. I opened a social media site and entered Michael Starke's name.

A page popped up with photos of Starke and a middle-aged woman with blond, Shirley Temple ringlets. According to the tag, the woman was named Dorothy Hastings. I scanned down. More pictures of Starke standing behind podiums and speaking.

"Except for that woman's photo," I said, "it's all professional stuff."

"Well, that's useless. Check out Aidan McClary."

I typed his name into the search bar and clicked on his page. Lots of pictures of Guinness and . . . I blinked. "Isn't that the same woman?"

"Yep. That's Dorothy Hastings." Charlene grabbed a pair of reading glasses off the end table and perched them on her nose. "And that's definitely not a professional photo."

Aidan and Dorothy wore bathing suits and embraced on a sailboat.

"Who *is* this woman?" Charlene asked.

"Abril might know." I found Dorothy's page, and all I learned was she worked at the college as an English and drama professor. I sat back on the lumpy sofa. "Hold on, didn't Abril say Starke's ex was an English and drama professor? That must be her."

"Yikes," Charlene said. "Right under Starke's nose at the college? He and Dorothy may have had a good post-marriage relationship, but that had to be awkward. Check out that Jezek fellow, the one who looked like a bilious vampire. Maybe she was dating him too."

"Piotr Jezek," I corrected, but I did as she asked and came up with zero. "There was a moment during the reading when I caught Jezek giving Starke an odd look, like he was angry or scared."

"So which was it? Angry or scared?"

"Um, I'm not sure." I clawed my hand through my hair. At least, I'd *thought* he'd been giving Professor Starke a weird look. "All right. Let's try something else."

I left the social media site and did a general search. Jezek had written letters to an online paper complaining about tree trimming and removal permits. He'd also demanded a new "view ordinance."

" 'When trees block views,' " I quoted, " 'property values fall.' "

"He's not wrong," Charlene said, sipping her root beer concoction. "Gimme." She set the computer on her lap. Through an excruciatingly slow process of hunting and pecking, she found a writing site that Starke had posted on. "This is strange."

"What? What?" I craned my neck to see.

"No poetry."

"Okay, that is strange. What's he writing about then?"

"They're a bunch of plays."

I yawned. "Send me the link, will you? I'd like to read them."

"Better you than me."

"Hold on," I said. "Let's check the college's website. It might have staff bios."

And it did.

RUDOLPH PROPHET

Under Dr. Prophet's ten-year stewardship as dean, the English department has substantially expanded its offerings with theater and poetry tracks, and with the establishment of the Theresa Keller Memorial Award for Creative Writing.

Charlene snorted. "Well, that's useless."
But I persisted.

DOROTHY HASTINGS

Theater has the power to build meaningful internal and external connections. It can be transformative. This is why English professor Dorothy Hastings teaches theater.

I continued down the list. But I learned nothing more useful than Starke had joined the college four years ago, and Aidan McClary a year before that.

Charlene shook her head. "Like I said, useless."

But was it? Uneasy, I shifted on the couch. An ex-wife. Her lover. Had Starke fallen afoul of a romantic triangle?

CHAPTER 4

It was a perfect lazy Monday morning. I sat at the picnic table outside my tiny house and sipped OJ. A warm, light breeze rippled the dried grasses at the edge of the cliff, and cartoon clouds floated between ocean and sky. There were lots of beautiful places in this world, and the California coast was but one. But wow. It was gorgeous.

Pie Town was closed Mondays, so I was brunching al fresco. A half-eaten slice of asparagus-and-mushroom quiche lay on a blue plate before me. I'd brought out the ceramic quiche dish as well, because you never know when you might want seconds.

A car motor rumbled up the twisting road to my house.

I sighed and dropped my head. It had been too much to hope that Charlene would let me take the day off from sleuthing.

But instead of Charlene's Jeep, my brother's black MINI Cooper emerged from the eucalyptus trees. He parked near the side of my blue tiny house/shipping container.

Grinning, I extracted myself from the picnic table and ambled to his car. It almost looked big beside my home.

Abril, in jeans and a blue, flowered blouse, exited from the passenger side. "Hi, Val. I hope it's okay—us bothering you like this. Doran said it was." She brushed a strand of long, black hair from her face and tucked it behind one ear.

Doran—black t-shirt, black jeans, black motorcycle jacket—popped up on the other side of the tiny black car. "Hey."

"Hey," I said. "What's up?"

"Did you find out anything about Professor Starke?" Abril asked.

"No. It's Monday morning," I said slowly. "He died last night."

She flushed, her dark skin turning scarlet. "Sorry. How's Charlene?"

"She's fine. Do you want some quiche? Orange juice?" I motioned toward the ceramic dish on the table.

"What kind?" Doran's almond-shaped eyes narrowed. He braced his elbows on the top of his low car.

"Asparagus-and-mushroom. Sorry, no meat." I was a flexitarian.

"I guess." He shrugged.

I hurried into my tiny house and to my kitchenette, which anchored its center. Grabbing plates, silverware, and glasses, I returned outside.

Abril sat at the table. Doran paced the cliff side.

"Have you heard . . . ?" Abril's hands fluttered helplessly. "I mean, has Detective Carmichael said anything?"

I sliced wedges of quiche. "No, and I can't—"

Another, louder motor growled up the drive.

Charlene's yellow Jeep exploded from the tree line and screeched to a halt beside Doran's car. She stepped from the Jeep, Frederick draped around the neck of her violet tunic like a stole. "Good. You're all here." She pointed a gnarled finger at the quiche. "Is that made with one of my piecrusts?"

"Of course," I said.

Doran ambled to the table.

"Then I'll have a slice." She sat across from Abril. "All right, young lady, spill. Tell us everything you know about Professor Starke. And not just the good stuff."

Abril laced her fingers together on the table and looked down at them, then blew out her breath. "That's the thing . . . Now, I'm not sure if he *was* a very good person."

"Excellent," Charlene said. "That's a start. Why?"

I passed out plates of quiche.

Abril flushed guiltily. "I mean, he was a great professor. And a great poet."

"But?" I asked.

"But there were a lot of rumors about his TAs."

"TAs?" Charlene asked.

"Teaching assistants," I explained, handing her a fork. "What sort of rumors?"

"I didn't want to say anything before," Abril said, "because . . ." She looked toward the cliff and the blue expanse beyond.

"It's okay," I said. "You knew and respected him, and of course you didn't want to spread rumors right after he'd died." Abril was the sweetest person I knew, but Charlene was right. It was time to talk.

"What rumors?" Charlene asked, leaning closer. "Occult ceremonies? Virgin sacrifices? Bodies in the basement?"

Abril looked everywhere but at us. "Every year he had a new TA, and they were all women."

"Aha!" Charlene pounded the end of her fork on the picnic table. "And he was schtupping his TAs?"

My face warmed with embarrassment, which was ridiculous. We were all adults. So why did I feel the urge to protect Abril's sensibilities?

Abril shifted. "That's what people *said*. But . . . I didn't want to believe it. I mean, I— He has such a good relationship with his ex-wife—"

"Professor Hastings?" I asked.

She nodded. "How'd you know?"

Charlene shrugged modestly. "The grass doesn't grow under our feet."

"You were saying?" I prompted.

"Anyway," Abril said, "I didn't think it was true. I mean, there are a lot more women than men taking upper-level English courses, so it sort of made sense he'd have female TAs."

"What's changed your mind?" I asked.

She looked up, her brown eyes serious. "Someone killed him. They had to have a reason, didn't they?"

"That's blame-the-victim mentality," Charlene said. "But in this case, you're probably right."

"Not necessarily," I said. "For all we know, the murder could have been a mugging gone wrong."

Charlene snorted. "In San Nicholas?"

"I feel terrible." A puff of wind tossed strands of Abril's near-black hair. "Professor Starke was looking for places to hold readings, and I suggested Pie Town. It was a bit far from the college, but he thought the space would be fresh."

"Our pies are always fresh," Charlene said.

"I meant emotionally fresh."

Charlene stared at her blankly.

"Cool," Doran translated.

"I know what it means," Charlene snapped. "I'm hip to the lingo."

"And now he's dead." Abril's knuckles whitened. "I was the one who pushed to come to San Nicholas. If we'd stayed on the other side of the hill, where the college is—"

"It wasn't your fault," Doran said.

"My brother's right," I said. "How could you have known?"

"I knew he and Professor McClary didn't get along. Everyone knew. They've always been competitive, and then . . ."

"Professor McClary started dating Professor Starke's ex-wife?" I prompted.

"You know that too?" she asked.

"We did some checking on the Internet," I said.

"But the Internet isn't enough." Charlene poured herself a glass of OJ and looked around. "Where's the champagne?"

"I don't have champagne."

"What's a mimosa without champagne?"

I crossed my arms. "I believe it's called orange juice."

"The point"—Charlene brandished her glass—"is, like this sad specimen of orange juice, we need more. More info, that is. And you two are going to get it."

Whoops. I had a sick feeling I knew where this was coming from. I cleared my throat. "Uh, Charlene—"

Charlene aimed a crooked finger at my brother. "Doran, I want you to help Abril put a list together of possible suspects from the college. Look for students and any teachers who may have held a grudge. Abril, cross-reference the list with your memory of who was at Pie Town last night."

I frowned. "Doran's not from the college. How's he supposed to—"

Charlene stomped on my foot, and I bit back a yelp.

"You're a graphic artist," she said to him. "You think differently. You can help prompt Abril."

"Sure," he said, a little too eagerly, "if you think it will help."

"Meanwhile," she said, "Val and I will . . . do something else."

"Right." I wasn't sure I liked this idea. "Um, Charlene, you know, I may have some champagne in my house after all. Will you help me find it?"

"Your house is less than five hundred square feet. How hard can it be to find a bottle?"

I ground my teeth. She was doing this on purpose. "I need your help," I said flatly. "Inside."

Feet dragging, she followed me up the two steps and inside my tiny house. "What?"

I shut the door behind us. "What are you doing?" I asked, backed up against the counter that marked off the kitchen.

"I'm finishing what you started—nudging Abril and Doran together—so you can keep him in San Nicholas." She stepped sideways, bumping a chair with her hip. Tiny houses are really only made for one.

"That wasn't— That seems kind of manipulative."

She arched a white brow. "And your point is . . . ?"

What *was* my point? "Let's go to the college."

"Why?"

"You told them we'd be busy doing something else, and the college is where all our suspects are."

It was time to do some real investigating.

Our heels clacked on the linoleum floor, the sound echoing in the dismal hallway. Fluorescent lights flickered dolefully in the white-tile ceiling. The hall smelled like old shoes and mildewed paper.

I loved it.

I'd been an English major myself, and the college reminded me of my old, underfunded state school. I still didn't know how my mother had managed to send me to college, and my chest grew heavy. I hadn't known of my mother's cancer then. She'd hidden it from me.

A door burst open ahead of us. The Shirley Temple blonde from the photos charged out, the hem of her brown corduroy blazer billowing in her wake. Dorothy jostled my shoulder in passing hard enough to knock me against the wall.

"Watch it!" Charlene shook her fist at the woman's retreating back.

"Ow." I rubbed my shoulder.

The rotund dean, Rudolph Prophet, stuck his graying head through the open doorway. His lips pursed, cherry red against his neat gray beard, and I was struck again by his Santa look. But when you live in a town named San Nicholas, you start seeing Santas everywhere.

"Dean Prophet!" I hurried forward. We didn't have an appointment (natch), and we'd located his office only by dint of the signboard at the end of the hall. I hoped he'd talk to us.

He adjusted his glasses and frowned, as if he was trying to place us.

"I'm Val Harris, from Pie Town. And, er, you remember Charlene?"

His ruddy face broke into a grin, and his stomach jiggled like the proverbial bowlful of jelly. "Ah, yes, the woman with the spatula! You have no idea how many times I've wanted to whack a professor." He sobered. "Apologies. I feel like I shouldn't be making jokes at a time like this. You've heard about Professor Starke, I presume?"

"Yes," I said, "it's why we're here."

"Indeed. Then come inside." He ushered us into an office overlooking an elm tree and overflowing with stacks and folders filled with paper.

Charlene rubbed her wrinkled cheek. "I see the paperless office hasn't made its way to academia yet."

"It has." His round face flushed. "But I'm a bit behind the times, I'm afraid. Perhaps it's the old English professor in me, but there's something tactile about paper and ink that I can't resist."

I smiled. I knew the feeling. As much as I loved my e-reader, there was something about flipping the pages of a book. . . .

Charlene pointed with her thumb over her shoulder, toward the closing door. "What was up with her?"

"Ah. Professor Starke's widow, Dorothy." He shook his head. "Sorry, that's not quite accurate. They were divorced. But still, she's taking it hard."

"So why's she taking it out on you?" Charlene's eyes narrowed. "You didn't have anything to do with his murder."

He started. "Murder? I thought— I mean, I knew he'd died, of course. But are you certain it's murder?"

"Stabbed with that sword he was carrying," Charlene said.

"Saber," he said absently, and dropped into the swivel chair. It made a pained shriek at the impact.

I shifted a stack of folders and took one of the gray chairs across from him. "Who do you think could have done this?"

"I have no idea."

"What were Professor Starke and Professor McClary arguing about?" I asked. The dean must have overheard—he'd been near enough to notice Charlene's spatula attack.

He stiffened behind his neatness-challenged desk. "I really can't say. I'm legally and professionally bound not to discuss matters of employee confidentiality."

"They were sure going at it in Pie Town," Charlene said. "There was nothing private about that conversation."

"But I'm afraid I didn't hear any more than you." He nodded to Charlene. "You got to the men before I could. You seemed to have things well in hand, so I thought it best to let it be. Sometimes a woman's touch is more effective than the heavy hand of authority. What did *you* hear?"

"McClary accused Starke of plagiarism," Charlene said, "and Starke called McClary a hack."

"Plagiarism?" He leaned back in his chair, and it creaked alarmingly. "It's the first I've heard of it. But tempers were high that night. I'm sure he was exaggerating."

"But *why* were tempers high?" I asked.

He lifted his thick hands in a helpless gesture. "As I said, I can't discuss employees of the college."

Oh, come on! I pressed my knuckles into the thighs of my jeans.

"An employee of your college was brutally murdered last night," Charlene said.

"And I'm sure the police are looking into the crime." He steepled his fingers. "The question is, why are you so interested?"

Charlene straightened in her chair. "Because we're the Baker Street—"

"Because we think Professor Starke may have left something behind at Pie Town and aren't sure whom to return it to," I lied.

He leaned forward and braced his forearms on the desk. "Oh? What?"

"I really couldn't say," I said demurely. *Take that!* "I suppose I should give it to Professor Hastings?"

"I don't know who his proper heirs are," the dean said. "As I mentioned earlier, Dorothy and Michael were divorced. But if you give it to me, I'll make sure it gets to the right people, along with the contents of his office."

I stood. "We didn't bring it with us today, but thanks for the info. You've been very helpful."

Forehead furrowing, he rose. "I have?" He opened his desk drawer and pulled out a card. "My number. In case I can be of further assistance."

I whipped out a Pie Town card—pink and white with our smiley face logo—and handed it to him. "Call anytime." I cringed. That had sounded like a pickup line.

Charlene made a disgusted sound.

"I'm, uh, sure we'll be seeing you." I wrenched open the door and collided with Gordon.

Heat washed my face. *Oh, crumb.*

"Hi, GC!" Charlene sketched a wave, and he flinched. "Fancy seeing you here."

Charlene knew he hated being called *GC*. Everyone knew it stood for Grumpy Cop, which he totally wasn't.

Most of the time. Judging by the thunderous expression on his chiseled face, now was not one of those happy times.

He blew out his breath. "I'd like to say I am surprised, but why aren't I?" He smoldered in a charcoal suit—his detective "uniform"—and I was smote with guilty lust.

"Um," I said, "I can explain."

"Why bother?" But he lightly gripped my elbow and steered me to an opposite corner of the hallway. "Seriously?" he whispered. "You do realize you're now interfering with an investigation, which is illegal."

"Is it?" I asked, my voice cracking.

Outside, the college's carillon bonged the hour.

"Look," he said, "it's one thing to listen for gossip in Pie Town or chat with people you know, but that's not what's happening here, is it?"

I shriveled inside. "Not exactly."

"You're lucky it's me on the case and not Shaw."

Due to a series of unfortunate circumstances, twice I'd managed to get Gordon kicked off murder cases. Since San Nicholas is a small town, Chief Shaw had taken over. It's not that Shaw was a bad guy, even if he had developed an unreasonable obsession with Pie Town. But to say he had a butter-knife wit would be too kind.

"I'm sorry," I said. "It's just that Abril was really shaken. That professor died leaving Pie Town, and with Chief Shaw . . ." I trailed off, realizing exactly how lame all those excuses were. "We won't interfere in your investigation."

"I know you won't. But I will arrest Charlene if I catch her sniffing around again."

"You know I can't control Charlene," I hissed, panicked.

"She doesn't get a pass because she's geriatric."

A student, shoulders rounded by a full backpack, ambled around us.

I lowered my voice. "But she's . . . You know how she

is!" Crazy in a good way. "That's got to count for something."

"I know she's managed to drag you into her insanity time and time again."

"This wasn't—" On second thought, maybe now wasn't the time to tell him coming to the college had been my idea. "I'll let her know what you said," I told him grudgingly.

He patted me on the shoulder and strode past Charlene and into the dean's office.

Charlene hustled to me. "Hoo-hoo! I saw the way you wrapped him around your little finger. Nicely done."

Ha. That's what *she* thought. "No. Charlene, Gordon told me we were interfering in a police investigation by talking to the dean. We could be arrested."

"Pshaw! He's not going to arrest you."

"He's a good cop," I said. "He'll do what he has to. And we need to confine our investigations to Pie Town."

"No can do. This case is rooted here in the college. Can't you smell it?"

All I smelled was floor polish and the faint scent of my own despair.

She rubbed her wrinkled hands together. "Now all we need to do is put the word out to the others that Starke left something in Pie Town last night and see who bites."

"Huh? I just said that to Dean Prophet because I couldn't think of anything else to say."

"But it was a good idea," she said.

"Charlene—"

"Carmichael said you could talk to people in Pie Town, right?"

"Not exactly," I said, worried. How far was she going to push this?

"Then the solution is simple. If we can't go to them, we'll get them to come to us."

"He didn't actually say we could talk to people in Pie Town."

"It's genius!"

I sighed and trailed after her down the hallway. *Get them to come to us?*

Sure. Why not? After all, what could *possibly* go wrong?

CHAPTER 5

Footsteps thudded above me. Frowning, I glanced at Pie Town's kitchen skylight. It glowed hazily in the afternoon sun. "Who's on the roof?" I asked Petronella.

My assistant manager slid a long, wooden paddle into the giant pie oven and snagged a pie off its rotating rack. "Charlene was saying something about UFO pictures." Her motorcycle boots matched her black jeans, but I'd no idea how she managed to stand in them all day, fatigue mats or no.

"Charlene's still here?" I tugged on my hairnet's elastic band. It was Tuesday afternoon, just after the lunch rush. My piecrust specialist was usually out of Pie Town by nine or ten a.m., having finished prepping her quota of piecrusts.

"She came back." Petronella whipped around and slid the pie onto a waiting tray, then adjusted her hairnet over her spiky black hair. The net might have ruined her dark, Goth vibe, but she managed to make it look cool.

"How did she get on the—?" I shook my head. *Never mind.* "I'll be right back."

Opening the heavy, metal door I stepped into the alley. A stiff wind off the Pacific tossed my hair, and I glanced up.

The sky was blue, but the news had said a storm was blowing in. "Charlene?"

"What?" she asked, appearing at my elbow.

I jumped a little, stumbling backward. "How—?"

A dark shape bulleted downward.

"Look out!" Charlene shouted.

I leapt sideways and yelped.

A ten-pound slab of plastic-wrapped chocolate slammed into the pavement, inches from my feet.

"What the hell!" I glared up at the roof.

Abril and our new busboy and dishwasher, Hunter, peered down at me.

"Whoops." Abril pressed a hand to her mouth. "I'm so sorry."

"What—? Why—? What—?" I sputtered.

"Did it break?" Hunter asked, his bronzed brow furrowing.

"You nearly broke me," I snarled at the teenager. "What are you two doing?"

"Sorry." Abril winced. "I was complaining to Hunter about how hard it is to break these big slabs of chocolate to melt. He thought dropping it from the roof might work."

Charlene bent to examine the chocolate. "It worked all right. Good idea."

"Except for the part about nearly bashing in my cranium." Death by chocolate might sound fun in principle, but the reality was just irritating. I blew out a shaky breath. "Next time, let me know what you're up to, and we'll get a spotter." And I'd go on the roof myself. I didn't want my staff risking their necks.

"Will do, chief," Hunter said, grinning.

Shaking my head, I returned inside the kitchen.

Charlene trailed behind me.

"I understand Hunter getting on the roof," I said, "but what was Abril thinking?"

Charlene nudged my side and leered. "She was probably thinking about getting on the roof with Hunter."

"He's a teenager." And okay, he was cute in a blond, blue-eyed, boy-next-door sort of way. But . . . a teenager!

Petronella snorted and rolled a rack of pie-filled trays across the kitchen.

"Abril's not that much older than him," Charlene said. "Not that I approve of those cougars like Marla," she said darkly. "But Abril's no Marla."

"No, but—" I thought my little brother kind of liked Abril, and I rubbed the back of my neck. I hoped he wasn't headed for heartbreak.

Abril hurried inside the kitchen, pulling the alley door shut behind her. "Val, I'm so sorry. We should have looked first. We just didn't think—"

"It's okay. But don't go on the roof again. If anyone needs to go up there, it'll be me. How'd you get onto the roof anyway?"

"There's a ladder to the roof on the gym next door."

Charlene canted her head.

I groaned. "I hope Heidi didn't see you." The gym owner hated being next door to a pie shop. But Pie Town had been here first, so she'd have to deal.

Hunter ambled inside, cradling the plastic-wrapped chocolate against his broad chest. "It's busted into at least fifty pieces." He thunked it onto the work island, and a cloud of flour rose into the air. Hunter coughed, rubbing his hands on his Pie Town apron. "This was tons faster than breaking it by hand."

"And more dangerous," I said. "Stay off the roof from now on."

His handsome face fell. "Seriously?"

"Serious as a heart attack," I said, and glanced at Charlene. I was still a little annoyed she'd been faking the other night.

"Can I talk to you and Charlene?" Abril asked. "Privately?"

"Yes, you can," Charlene said. "In my office." She strode to the door of the flour-work room and went inside.

I shrugged. Abril and I followed her, and I shut the heavy door behind us.

Charlene leaned against the long, butcher-block table in the center of the room. Light glittered off the metal counter on the opposite wall lined with mixing equipment. The flour-work room was climate controlled, and I shivered in the cool air.

Abril hugged herself, goosebumps cropping up on her bare arms. We all wore Pie Town t-shirts except Charlene, who had an exemption.

"It's about Professor Starke," Abril said. "Doran and I talked to a TA who worked for him."

"*What?*" White curls quivering, Charlene straightened off the counter. She buttoned her hip-length, orange knit jacket to her chin. "This is the problem with bringing in amateurs. You don't interview suspects! Not without us."

"I'm sorry," Abril said. "But we were on campus, and she was there, and . . . we talked to her."

"Who was she, and what did she say?" I asked.

"Her name is Genny Glasspool. She said . . . she and Professor Starke dated, and she was really angry."

"Because he broke it off with her?" I asked.

"Because he gave her a lame recommendation for her application to transfer to a university. She wasn't supposed to see it, but her adviser, who did see it, recommended against using it because it was only one sentence. She was furious. Everything he'd told her about being a great student and great TA were lies." Her face fell.

"So this young woman had motive," Charlene said.

"I don't think she could have killed him," Abril said. "Genny was in Pismo Beach on Sunday and didn't get back until Monday afternoon. I checked her social media accounts, and it all corroborates."

"And we're back to square one." Charlene made a face.

"Not completely," I said. "Now we know the rumors about the professor were true."

The counter bell rang.

"I've got it." I said, pushing through the swinging kitchen door and into the dining area.

Joy, who owned the comic shop next to Pie Town, stood expressionless on the opposite side of the register. Her long, pale coat hung on her like a depressed spirit. "Hi, Val," she said in a low monotone.

Since this was normal for Joy, I smiled. "Joy! How's it going?"

She shrugged. "The usual," she said in her flat voice, and glanced at the gamers who'd taken over my corner booth. "Superheroes are still selling."

At the counter, Tally Wally snorted into his coffee mug.

His best friend, Graham, choked back a laugh, his broad stomach jiggling.

I sold Joy a chicken curry pot pie to go and ambled down the counter to my regulars.

"Hey, guys. What's going on?" I asked, watching them carefully for tells. The two senior citizens were here every morning for the serve-yourself coffee and day-old hand pies. But it was nearly three in the afternoon. They were up to something.

Graham shifted his checked cabbie's hat on the counter. "Word is, you and Charlene are chasing another killer."

"Word?" I shot a look at Tally Wally. "You mean Wally?"

"He can't help it if a man was skewered outside his house." Graham shook his balding head. "Neighborhood's going to pot."

Charlene joined me behind the counter. "What do you two know about all this?"

"Professors at the college aren't our crowd," Tally Wally said. "Don't suppose aliens did it, eh, Charlene?"

"With a sword?" she asked, peeling off her soft jacket to reveal the brown knit tunic and matching leggings beneath. "Not likely. A vampire might though," she mused.

"Who kills someone with a sword?" Graham said.

"Errol Flynn," Wally said.

"Errol Flynn never actually killed anyone with a sword," Graham said. "He was an actor."

Tally Wally brandished his mug. "Actors can kill people."

"Okay," I said. "I'm going to get back to the kitchen."

"Wait, wait, wait," Graham said, laughing. "I have a clue." He reached into the pocket of his stained jacket and pulled out a familiar piece of goldenrod paper. Unfolding it on the counter, he stabbed one of the grainy photos with his broad finger. "I know this guy."

I turned the flyer toward me. "Aidan McClary?" I asked, interested. The sexy Irishman who'd been arguing with Professor Starke and dating his ex-wife was my prime suspect. "How do you know him?"

"He's my neighbor. He's always having his hoity-toity faculty friends over for drinks at all hours. Won't cut back his damn ivy, even though the rats love it. He says it looks *nice*."

"What can you tell us about him?" I asked.

"I just told you. He won't cut his damn ivy."

"That's helpful," I lied.

"Don't look at me like that, Val. How would you like rats tramping through your yard?" he asked.

I didn't even want to think about the wildlife in the overgrown tangle behind my tiny home. "I wouldn't. Thanks for letting me know." But I kept my hand on the flyer. There was a tiny symbol in the lower-right corner I hadn't noticed before, and I squinted at it. A snake coiled around one spoke on a crude, five-spoked wheel.

The bell over the front door jingled. Gordon walked in,

and my heart jumped with nervicitement. I hoped the detective wasn't still annoyed with me.

The wind caught the glass door, and Gordon turned to pull it shut, his charcoal suit jacket flapping in the breeze.

I bustled around the counter. "Hi!"

He kissed me lightly on the mouth, garnering whistles from the peanut gallery.

I smothered a delighted sigh and inhaled his woodsy cologne.

"Hi back." He took in the gamers in their corner booth, Tally Wally and Graham at the counter, Charlene. "I see the gang's all here. Got anything interesting for me?"

"Aidan McClary won't cut his damn ivy," Graham shouted, swiveling on his pink barstool.

"Not much I can do about that." Gordon ambled to the high counter and braced his elbow on it.

"It attracts rats," Graham said.

"In other words," I said, "we've got nothing. Sorry."

"Don't be sorry," he said. "Hey, I'm actually here on a call. Your neighbor phoned in a complaint about people on the roof of her gym. Your roofs connect. Did you notice any strangers up there?"

Hunter! "Strangers on my roof? Nope. No strangers." No, siree. I *knew* Hunter and Abril.

His jade eyes narrowed. "You know, going up on her roof would be trespassing."

Only if we're caught. "That is good to know," I said. "Was that all?"

"No," he said. "Are you free Thursday night?"

Charlene rubbed her chin. "I suppose I could power-wash my windows on Friday instead."

"I meant Val," he said.

"I don't have any pie-making classes this Thursday," I said. "I'm free."

He broke into a smile. "Then may I take you to the White Lady?"

"It's my favorite spot." And I loved that he knew the difference between *may* and *can*. Common usage had blurred those meanings, and I could be free with them myself. But I liked that he knew.

"It's my favorite too," Charlene said meaningfully, and I glared at her. She was so not going to horn in on my date.

"I'll pick you up at seven." Gordon kissed me again and walked out of the restaurant. We watched his tall form stride down the sidewalk, past baskets of impatiens swaying from the lamp posts.

"So your young man hasn't found the killer yet," Graham said.

I sucked in my cheeks. "It hasn't even been two days. Give him a chance." *Sheesh.* Talk about unrealistic expectations.

"Well," Graham said, "if *someone* wanted to meet that Aidan McClary character, and *someone* brought a free pie by my house tonight—as a gift, for example—and accidentally went to the brown house next to mine instead, they might meet him."

"That's not a bad idea," Charlene said. "Except it's supposed to rain tonight. I'm not catching pneumonia because you're too cheap to buy an entire pie."

"Neither rain nor gloom nor any of that other stuff shall keep pie deliveries from their appointed rounds," Wally boomed. "And I want half of that pie."

I left them to argue about what kind of pie they wanted and returned to the kitchen. Of course we were going to Graham's with pie.

Petronella abandoned us to go to her funeral services classes—yes, there's a degree for that. Abril took over kitchen duties—she was more comfortable out of the limelight—and I worked the dining area.

About an hour later, I was wiping down a booth Charlene had claimed when my brother walked into Pie Town.

I grinned like an idiot. Three visits in three days? This had to be a record. "Hi, Doran."

Charlene looked up from the table and sipped coffee. "Look what the cat dragged in."

He looked around. "Hey. Is Abril here?"

My heart plummeted. "Yeah, she's in the kitchen." Okay, I understood that a sister wasn't going to be as exciting as a potential romance. I needed to get over it. Or be more exciting.

"Do you mind?" He angled his head toward the swinging kitchen door.

"No," I said. "Go ahead."

He moved to pass me.

Exciting, exciting . . . What was exciting? "Wait," I said.

He turned.

"I can see you're worried about Abril," I said in a low voice.

"Of course I'm worried." His blue eyes, so surprising in his Eurasian face, flashed. "Her professor was murdered. She's upset and needs help."

Charlene arched a brow.

"I'm going to try to meet one of the suspects tonight," I said, "a professor who was at the poetry reading. Do you want to come?" My little brother might not be interested by the pie life, but he'd definitely gotten intrigued by the murder.

Charlene stiffened.

"Me and Abril?" he asked.

In the corner booth, the gamers' dice rattled.

"It might be safer if Abril has some distance from the investigation," I hedged.

The corners of his mouth pulled downward. "You may be right. What time?"

"Meet me here at seven?"

"I'm in." He strode into the kitchen.

"You're taking Doran to Aidan's?" Charlene whispered angrily. "What did we just say about amateurs?"

"You said you didn't want to go out in the rain."

"I said Graham could buy his own pie."

"I don't think that's what you said."

"Fine." Her smile looked forced. "Your brother can come with us."

"Well, actually . . ." I winced. "I thought just me and Doran could go."

"What?"

"Just this once," I said quickly. "He's leaving soon, and I'd like some brother-sister bonding time. Please?"

She leaned back in the booth and folded her arms. "This stinks."

"He's the only family I've got." Because my wayward father didn't count.

She grimaced and looked out the window. "Okay. But just this once."

My muscles unknotted. "Just this once. Thanks, Charlene."

The front bell jangled, and Marla Van Helsing strolled into Pie Town. Drops of rain darkened the shoulders of her elegant trench coat. Thunder rumbled in the distance.

Charlene leaned her head against the rear of the booth. "Can this day get any worse?"

Since I'd skunked Charlene out of playing detective tonight, the least I could do was face her archnemesis. "Hello, Marla. What can we get you?"

"Coffee. Black."

"The coffee's self-serve—"

Marla sat across from Charlene and placed a hand atop hers, angling her diamonds for the sparkliest effect. "Dear Charlene. I've come to help you in your hour of need."

Charlene jerked her hand free. "What hour of need?"

"Another Pie Town murder. How utterly dreadful." She looked around the shop, empty except for the gamers and our regulars at the counter. "I can see it's already affected business."

"Business is always slow at this time of day," Charlene said. "The lunch rush is over."

"That's right." She patted Charlene's hand. "Be brave."

"And it's not a Pie Town murder," I said. "It didn't happen in Pie Town."

Marla fluffed her platinum-blond hair (heavy on the platinum). "But it happened after an event here, while poor Professor Starke was leaving Pie Town. And that's what I'm calling it on my channel."

"Your video channel is all about self-help and decorating," Charlene snarled. "There's no reason for you to be talking about that murder."

"I can't ignore human interest," Marla said sweetly. "Especially when Chief Shaw himself admitted the Pie Town connection. And *where* is that coffee?"

"In the urn on the counter," I said. "You *know* we're self-serve. We've always been self-serve."

"It's true," Graham said. "They have."

"What did Chief Shaw say?" I asked.

"I can see you're distraught." She rose. "Remember, anything I can do." She glided from the restaurant.

"She probably didn't really speak to Shaw," I said uncertainly. "I mean, why would he let her interview him?"

Charlene growled, her hands fisting.

"It doesn't matter what she says," I said. "Hardly anyone watches Marla's online videos."

Lightning cracked, and the skies broke open.

CHAPTER 6

Because for some reason my brother objected to riding in my roomy pink pie van, I sat squished in his teensy car, pie sampler on my knees.

I stared unenthusiastically out the window. Curtains of rain flowed down the windows and flooded the yards of two near-identical Victorians. A wide strip of waterlogged ivy lay between both the yards.

A gust rocked the small car and slapped a wave of rain against the windshield.

Doran, in a black windbreaker, which I hoped was waterproof, leaned across me and squinted out the window. "He said it was the brown one?"

"Yeah," I said, dragging out the word. *Both* Victorians were brown. Creepy Monterrey cypresses flanked them both. The trees dripped with gray-green trailing moss, blowing sideways in the gale. Candlelight flickered in the front windows above both porches. It wouldn't be hard to honestly confuse Graham's house for Aidan's. That was the whole point of this pie-delivery exercise. Not knowing the actual house bothered me though. "Well, it doesn't matter. If we go to Graham's house, he'll just send us to the other."

But Doran and I sat in the car, unmoving. I was starting to sweat in my raincoat, even if I was wearing only a t-shirt beneath.

"So what are we expecting to get out of this?" Doran finally asked.

"Take advantage of this weather to get inside Aidan's house, ask questions about the murder, and snoop."

"Oh." He drummed his fingers on the wheel. "How do you usually do that?"

"I'm glad you asked, because I have a cunning plan. As Aidan's shooing us from his door, I'll twist my ankle and fall into the house. He can't turn away someone with a sprained ankle in this rain."

He angled his head and pursed his lips. "Hm . . ."

"Or, if Aidan's nice, I'll give him the pie sampler but ask to come inside so I can write down the reheating directions."

"These don't sound like very good plans."

They were better than most of the schemes Charlene and I came up with. "Okay, let's do this." I flipped up the hood on my raincoat and stepped from the car. A blast of wind caught the door, blowing it shut on my legs and chest. "Oof." I fought my way free of the car and stared at the lake of water between us and the front porch steps. There was no way through without getting our ankles soaked.

Doran made his way around the car. "So?" he shouted over the wailing wind.

"I guess we make a run for it."

"But which house?"

"The closest one!"

Headlights swept across us, and we froze like the guilty criminals we were.

Charlene's yellow Jeep roared through a puddle, spraying us with muddy water, and screeched to a halt.

"Gross!" I shook the schmutzy water from my raincoat, while Doran swore.

Looking like the guy on the fish-stick packages, a Frederick-free Charlene stepped from the Jeep in a yellow rain jacket and matching hat. She arched backward, cracking her spine, then stomped through the muck to us.

"I thought you were staying in tonight," I sputtered, annoyed. Couldn't I have *some* alone time with my long-lost brother?

"There's no power at my place," she said. "A tree knocked down a line. So I figured I'd come here."

Augh. "The electricity's out here too," I shouted, motioning to the windows of the twin brown Victorians. "They're using candlelight."

"Rats," she said. "I was hoping to watch Graham's TV. *Ghost Hunters* is on."

"Which is Graham's house?" I asked.

"Funny." She rubbed her chin. "You know, I've never been to his place before. It's a little weird now that I think of it. I don't have his phone number either."

Doran shifted his weight and glared from beneath his black hood. Water streamed down his face. "Can we get this over with before I drown?" He grabbed the pink box from my hands. "I'm going."

Charlene's head turned. Her eyes widened. "No, don't!"

Doran moved toward the Victorian.

Instinctively, I grabbed Doran and yanked him backward.

He shook me off. "What are you doing? I nearly dropped the pie."

"Charlene—" What *was* I doing?

"Jiminy Cricket," she said, pointing. "Look!"

I followed her gaze. Tentacles of black cable writhed atop

the pool of water flooding the yards. The lines sparked menacingly.

"The whole yard's an electrocution hazard," she continued. "Both their yards are."

Doran cursed. "I knew this was a bad idea."

"We've got to warn Graham," I said.

"I told you," she said, "I don't have his number!"

This was bad. "Well, call the electric company."

The squall sent a wave from the yard rippling toward us.

Doran tugged us backward and to Charlene's Jeep. Dripping and fumbling, we got inside and slammed the doors.

We shivered and rubbed our hands together while Charlene called.

She shook her head. "I can't get through. Everyone and his mother must be calling the electric company right now."

"We've got to let Graham know about that wire." I clutched the pink box, my gaze darting toward the sparking wire. "And Aidan too."

Rain drummed hollowly on the Jeep's canvas roof.

"It's not likely he or that professor are going to come outside in this weather," Doran said.

"Yeah, but what if they do, or if it's still down tomorrow?" I asked, worried.

We sat in glum silence, pondering that.

"There's got to be a way to get to one of their porches," I said.

Doran pulled his phone from his pocket and fiddled with the keypad.

"We can throw pebbles at their windows to get their attention," Charlene said.

I shook my head. "What if they come outside because they can't hear us over the wind?"

"We could fly a paper airplane to them," she said.

"In this hurricane?" I asked.

"Hey," Doran said, "I'm on hold with the electric company."

"Good man," Charlene said.

"I'm going to take another look outside." I stepped from the Jeep. The wind tugged my hood, and I made a grab for it before it could fly off. I sloshed to the gravel trail that made up a sidewalk and studied the two homes.

A car door slammed.

I canted my head. In front of the Victorian without the downed power line were thickets of lavender, a tree stump, and a bench. Some midsized boulders stuck up from the growing pool of water.

Charlene came to stand beside me. "Got any ideas?"

"I think I can make it to that Victorian's front porch without stepping in the water." I gestured to the nearby tree stump.

"You're a baker, not a gymnast," she growled. "It's not worth the risk."

"The biggest jump is from the bench to the front porch. But if I slip up on the porch, I'm still on the porch."

"Let Doran do it," she said. "He's nimbler."

"I'm not going to put my brother in danger."

"So you admit it's dangerous!"

In answer, I clambered onto the stump.

"Come back here, young lady!" she shouted.

I rose to my feet. *Don't think about falling off. Just go!* I took a big step onto a small rock, just above the waterline. It wobbled beneath my feet, and my heart jumped. I moved hastily to the next, slightly larger stone, and then the next. I was doing it!

"Doran's on hold," Charlene shouted. "There's no point to going any farther!"

But there was, because who knew when the utility company could get the live wire fixed and inform Graham and Aidan of the danger?

By the third heart-poundingly wobbly stone, I thought this might have been one of my stupider ideas. By the fourth stone, I was certain of it.

I climbed onto the largest boulder and surveyed my path. All I had left was the bench, a couple of feet away, and then from there, the porch. I reached with one foot for the bench. With a grunt, I clambered onto it and grabbed its back for balance.

Charlene shouted something, but the wind carried her words far away.

I gripped the back of the wood-and-concrete bench. It faced the street, and I realized my problem. Its back was standing in my way, between me and the porch. I shifted my weight, testing how well the bench was anchored into the ground. It didn't budge.

Okay, I can do this. I'll just step on its back really quickly and launch myself onto the porch. No problem. I blew out my breath and braced one foot on the top slat. One . . . two . . .

I jumped. The bench tilted beneath me, and I was flying. Charlene screamed.

I hit the front porch. There was a huge splash.

My foot slipped on the top step, and I jounced downward. I grabbed the banister and righted myself on the bottom step.

Slightly dizzy, I looked behind me. The bench had tipped onto its side. Ripples of water spread from its concrete seat.

I trotted up the steps and banged on the front door.

No one answered.

I knocked again, scuffing my knuckles. "Ow."

The door opened, and Graham peered out at me. He adjusted his spectacles. "I don't see pie."

"That's because it's in the car."

"It won't do me any good there." He made a face and opened the door wider. Graham's relaxing-at-home wear wasn't any different from his man-about-town clothing. His beige, button-up sweater vest strained over a short-sleeved checked shirt and matching khaki trousers. "You're not going to make an old man go out for pie in this weather?"

I shook my head. "No. There's an emergency—a downed power line in Aidan's yard." I pointed.

He walked to the edge of the porch and peered over the railing. "Damn. Has anyone called the power company?"

"Doran's on hold, but someone needs to warn Aidan."

He turned and frowned. "What's my bench doing on its side?"

"I—" Shamefaced, I shuffled my feet. "Maybe it was the wind?" Or maybe it was a baker who'd left her pie sampler behind. "Look, both your yards—"

"Yes, yes," he said testily. "I'll call Aidan. Come in."

I followed Graham, muttering about lost pies. In his kitchen I waited, teeth chattering, while he dialed Aidan on an old Bakelite wall phone.

"Aidan, it's Graham . . . There's a live wire in your front yard . . . Yep . . . Yep . . . If I find electrocuted rats in my lawn, we're going to have another talk about that ivy!"

I rolled my eyes. "Ask Aidan if he left anything behind at Pie Town on Sunday," I whispered. My pie plan of attack tonight had gone kablooey. But I'd already planted the seed with Dean Prophet that Professor Starke had left something in Pie Town. Now I could do the same with Aidan and see how he reacted.

Okay, it wasn't the best plan. But I was desperate. And cold. And wet.

"The owner of Pie Town wants to know if you left anything there on Sunday." Graham covered the receiver with his hand. "He says no."

"It must have been that other professor then," I said loudly, hoping Aidan would hear.

"I warned you about that power line," Graham said. "Now we're both trapped inside until someone fixes it." He banged down the receiver. "Idiot."

"You warned him?" I asked, my scalp prickling.

"He was getting a sofa delivered last December—nearly a year ago. The top of the delivery truck rammed into the metal thingummy on his roof that the power line runs into. So some genius just wrapped the line around a branch of his plum tree. A plum tree!"

"The wind must have snapped the branch," I said. "Have you got a flashlight?"

He opened a kitchen drawer and handed me a heavy flashlight.

"I'll be right back." I returned to the front porch and shone the light in Aidan's yard. The plum tree's leaves were gray burgundy beneath the artificial light. I could see now that a slim branch was tangled in the dangling line.

I aimed the light higher and found the broken branch. Frowning, I studied it. It had broken in the middle. Was that natural? Or was I seeing something sinister just because it was the proverbial dark and stormy night and I had murder on the brain?

I glanced toward the road. Charlene had vanished. I guessed she was in the Jeep with Doran.

My cell phone vibrated in the pocket of my raincoat. Tucking the flashlight beneath my arm, I dug it out. *Doran.* I answered.

"Hey, genius," he said, "you realize you're stuck there until someone fixes that cable, don't you?"

Oh, crumb. "Um, did you get hold of someone at the electric company?"

"Yes."

"How long did they say they'd be?" I asked.

"Maybe four or five hours."

I groaned.

Graham emerged on the porch and frowned at the cars on the street. "So who's going to bring me my pie?"

CHAPTER 7

Utility company staff arrived only an hour later. Men in hard hats and raincoats spilled from white trucks. They fanned across the neighborhood, and soon the cable stopped sparking.

One of the men pounded on Aidan's door.

Graham chuckled and let the drapes in the kitchen window fall. "Wrapping that cable around a branch doesn't seem so clever now, does it? *Intellectuals.*"

I retrieved the pie sampler, delivered it to Graham, then got into Charlene's Jeep and sank low in the front seat. Doran had abandoned the expedition as soon as he'd been certain the electric company was on its way.

Bracing my elbow against the window frame, I propped my head in my hand. I couldn't blame my brother for bugging out. The weather was miserable, and who wanted to just sit around watching a house?

Rain lashed the Jeep's windows. *"Stargate?"* Charlene asked.

"Why not?" I said. After listening to Graham reminisce about the Korean War, I needed something fun and mindless.

We drove to her wooden two-story. Wind tossed the exuberant garden, hemmed by a picket fence.

In her living room, I slumped on Charlene's floral-print couch. "I didn't get a good look at the tree limb. And even if I had, it's not like I'm an expert in tree-limb breakage. It *could* have been an accident."

My rain slicker dripped from the coat-tree near the front door. The TV flickered, illuminating the living room in shades of gray, a *Stargate* rerun playing silently.

She sipped her Kahlúa and root beer and watched the screen. "But what are the odds?"

Yeah. I didn't really believe the accident theory either. Wrenching free the hard pillow behind me, I clasped it to my chest. "It's a weird way to try to kill someone though. I mean, first, the killer would have to know that the line had been wrapped around a tree limb."

"You said Graham knew."

"I doubt Graham's the killer. Anyway, next there'd need to be a convenient storm for our hypothetical murderer. Finally, they'd have to somehow break the limb *and* drop the power line onto the lawn. And they'd have to do all that without getting themselves electrocuted in the process."

"Maybe they broke the limb before it started to rain." She gestured toward the night-blackened window.

"In the daytime?" My face tightened, and I ran my fingers along the pillow's seam. "In Aidan's front yard?"

"It's a quiet street," she said, still not meeting my gaze, "and the houses are set far apart."

"Except for Aidan's and Graham's. And you're mad at me for bringing Doran, aren't you?" I bit the inside of my cheek. I'd also nearly gotten my brother electrocuted. If she hadn't arrived in the nick of time, he might have been hurt or killed.

And if Charlene and I had been on our own, who knows

what would have happened? Bottom line: I wasn't happy with myself.

Also, my feet itched from all their time spent in damp shoes.

"I'm not mad." She sighed. "I understand wanting to spend time with your brother."

"But?"

"But I'm worried about you."

"Me? Why?"

She met my gaze, her blue eyes weary. "Because I don't think you can force a relationship, and I don't want you to get hurt with unrealistic expectations."

That was surprisingly sensitive of Charlene. Was she thinking of her own estranged relationship with her daughter? I had faith they'd patch it up. Who could resist Charlene? But I knew the separation was hard on my friend.

"What are you thinking?" she asked.

"About my brother," I lied. But *were* my expectations for him unrealistic? "Doran did come to San Nicholas to get to know me." And now that he had, did he think it had been a bad idea? I gnawed my bottom lip. Was I pushing too hard, driving him away?

"Did you two talk while I was in Graham's house?" I asked anxiously. "Did he say anything?"

"There wasn't much else to do but talk," she said.

"And?"

"And what?"

"What did he say?"

She rubbed her wrinkled chin. "We talked about the weather. He doesn't like it. Too cold and damp."

I collapsed back on the sofa and burrowed deeper into my borrowed Pie Town hoodie. "Another reason to return to sunny SoCal." The irony was, I was from Orange County. Doran and I had been so close for years and not known it, and then I'd moved here.

"He also asked about Abril." She smiled craftily. "Our plan there is working. That young man's not going anywhere as long as he's got a shot at rescuing the damsel in distress."

"That's your plan, not my plan. Whatever happens between Abril and my brother has nothing to do with me." I crossed my fingers beside my thigh, where she couldn't see.

"What's wrong with playing cupid?" she asked.

"It's for entirely selfish reasons."

"Yours may be selfish. I'm doing it for you."

"Oh," I said, trying to find a hole in her logic and failing. "I'll lower my expectations about Doran." And definitely *not* think about him and Abril.

"As long as you admit you were wrong," she said.

My eyes narrowed. "Wrong about what?"

"About bringing a noob on an investigation without me." She tilted her chin down and stared, her white brows lowering. "You realize I saved your brother's life. You owe me."

"I promise that, henceforth, when there is something or someone to investigate, you will be the first person I call."

"Good enough. Now about that power line . . . Starke's ex-wife was dating Aidan."

"Which means she may have gone to his house and seen that cable wrapped around the branch."

"And as the ex, she had motive to kill Starke."

"But why go after Aidan?" I asked.

"Maybe he knew too much? Maybe the lovers were in on Starke's murder together, and now she's getting rid of her accomplice?"

The *Stargate* credits rolled down the screen.

I shook my head. "That would make a good movie, but we're guessing. We know hardly anything about these people."

"Then it's time we find out."

"Gordon told us we can't investigate outside of Pie Town without being guilty of interfering," I warned.

"Telling them Starke left something behind doesn't seem to be getting them into Pie Town. We need to be more aggressive with our invitation."

Eureka! I snapped my fingers. "We could invite them to our new pie-making classes."

"No," she said dryly, "that won't look suspicious."

"What if we told Aidan and Piotr we held a giveaway for attendees of the poetry reading, and they won?"

"Why would two English professors be interested in a pie-making class? They might give their tickets to someone else."

"You never liked the idea of those classes." I tossed the pillow to the sofa cushion beside me.

"They're interfering with our *Stargate* nights!"

Ah. Charlene was lonely. I turned my glass in my hands. "I'll always make time for *Stargate*. I want to get to *Stargate Atlantis*."

"And don't forget the movies," she said, seemingly mollified.

"What if we give our winners two tickets, so they can bring dates? And don't forget Rudolph. We need to get him to the class too."

"It won't hurt to try."

"What about Dorothy?" I asked.

"Hm. Maybe we would increase the odds they'll attend if we give the tickets to Dorothy instead of Aidan."

"But she wasn't at the reading," I said. "What's our excuse for giving her a free pie-making class?" I yawned, out of ideas and out of energy. "I'll think on it."

"We can brainstorm—"

"Let's do it independently. I'm exhausted. Do you mind giving me a lift home?"

Grumbling, she drove me back to my tiny house. I changed into my pie pajamas and went to my kitchen for a drink. In the cupboard, I drew out a green water glass I'd brought from my mom's house.

Unexpected loss welled from my heart to my head, making me gasp. I ran my thumb along the bevels and blinked back unwanted tears. It was such a stupid thing. Only a cheap glass. I think my mom had won the set or got coupons for it. But my tiny house that usually felt so contained and cozy now felt empty and small and isolated.

Charlene wasn't the only one who was lonely.

I forced myself to fill the glass with water and drink. Finally, I fell asleep to the rain pattering against my home's metal sides, branches scraping and creaking against the roof.

I crawled from bed at my usual horrible baker's hours. The rain and wind had stopped, but the power had gone off some time during the night, leaving my stove clock and microwave blinking. I only hoped we had power at Pie Town. I hadn't gotten around to buying a generator, because I couldn't afford one yet.

In the dark, I fumbled into jeans and a *Turn Your Frown Upside Down at Pie Town* tee. I shrugged into a matching hoodie and stepped outside.

A beam of light arced upward, illuminating a wavering, metallic disc. It zipped toward me, making an odd, whistling sound.

I gasped and hopped backward, tripping over the bottom step and falling on my butt inside my front door.

An eerie cackle drifted across my front yard.

"Charlene!" Scowling, I leapt to my feet and brushed off the seat of my jeans. "That was just mean."

She strolled around the corner of my tiny house, a fishing

pole in one hand and flashlight in the other. From the end of the pole dangled a flying saucer made of two pie tins glued together.

She tut-tutted. "Looks like someone still hasn't gotten over their fear of UFOs."

"I am not—" I breathed heavily. "My reaction had nothing to do with UFOs and everything to do with something flying at me from out of nowhere."

"But my pie-plate UFO is more realistic than you thought." She bobbled it toward me, and I sheered away.

"Yes," I said with my usual pre-five-a.m. testiness. "You got me. Is the power on in town?"

"Yep. It went off for a couple of hours last night, but it's back." She frowned. "Your trailer's awfully dark. Are you telling me you don't have any electricity?"

"Not yet." I zipped my hoodie higher. "I'm sure it will be fixed by the time I get home." But I hoped it came on soon. I didn't want to return to a dark house. I'd spent enough time last night freaking myself out over all the creaks and scrapes outside.

We drove to Pie Town in our separate vehicles, and sunrise turned the eastern hilltops gray.

In the Pie Town kitchen, morning was its usual whirl of prep work, taking deliveries, and baking, baking, baking. I was slowly building my staff and still didn't have as many people as I'd like. So I had a hand in pretty much everything we made except the piecrusts. That was Charlene's sacred domain.

At six a.m., I set out the coffee urn and turned the sign in the front door to OPEN. I surveyed the dining area. The neon smiley face above the order window grinned rosily. The glass display case was fingerprint-free. The checkerboard floor gleamed. We were ready for business.

The door jangled open, and Graham doddered into the

dining area. At his usual counter spot, he regaled my assistant manager, Petronella, with tales of electrocution victims he'd known. "Val was nearly one of 'em," he finished.

I shooed a fascinated Petronella, no doubt wondering about how morticians dealt with deep-fried corpses, into the kitchen. The morning rolled on.

Finally, at ten o'clock, Charlene emerged from the flour-work room and whipped her apron over her head. "Have you called our winners yet?"

"Win— Oh!" I whisked a pie from the rotating racks in the giant oven and set it on a wheeled set of stacked trays. "No, but no time like the present. Er, have you got their numbers?"

She rolled her eyes and plucked a piece of paper from the pocket of her burnt-orange tunic. "I came prepared."

I glanced around. We were alone in the kitchen, Petronella working the counter.

Stomach fluttering, because I wasn't a very good liar, I called Professor Jezek.

"This is Piotr Jezek," a funereal voice intoned and hiccupped.

"Hi, this is Val Harris from Pie Town."

"What can I do for you?" The last word trailed off mournfully.

"We've had some cancellations for this week's pie class. I thought we'd give the classes away to randomly drawn guests from the poetry reading. You won."

"I find that hard to believe."

My breath caught. Was my offer that transparent? "Why?"

"Because I never win anything." He sighed, a ghostly sound.

"But you did! I know it's short notice, but I've got two tickets for you and a guest Thursday. Next Thursday," I amended, because I had a date with Gordon tomorrow night.

I crossed my fingers. "Would you like to come? It's a three-hour class in the Pie Town kitchen. You'll get a behind-the-scenes—"

"I'll—I'll do it." His voice trembled.

I blinked. "You will?"

"As a writer, it's important to experience different walks of life." He spoke rapidly, as if taking a plunge. "May I take notes and photos?"

"Of . . . course," I stammered.

"Send me the details." He rattled off an email address.

"Great," I said. "We'll see you next Thursday."

"No substitutions!" Charlene shouted into the phone.

"What?" he asked.

"Nothing," I chirped. "Bye." I hung up. "That's one suspect down. Three more to go." But Aidan and Rudolph didn't answer their phones, and we didn't know Dorothy's number.

"We'd better round up those suspects," Charlene growled, "or our investigation is DOA. Either that, or you can dump your boyfriend, so we can do some real investigating in the field."

I dropped the phone in my apron pocket and grabbed a ticket off the wheel in the order window. "That wouldn't help. He'd still arrest us for interfering. Besides, Gordon's on our side."

"Mm," she said, skeptical. "In any case, we need to step up our game, my girl."

The order ticket crumpled in my hands. Hastily, I smoothed it on the metal counter. Charlene was right. But how was I going to interrogate suspects without falling afoul of the law?

CHAPTER 8

The wind had blown away the clouds, leaving a tattered pink and tangerine sunset floating above the Pacific. Gordon and I sat on the White Lady's cliffside patio. Our feet rested against the edge of the brick firepit, a cozy blanket wrapped around our shoulders. The remains of our dinner lay on a nearby low table.

Wineglass in hand, I shivered and huddled closer to him on the bench, but not because I was really cold. The cardigan I wore over my blue dress was enough, but his ivory fisherman's sweater was super soft. Plus, I'd pretty much take any excuse to get closer to Gordon.

"Alligator," I repeated, trying not to laugh. It had to be a joke. "An alligator at the drive-through?"

"Not *at* the drive-through, *in* the drive-through. The woman shoved the gator through the window when the guy was handing her a bag of burgers."

"Oh my God." I stiffened on the bench, glad I hadn't laughed. "Was anyone hurt?"

"Not by the gator, but someone turned their ankle in the

stampede from the kitchen. And no alligators were harmed in the perpetration of this crime."

"That's good news." I choked back another laugh, relieved. "But what did you do?" And how did Gordon get stuck with that call? Wasn't he supposed to be investigating Michael Starke's murder?

"It wasn't a very big alligator. I just picked it up and held its jaws shut."

"How big is not-a-very-big alligator?"

He held his hands two feet apart.

"And the woman?" I asked, grinning.

A couple wandered behind us, and the glass door to the restaurant slid open and shut.

"Said it was revenge. The guy working the drive-through broke up with her by text."

I folded my arms. "Then he totally deserved an alligator through his window."

He raised a brow. "I can't tell if you're joking or not."

"That's all right," I said. After all, he *was* a detective. If I couldn't keep Gordon on his toes, there was no way I was going to keep him around.

"No." He chuckled. "It's a little disturbing."

"Where'd she get the alligator?"

"It was a pet. It wasn't legal."

I shook my head. "So how did you get roped into this?"

"I caught the call."

My stomach lurched. Gordon was a detective, not a gator wrangler. I hadn't gotten him thrown off a case again, had I? "But aren't you, I mean . . . Chief Shaw hasn't—"

"He hasn't pulled me off the murder investigation."

I relaxed, then straightened. The gray blanket slid from my shoulder. "But that's weird. He's always trying to showboat the interesting cases."

He adjusted the blanket over my shoulder and pulled me closer. I snuggled against his warmth, hard and muscular.

"Shaw's supposed lack of interest is . . ." He hesitated. "Let's just enjoy the mystery. Much like the San Nicholas pie-plate UFO photos that have been cropping up all over the Internet."

Supposed lack of interest? But I knew a diversion when I heard one, and I rolled with it. "Those are Charlene's, as I'm sure you've already deduced. She claims the photos are a promotion for Pie Town, but we both know she just likes flying tiny UFOs around town."

"She's lucky they're obvious fakes. We've had a few alarmed calls to 911."

"About her pie-tin UFOs?" I asked, chagrined. "But you said they were obvious fakes." Were we in trouble?

"Obvious to the police department and to most people with any brains. But she's been posting them on Twitter. Fortunately for you, she hasn't put the Pie Town name on them. But she needs to be careful."

Like *that* would ever happen. "I'll let her know. How's the murder investigation going?"

"Mm." He nuzzled my neck. "You know I can't talk about that."

"You can't distract me with sexy fun." I gasped, my skin prickling with the heat of his touch. "Not on a public patio." But he was getting darned close to succeeding.

He sighed and sat back against the bench. "I guess not. Actually, there is something—"

Someone banged on the window behind us. My shoulders jerked, and we turned toward the white-painted two-story. A few other couples craned their necks, searching for the source of the noise.

The banging grew louder, and I looked up.

Charlene stood framed in the second-floor window like Dustin Hoffman in *The Graduate*. Frederick curled around the neck of her sky-blue tunic. She pointed behind her and made a "Come on" motion with one hand, then disappeared.

Seriously? I forced a smile. "If I don't see what she wants, she'll just come down to the patio." I *knew* he shouldn't have blabbed about our date in front of her. Charlene had busted up more than one of my rendezvous with Gordon before. And there were several dogs on the patio who Frederick might not get along with.

He laughed. "Go on."

Reluctant, I shrugged out of the warm blanket and trotted across the patio and upstairs.

Charlene waited for me at the top of the steps. "Get anything from your detective about the murders?"

"No," I grumped. "He won't talk about the case." I loved that he was so professional, but it could also be super irritating.

"No worries. I've got a lead." She strolled to the old-fashioned bar—of dark wood, its rounded edges chipped with age—and sat on a high stool.

"Can this wait?" But I followed, of *course* I followed.

"No," she said, stroking the white cat on her shoulders.

"You came all the way to the White Lady to tell me. So hurry up, because Gordon's waiting."

"He should get used to waiting. It's like that country song. Waiting . . ." She crooned. "Something, something waiting . . ."

"What's going on?"

Crossing her legs, she exposed the white-and-blue-striped socks beneath her loose leggings. "And even though you abandoned me for your brother—"

"I already apologized for that. Plus, you said it was okay!"

"—when I caught a lead," she plowed onward, "I came right to you. My partner."

"All right."

"A fellow Baker Street Baker."

"I get it," I said testily.

"Even though it was awkward, breaking in on your PDA."

"We were not—" Okay, we *had* been publicly displaying affection, but nothing over the top.

"But I soldiered through."

"Charlene."

"Yes?"

"What's the lead?"

The bartender Patel strolled along the bar to us. "Hey, Val. What can I get you? Another glass of the Cab?"

"Um, sure." Why not? It was only my second, I wasn't driving, and I had a feeling I'd need one to get through this conversation.

Patel gave the cat a wary look. Drifting to the other end of the bar, he pulled a bottle from beneath it.

"So?" I asked Charlene.

"Hm?"

"The lead, the clue, the lowdown. What is it, before Gordon comes looking?"

"Patel."

"The bartender? Why didn't you—?"

Patel sat the glass in front of me on the bar. "Here you go. Same tab?"

"Yeah," I said, frowning.

He turned to the mirrored shelves and studied the bottles there. "You know, pets aren't allowed in the restaurant."

"What pet?" Charlene asked baldly. "Now, Patel, please tell Val what you told me about Professor Dorothy Hastings."

"What?" he asked. "That she comes in here a lot?"

"Everyone comes in here," she said. "It's the most interesting restaurant on this part of the coast. No, the other stuff."

"About her boyfriend?"

"Yes," she said. "Aidan McClary."

"They come here a lot together." He picked up a beer glass and rinsed it in the metal sink. "Why? Are you two investigating the murder of that professor?"

"No," I said.

"Yes," Charlene said.

"No," I ground out, "because interfering in an investigation is illegal. The nice policeman downstairs will tell you all about it."

Charlene rocked her head sideways and back. "Mm . . . Not so sure about that. The law's not really clear—"

"Thank you, Pa— Wait," I said. "Why would you think we were investigating?"

"Because someone told me the murder was connected to Pie Town."

What? It totally was not! "Who told you that?"

"That friend of yours." He nodded to Charlene. "What's her name? Mary?"

"Marla!" Charlene slammed her hands on the damp bar. "That harpy won't be happy until she has ruined everything that is good in my life."

"Okay," I said, "that's not—"

"The Ice Capades, the YouTube channel—"

"Well," I said hurriedly, "thanks, Patel. If you do hear anything pertaining to the murder, let us—I mean the police—know."

Charlene growled. "I'm flying my UFO straight over her fancy beach house."

Patel rubbed the back of his neck. "Well, there *is* something else."

"That rat, that—" Charlene stopped midstream. "I thought you said that was all you knew?"

"But not about the murder," he said. "You didn't ask me about the murder."

Her eyes bulged. "I was trying to be discreet!"

Heads swiveled in our direction.

"Patel," I said, "hold that thought."

I trotted down the steps. Pausing inside the glass doors, I smoothed my dress. I slid them open, and a blast of salty air tossed my hair. The sun had settled deeper to bed, the cobalt ocean blanketing its blazing rim.

Gordon smiled warmly. "Hey, beautiful. What kept you? Has Charlene got another paranormal caper brewing?"

I let him tug me to the bench and sank into his embrace. He looked so good in that sweater, I hated to ruin the mood. "Yes, I mean no. Gordon, Patel says he might actually have some information about the murder."

"And he told you, because . . . ?"

"He didn't tell me. I asked him not to tell me. I asked him to tell you. I have no idea what the information is, or whether it's of any interest. But if you don't get up there soon, Charlene will wheedle it out of him, and then you'll have her on your hands and in your jail."

"Save me." He leapt from the bench and hurried past me and indoors.

I dithered for a moment on the bench, grabbed my sequined clutch off the table at my elbow, and followed.

Gordon leaned one elbow on the bar. "What's the word, Patel?"

The bartender set down the beer glass. "Professor Hastings's boyfriend, that Aidan fellow, has been pushing for marriage. But she's not interested."

"And?" Gordon asked.

"And that's it. But they were pretty hot and heavy. Well, as much as you can get at a place like this." Patel motioned with the empty glass around the bar, filled with the low murmurs of couples at square tables.

I slumped, disappointed. We'd already known Aidan and Dorothy were dating. Charlene had dragged us up here for this? Though in fairness, this time, I'd been the one doing the dragging.

Charlene rubbed her jaw. "Suspicious."

"Anything else?" Gordon asked briskly.

"Nope," the bartender said. "That's it."

"Okay. Thanks." He handed Patel his card. "If you think of anything else, let me know."

I motioned for Charlene to stay. Cheeks burning, I followed Gordon downstairs and to the patio. "I'm sorry," I said.

"I always welcome tips."

"But that one was weak."

"Look," he said, "I know you and Charlene are friends, and I know you do a lot for her—"

"Not really." She'd done more for me. Finding me a home. Getting me involved in the community. Being a friend.

"But you need to be careful."

"Careful? I mean, okay, that so-called tip was embarrassing. But Patel said he had information, so I passed it on to you."

"That's not what I'm talking about. You two have been lucky so far."

I preferred to think that my keen instincts and amazing skills as a detective had kept us safe and successful. My eyes narrowed. "Oh?"

He pulled me close. "She's going to get herself into trouble," he murmured into my hair. "I just don't want you to get drawn in."

"Charlene's not as crazy as she likes to let people think."

He hesitated. "It isn't only Charlene."

I pulled away. A gust of wind blew off the Pacific below and shivered my skin. "What's that supposed to mean? You think I'm crazy?"

"No," Gordon said quickly. "Well, a little. In a good way. Anyone who starts a business has to be a little crazy. It's a huge risk."

I folded my arms, partly from annoyance, partly because I wanted my patio blanket back. The cliff was chilly.

"I wasn't talking about you," he said. "Listen, this needs to be completely confidential. You can't even say anything to Charlene."

"Okay," I said slowly.

"I shouldn't be telling you this, but—"

"But what? Telling me what?"

He clawed a hand through his thick hair and blew out his breath. "I'm bringing Abril in for questioning tomorrow."

CHAPTER 9

I gaped. A bitter wind moaned through the ocean cliffs below. The sun vanished beneath the waves. Gray darkness fell, turning the Pacific to pale lines of white foam stretching toward the shore.

I shook my head. "Question . . . You mean, not as a witness? As a suspect?" My voice rose on the last word.

Couples at the patio tables nearby glanced our way.

He nodded, his expression sympathetic. "I'm sorry."

A log shifted in the firepit. Sparks shot upward, our shadows dancing weirdly across the patio.

This was crazy. "But . . . Abril! She couldn't hurt a fly. She instituted a catch-and-release program for the Pie Town spiders." Not that we had much of a bug problem. Since we were food service, I was militant about pest control.

"There's a chain of questioning that I have to pursue."

"What questions?"

"You know I can't tell you. I shouldn't have told you this much."

The wind whipped hair into my eyes, and I pushed the

wayward strands behind my ears. Another gust immediately freed them, slapping my face.

I took deep, yogic breaths. Gordon was a good cop. Abril was innocent, and I had to trust that he'd prove that. Bringing her into the station was just one more step in the investigative process. "Okay. I know you're doing your job, and she'll be all right. Abril's got no motive."

He shifted his weight, his arms loose at his sides, and said nothing.

"She has a motive?" I whispered, horrified.

He gazed at me, his emerald eyes glittering with sorrow.

"No," I said. "There are other, better suspects than Abril. There was a student TA Abril and Doran talked to—Genny Glasspool. She worked for Starke, and they had an affair. He gave her a bad recommendation, and she was furious."

He lowered his head and grimaced. "I know."

"You know?" My shoulders collapsed. "But . . ." This made no sense! How could Abril have a better motive than Genny, unless . . . I remembered Abril's eagerness to bring the reading to Pie Town, her enthusiasm over Starke.

Unless Abril had been romantically involved with him too.

I shook my head. *No*. Abril was smarter than that. I didn't believe that was the answer.

The phone buzzed in Gordon's pocket, and he clapped it to his ear. "Carmichael . . . I'll be there in ten." He pocketed his phone. "I'm sorry, Val, it's an emergency—not the murder."

"And you've got to go," I said dully. "It's okay."

"I'll get the check on the way out." He kissed my cheek and jogged inside the white stucco building.

The fire popped, and I jumped. I needed to talk to Charlene—no, I couldn't talk to Charlene. I'd promised Gordon to keep my mouth shut. If I told Charlene, she'd go tearing off to Abril's to learn the truth.

Pasting a smile on my face, I walked inside and up the stairs, to the gleaming wooden bar. As I'd half hoped, half dreaded, Charlene still sat on one of its high, leather stools.

I slid onto an empty seat beside her and adjusted my dress. "Gordon had to leave for a police emergency." I dropped my sparkly white clutch onto the bar.

"Ah, the life of a copper. Fast-talking dames, fog, and fisticuffs."

"That's a Sam Spade movie, not San Nicholas."

"In the first place," Charlene said, "Sam Spade roamed all over this coast. In the second place, they wouldn't call Gordon in for another surfer dispute. What was the emergency?"

I shrugged off my guilty conscience. "I don't know. Did you hear about the alligator at the drive-through?" I asked, trying to change the subject.

"Was it the ghost alligator?" she asked, breathless.

"A real one. Wait, there's a ghost—" I shook my head. *Not important.* I told Charlene and Patel the story of the gator in the drive-through.

"What are you drinking?" I asked her.

"Same thing I was drinking before." She raised her sidecar, amber in its cocktail glass. "I suppose you'll need a lift home."

I sighed. "If you don't mind."

"I'll need to finish my drink first."

I eyed the near-full glass. Charlene was a slow drinker, and she filled in the gaps with plenty of pretzels between sips, so I wasn't worried about her driving. "In that case, I'll have another glass of wine." I motioned to Patel, and soon I had a full goblet in front of me.

Patel drifted to an elderly couple. They held hands atop the bar and spoke in low voices, laughing. My chest squeezed with longing. Would I ever have that?

"What's wrong?" Charlene asked. "Murder got your tongue?"

"Why are all the men in my life always in such a hurry to go?" I blurted. It was enough to make me want to pack it in and join a monastery, or whatever it was women joined. I could never remember that word.

"That detective would have stayed if he could. I see how he looks at you." She stared at her reflection in the mirror behind the bottles.

"I guess I wasn't entirely thinking about Gordon," I admitted.

"Your father is a special case. And Doran hasn't left yet. At least he's trying to stay."

My breath hitched. I wasn't the only one who'd been ditched. Charlene's daughter lived somewhere in Europe. And like Charlene had said, at least Doran was trying. Her daughter seemed to have said *good riddance* to their relationship.

"Ah, family." Polishing a glass, Patel wandered to our end of the bar and carefully did not make eye contact with Charlene. "Can't live with them, can't avoid them at the holidays. But even though I find myself thinking homicidal thoughts whenever my auntie makes me wear one of her awful Christmas sweaters, I know they will always be there for me." His brows drew together. "Except for that time they left me behind in Yosemite and I was nearly eaten by coyotes."

"As a child, I was raised for a time by coyotes," Charlene said. "It's why I have such an instinctive connection to Bigfoot."

"I spent three hours in a pine tree before the rangers rescued me." Patel rubbed the glass more vigorously.

"I spent five hours in a redwood once," Charlene said, adjusting Frederick over the collar of her sky-blue tunic. "Bigfoot hunting."

I cleared my throat. "Moving on, Gordon told me there have been some 911 calls about your UFO pictures."

"What UFO pictures?" Patel asked, his brown eyes widening.

"My pie-plate UFOs." She pulled her phone from the pocket of her knit jacket and clicked on a photo, expanding the image. "It's a promotion for Pie Town. If you enlarge it, you can even see the Pie Town logo on the back. See?" She handed the phone to Patel.

He tugged his ear. "Is that UFO over the White Lady?"

"Yup," she said. "I took a snap before I came in tonight. Nice lighting, don't you think?"

"The hours around sunrise and sunset are best for photography," he agreed.

While they chatted about exposure and contrast, I dug out my own phone and checked Charlene's Twitter feed. She'd already posted the UFO over the White Lady photo with the text: UFO SPOTTED OVER WHITE LADY! #SANNICHOLAS

I scrolled through her other posts. They all treated the pictures as the real deal. And there were comments. So many comments. Most seemed to take the pictures at face value.

I groaned. "Charlene, some people are taking these pictures seriously. You've got to say they're fake."

"Everyone knows they're fake. They're obviously fake. The tins say Pie Town on top."

"Yeah, but you don't see that at this size."

"Besides," she said, "I'm limited by the amount of characters I can include, and brevity is the essence of wit."

"People have been calling 911," I repeated.

"People are crazy."

Briefly, I closed my eyes. *It takes one to know one.* "Yes, Charlene. *People* are crazy."

"Oh, hey." Patel angled his dark head toward the other end of the bar. "There's Professor Hastings."

A sadder and wiser-looking version of Shirley Temple sat alone on a corner barstool. She crooked a finger at Patel.

He glided to her end of the bar.

"This is too good an opportunity pass up," I said.

"Definitely kismet," she agreed.

I rose and sat again. "Um, we don't actually know her. What's our approach?"

"The whole point of coming to a bar is to get to know the other people in it. And this is a good chance to give her two tickets to a pie-making class."

"And it's not interfering in an investigation," I rationalized. "It's not our fault she sat down at the bar beside us. If Gordon hadn't left early, he could have talked to her." That's what he got for ditching me to save lives.

Dorothy's scowl settled deeper into her skin.

"Maybe we should let her get a drink or two under her belt first," Charlene said in a low voice.

Professor Hastings raised a beer bottle to her lips and chugged it down in one go.

"Or we could talk to her now." I grabbed my clutch and walked to her end of the bar. "Professor Hastings?"

She belched and shook her blond ringlets. "That's me."

"Um, I just wanted to say how sorry I am—"

"We are," Charlene said.

"—about the death of Professor Starke."

She eyed Charlene. "Is that a cat around your neck?" A multicolored silk scarf hung limply around the collar of her denim jacket.

"Maybe," Charlene said.

"Is that animal alive?"

"Definitely," I said. "Frederick's narcoleptic. May we join you?"

The professor shrugged and motioned with her empty bottle. "I don't own the barstools." Patel put another opened bottle by her elbow, and she took a swig.

I stuck out my hand and sat. "I'm Val Harris. This is my friend, Charlene McCree."

She shook my hand warily, her silver rings biting my fingers. "And you already know me. The question is, how?"

"We ran into you leaving Dean Prophet's office the other day," I said, "after Professor Starke's death."

She rested her forehead on the bar, and an anguished sound escaped her throat. "I didn't do it."

"Coppers been giving you the third degree?" Charlene said, tone sympathetic.

"You have no idea," she mumbled into her elbow.

"The lead detective knows what he's doing," I said. "He'll figure it out."

She bolted upright and fixed me with a gimlet eye. "Oh, he will, will he?"

"Yes!" I said, and crossed my legs on the barstool. Though he did seem somewhat jinxed when it came to cases connected to Pie Town. *Augh!* Even I was connecting the murders to Pie Town now.

"It doesn't look like it from where I'm standing," the professor said. "He's obsessed with that damn sword. Just because it's mine—"

"Wait, are you talking about the sword that killed Professor Starke?" I asked.

She nodded and took another pull on her beer. "Everybody knows it wasn't in my possession. I *lent* it to Michael. It's not my fault the idiot got skewered with it."

"It sounds like your feelings for the man were . . . complicated." Charlene rolled her hand in front of her heart. "Get it off your chest. We're good listeners."

Dorothy's blue eyes flashed. "My feelings for that detective are crystal clear!"

"I meant your ex," Charlene said.

"Look. Michael and I worked together. We were colleagues, that was all. And I didn't want him dead, and I certainly wouldn't have wrestled my own sword away from him to stab him with it."

"You couldn't have," I said, probing, "not when you were so far away from the crime scene." Where *had* she been?

"That's right." She waved her empty bottle at Patel. "I was at home."

"Alone?" Charlene asked hopefully.

"Another?" Patel asked.

"Yes." Dorothy held out her empty bottle. "Please."

Patel took the bottle and glided to the other end of the bar.

I cleared my throat. "You were saying about being at home?"

Dorothy slumped. "I should have gone to the stupid reading. If I had, maybe none of this would have happened. And now Aidan . . ."

"You mean your boyfriend, Professor McClary?" Charlene asked brightly.

She nodded, fuming. "I really dislike that word when applied to adults."

"What word?" Charlene asked. "*Professor*?"

"*Boyfriend*," she said. "It sounds juvenile. But everything else sounds sterile or melodramatic. I loathe the word *partner*. And *lover* is even worse. Ugh. It's like something out of *Valley of the Dolls*."

"The only other alternative for adults is *um-friend*," I said.

"Um-friend?" Dorothy asked.

"As in, this is my, um, friend."

"Did you know," Charlene said, tapping one finger on the bar, "that in Kyrgyz, *um* is the word for a lady's private bits?"

Charlene!

"I'm in the English department," the professor said, "not the Kyrgyz department." She turned to me. "Val Harris . . . Where do I know that name?"

"I own Pie Town."

She drew back on her barstool. "Oh. Then . . . you were there." Her expression grew anxious. "Did the reading go well? How was he?"

Aside from the murder? "You mean . . . Professor Starke?"

"No, Aidan. Michael always does well at those things. He's such a—" She looked down. "He was such a ham. But he knew how to work a crowd. Aidan on the other hand is a typical Byronic hero—his passion is as changeable as coastal weather."

"They both did great," I lied, since I hadn't been paying much attention.

"I'm glad," Dorothy said. "And I'm glad for Michael as well. Even though these things were old hat for him by now, at least he went out on a high note, doing what he loved."

I fiddled with my wineglass. "You know . . . I had some cancellations for a pie-making class next Thursday. Would you like two tickets? For you and Aidan? It's a fun class, and you get to keep the pies."

She was silent for a long moment. "Yes. I can't speak for Aidan, but I'll ask him if he wants to come with me. I could use the distraction."

"Great!" I dug a business card from my clutch and wrote the time and date of the class on the back. "If you can't make it, please let me know, so I can give the tickets to someone else."

"I will. Thanks."

We finished our drinks and said our goodbyes. Charlene and I walked into the parking lot, and the wind tossed my dress. I pressed it against my legs with my white clutch.

"I liked her," Charlene said.

"Me too. But I don't suppose we can count her out."

"No. We should have pushed her harder, but . . ."

"But we liked her." Gordon would have done better. He wouldn't have cared if he liked her or not. *The police really were better at these things,* I thought glumly. They knew to separate witnesses when questioning them and . . .

Oh.

"What's wrong?" Charlene asked.

"Maybe we should invite our suspects to Pie Town on separate days?"

"Why?"

"Because by throwing all our suspects together in one kitchen, we're creating a powder keg."

She smiled. "Isn't that what we're counting on?"

CHAPTER 10

There are no wimps in bakeries. The bags of flour and sugar weigh fifty pounds each. All of us (except Charlene) were used to hefting them around.

And then came Hunter.

My assistant manager, Petronella, watched the bronzed teen. Hunter easily lifted a sack of flour onto his shoulder and strode through the kitchen. Muscles bulging, he ripped open the bag and dumped it into the bin, a barrel on wheels that could hold four sacks of flour.

Hunter dumped too fast. A cloud of flour filled the kitchen. The teenager vanished into the cloud that coated the net over Petronella's spiky black hair like snow.

He emerged coughing and covered in white stuff. Hunter blinked, his startling blue eyes giving him a china-doll look. "Whoa. This isn't toxic, is it?"

"It's flour," I said through clenched teeth and glowered at the mess.

Petronella shook her head, and flour drifted to the shoulders of her *Pies Before Guys* t-shirt. "You know where the broom is." She sighed and brushed flour off her hairnet and shoulders as he ambled from the kitchen, leaving a white trail of footprints. "Honestly," she said, "he does this *every* time. Is he making more work for himself intentionally?"

I pulled a slice of strawberry-rhubarb pie from the microwave. "He's learning." And he was the only person willing to work cleanup for the pay I was offering.

Petronella threw up her hands and took the pie. She stomped into the dining area, her motorcycle boots making more tracks on the linoleum.

Worried, I turned off the big oven with the rotating racks. Abril had today off, so I hadn't expected to see her. But it was late in the day, and if she had been questioned by the SNPD, surely she'd be free by now? I smoothed my apron and took the slice into the restaurant.

Pie Town was delightfully crowded this Friday afternoon. It had been a warm, sunny day. A good portion of the Bay Area seemed to have shifted to the coast for one of the last glorious beach days of the year. My heart swelled. I loved September—summer's last hurrah before fall and all things pumpkin spice took over.

I brought the strawberry-rhubarb to the gamers' pink corner booth. The engineering students argued good-naturedly with their pudgy ringleader, Ray, who'd apparently done serious damage to their gaming characters.

"Here you go." I slid the pie in front of the burly redhead.

Ray flushed, turning crimson beneath his freckles. "Um, I'm sharing with Henrietta."

Henrietta, in khakis and a shapeless t-shirt, nudged him and grinned.

Ray, sharing? Had the world gone topsy-turvy? I handed her an extra fork from my apron pocket. Maybe he was trying to lose weight? "Here you go."

"What's happening with the murder?" Ray asked. "It was our college too, before we transferred, even if we weren't in the English department. Maybe we can help, like before?"

Ray and Henrietta had once become honorary members of the Baker Street Bakers on a case Ray had brought us. (So there was totally precedent for my brother helping out.) But I shook my head at Ray's offer. "Only if you know any of Professor Starke's teaching assistants."

The twentysomethings glanced at each other across the table.

"I know an ex-TA," Ray said, "does that count?"

"An ex-TA of Professor Starke's?" I asked.

He nodded. "Yeah, her name's Brittany." His broad brow creased. "I don't know her last name. Do any of you guys?"

They shook their heads.

Ray brightened. "But I know where she'll be tonight."

"Where?" I asked.

"The Father Serra statue off Two-Eighty."

"That's . . . a weirdly clandestine spot," I said.

"You know," he said, "because of the hat."

"I'm not from around these here parts." I braced my fists on the hips of my apron. "You'll have to explain."

"They do it every year," Henrietta said. "Before the big robotics competition, the engineering team puts a hat with the college colors on the statue."

"What time will they be there tonight?" I asked.

He shrugged. "Some time after dark."

My brother walked into Pie Town, the bell over the door jingling. He looked around, his dark brows slicing downward.

Charlene followed close behind him, and my breath quickened. What were *they* doing together?

I dragged my gaze back to the gamers. "Some time after dark because they're not supposed to be putting a hat on the statue. Got it. Thanks." I hurried to Doran and Charlene. "Hey, what's going on?"

"Have you heard from Abril?" he whispered.

"Um, no. She's not working today, but—"

"She was arrested," he said.

"What? No. She was only brought in for questioning. There's a difference."

"You knew?" Charlene glowered and adjusted Frederick, hanging limp over the shoulder of her mustard tunic.

Uh-oh. "Abril set up the poetry reading in Pie Town," I hedged. "She knew Professor Starke. It's not that strange for the police to want to talk to her."

"All day? We've got to get her out," Doran said.

"You mean she's not out yet?" I asked.

He folded his arms across his chest, and his leather jacket squeaked. "Why do you think we're here?"

"Gordon's in charge of the investigation," I said. "He'll be fair."

Charlene's mouth flattened.

I could see I was losing control of the situation. "The best way we can help Abril is by following our new lead."

"You follow it," Doran said. "I'm going back to the station." He strode from the restaurant, and the front bell jangled violently.

"What new lead?" Charlene asked.

What was he going to do? Glancing toward the closing door, I explained about Brittany and the engineers.

Charlene nodded. "It's a stakeout. I'll get the chips and root beer."

Charlene munched a chip, shooting barbecue-flavored shrapnel across the seat of the Pie Town van. I was starting to understand why she'd agreed to let me drive for once.

We sat parked, lights off, at the rest stop. Low spotlights in tufts of ornamental grasses up-lit the adobe-colored statue of Father Serra. The tonsured saint stretched one arm to the west, toward the black reservoir and the curves of dark hills and the ocean beyond.

Pulse speeding, I shifted in my seat. I wasn't worried about the engineering students. But we'd ignored the sign saying the rest area was closed after sunset.

It was after sunset.

We were scofflaws.

"So," Charlene said for the eighth time. "Abril's being questioned by Gordon."

"Okay, fine." I glanced in the rearview mirror, searching for red and blue lights. "I knew he was questioning her in advance. But he told me not to tell anyone."

"Why didn't you tell *me*?"

"Because you would have told Abril. Then we really would be in jail for interfering in an investigation, and Gordon would have gotten in trouble too."

"Traitor," she mumbled through a mouthful of chips.

I sputtered. "That's not fair. I trust Gordon, and you do too. It's not like he's giving Abril the third degree. And why did you bring that fishing pole?" I jerked my head toward the back, where the pole lay between racks for delivering pies.

"Not only the pole." She unzipped the backpack at her feet and pulled out her pie-plate UFO. "I want a shot of a Pie Town UFO over Father Serra."

"At night?"

"My phone takes excellent night shots."

Headlights streamed up the freeway exit, and my heart frog-jumped into my throat.

Charlene's arm jerked. Chips flew through the air. "Duck!"

We scrunched down in our seats, and the lights swept across the dashboard.

Car doors slammed.

Charlene and I inched upward in our seats and peered through the windshield.

Two students awkwardly opened a giant, green-and-white

baseball hat between them. The thing was huge, but so was Father Serra's head.

I squinted up at his tonsured skull. His head was also at least twenty feet off the ground, and I didn't see any ladders.

"Let's go." Charlene opened her door and clambered from the van.

I followed, quietly shutting my door.

We approached the students, who seemed to be assembling some sort of cable and pulley system.

"Where's Pole C?" a slender young man whose head seemed too big for his body asked. His long fingers twitched. He reminded me of a praying mantis.

His five friends looked at each other.

"I thought you brought it," the only woman in the group said, and she adjusted her green-and-white college hoodie.

Brittany?

"Hello," I said, and they started.

"We're just putting a hat on Father Serra's head," Praying Mantis said. "It's an innocent stunt. No one gets hurt."

Charlene snorted. "Not without Pole C, you're not."

"We don't care about the hat," I said. "We—"

"We have to go back for the pole," the young woman said. "The pulley system won't work without it."

"No," Mantis said. "I'll go back. You get the rest of the system assembled."

"And waste all that time?" Charlene asked. "Why don't you just climb up there?"

We craned our necks at Father Serra. A rough, low fence surrounded the statue, kneeling amid the ornamental grasses.

"Are you Brittany?" I asked the girl. She was attractive in a dangerous sort of way, with deep-set, coffee-colored eyes; a long, straight nose; and olive skin. I blinked, suddenly recognizing her. She'd been at the poetry reading.

She dragged a hand through her thick, black hair. "Yeah. Why?"

"We're friends of Ray MacTaggart," I said.

"Just climb onto the statue's lap," Charlene told Mantis, "then the arm, and from there you can easily get to his shoulder. Then the ear, and then the head. Easy-peasy."

"Or we can get Pole C," he said.

"Sure," Charlene said, "stay all night. I'm sure none of the highway patrol will notice."

"I heard you worked for Professor Starke," I murmured to Brittany.

Brittany stiffened. "Yeah?" she asked cautiously.

"We'd like to talk to you about him," I said, "if you don't mind."

"I do mind," she said. "And we're busy." She turned away from me and to the rest of the group.

"What's wrong with you boys?" Charlene jammed her hands on her hips. "When I was your age, I was getting up to all sorts of hijinks." She flexed her arms.

"We're engineers," a portly young man said. "We build things so we don't have to get up to hijinks."

"You're all chicken," she said. "Why, Val could get up there in nothing flat."

I'd rather slam my hand in the pie oven. "No, I really don't—"

"And look at her," Charlene continued. "No one could say she's in shape."

"I'm a normal weight," I said, my voice shriller than I liked.

"Making the climb would be quicker," Brittany said. "And it would reduce the odds of us getting caught."

Cars rumbled past on the nearby freeway below.

"Then it's agreed." Charlene nodded. "Val will get your hat up there, and you'll spill the dirt on Professor Starke."

"*What?*" I said. "I didn't agree to that."

"Hm . . ." Brittany shook her head, her long hair cascading over her shoulders.

Charlene grasped my elbow and tugged me toward the low fencing surrounding the statue. "It's not that hard. Look. Just climb onto his lap, then the arm—"

"I heard you the first time," I said. "And I'm not spelunking on Father Serra's statue. He's a saint. It's desecration or something."

She lowered her head and glowered beneath her white brows. "Oh, so all that talk about helping Abril was just talk. Abril, who's sitting in jail. Abril, who's never done anything bad to anyone. Abril, who bakes your—"

"Okay, fine. If Brittany agrees, I'll do it." Stupid guilt.

I looked a question at Brittany.

Slowly, she nodded. "Deal."

I tugged down the hem of my Pie Town hoodie. Clambering over the fence, I strode to Father Serra's sandaled feet. "I need a boost."

The engineers looked at one another.

I rolled my eyes. "Oh, come on."

"Well, you have put on a few pounds, Val," Charlene said.

"I have not! You"—I pointed to the largest engineer—"get over here."

He trudged closer.

I climbed onto the statue's foot and stretched, grasping the fold of Father Serra's robe between his knees. "Let's go." I raised one foot.

The engineer latticed his hands together and boosted me.

Huffing, I wriggled onto the folds of the statue's lap robes. I'd done it! I was a third of the way there. I turned. "Okay, hand me the . . ." And then I realized the problem. There was no way I could carry the hat onto his shoulder.

"Someone else will have to get on the lap too," Charlene said, "and hand you the hat when you get high enough."

There was some muttering. Finally, Brittany volunteered.

I moved to the edge of the statue's thigh and hauled myself onto his outstretched arm. I looked down and gulped.

"Don't look down," Charlene called unhelpfully from below.

I inched toward the shoulder and slowly stood, grabbing the statue's earlobe. "Okay. Hand me the hat."

Brittany stretched, shoving the green-and-white fabric up to me. Keeping a vise grip on the rough earlobe with one hand, I leaned down and grabbed the hat.

The engineers cheered.

"Are you okay up there?" Brittany asked. "You look a little pale."

"It's the spotlight," I lied. "I'm fine." Or at least I would be once this stupid hat was in place. I pressed closer to the giant ear and blindly tossed one end of the fabric onto the head. It slipped down and crumpled atop me.

"A little more to the left," Charlene shouted.

After three more attempts, I got the hat on and adjusted to everyone's satisfaction. Grinning with relief, I turned and looked down at the group.

"Catch!" Charlene hurled a spinning silver disk.

Automatically, I lunged for the pie-plate UFO. It pinged off my fingertips, and I lost my grip on the ear.

I staggered onto the statue's arm and scrambled to get my footing. One foot skidded into empty air. I was falling.

My shoulder hit something hard. Too terrified to scream, I gasped, grasping for a handhold. Rough concrete scraped my palm. I caught hold of something between two hands. My feet swung in empty air.

"Ah!" Heart hammering, I dangled from Father Serra's pointing finger.

"Oh," Charlene said. "That's not good. Hold on, Val! Quick. One of you boys get on the lap. Get on the lap!"

A siren wailed.

"The cops!"

The engineers scattered, leaping into their cars. They roared down the exit, Brittany's silver Mustang the last in the line.

A black-and-white police car and a familiar sedan rolled to a halt at the base of the statue.

Gordon emerged from the sedan and looked up at me. "Let me guess. Someone left you hanging?"

CHAPTER 11

"There's something I don't understand." Charlene perched on her wooden stool beside the door to the flour-work room. Afternoon sunlight streamed through the skylights and glittered off the metal counters. Cheerful Saturday chatter drifted from the dining room and into the kitchen.

"Like, why weren't we arrested?" I asked. "Or maybe, what made you think I'd catch that UFO? Or, why did I let you talk me into that stunt?" Movements jerky, I arranged a tongful of salad beside a slice of quiche Lorraine.

"No, I understand all that. You parkoured through Graham's front yard. Of course you'd climb Father Serra." She ripped a loose thread from the cuff of her violently violet tunic. "What was Gordon doing at that rest stop? It's miles outside his jurisdiction."

"Same thing we were doing. He got word an old TA of Starke's would be there. So he contacted a friend of his in the local PD, and they came." Fortunately, the other cop was a good friend of his, or we'd have been arrested for trespassing.

The alley door to the kitchen rattled and swung open.

Abril, wisps of near-black hair escaping from its thick knot, slipped inside the Pie Town kitchen.

"Abril!"

Charlene and I hurried around the butcher-block work island to hug her.

"Are you okay?" I asked.

She laughed unevenly. "You heard?"

"Yeah."

"It was okay." She gulped, grabbing a hairnet from the box. "Just some questions."

"They sure took a long time," Charlene growled.

Abril adjusted the hairnet over her glossy, black bun and slipped a Pie Town apron over her head. "The police were thorough."

"But why focus on you?" Charlene asked.

I nudged Charlene's tennis shoe with mine. I'd gotten the distinct impression Abril had become a suspect for good reason. Gordon thought she'd been romantically entangled with Michael Starke.

Abril colored. "It's embarrassing."

"It's okay," I said. "You don't have to tell us."

"Yes, she does," Charlene said.

"It's just—I'm so ashamed."

"Never mind," I said.

Charlene's eyes narrowed. "Ashamed about what?"

Abril tied the apron behind her back and didn't meet our eyes. She closed her eyes, her nostrils flaring, and nodded. She met my gaze. "You should hear it from me, because you'll find out soon enough."

"Maybe not," I said with increasing desperation. Couldn't Charlene just leave it?

"Professor Starke hired me to be his teaching assistant this year."

I stared. If Starke hit on all his assistants, it explained why Gordon had thought them romantically involved.

"Going to class, working at Pie Town, *and* being a TA?" Charlene asked. "That's a lot of hours."

Abril's flush turned a deeper shade of crimson.

"Oh," I said, cast iron weighting my stomach. "You were planning on quitting Pie Town."

"It's not that I don't love this place," she said hurriedly. "But I want to be an English professor someday. Working as Professor Starke's TA would have looked great on my application when I transfer to a university. It was an opportunity I couldn't pass up. You understand, don't you?"

"I do." My voice lowered, and I looked away. Well, of *course* she didn't want to work here forever. This was my dream, and she had her own, and I needed to cowgirl up. I patted her upper arm. "Honestly, it's okay. Petronella wants to become a mortician. I get that Pie Town isn't a lifetime career for most of the staff." Or for anyone but me.

Charlene coughed. "Well, at least you came clean." She took the plate from my hand and gave it to Abril. "Table twelve."

Abril bustled into the restaurant.

"Pie Town's *my* career," Charlene said.

I smiled. "Thanks."

She looked at me expectantly.

"Good thing your piecrust is the best on the coast," I added.

"But Pie Town's really just a cover for my work as a secret agent," she whispered.

"I suspected as much."

"Order up," Petronella called through the window to the dining area and spun the ticket wheel.

I pulled the ticket—an order for a banana cream pie—plated a slice, and set it on the window.

An hour later, Abril, Charlene, and I were lounging at the counter. We'd hit one of those four o'clock ebbs—the beachgoers on their way home for the day, and the locals finding it too early for pie.

"I still can't believe it," Abril said. "Professor Starke was here, right here in Pie Town. And now he's gone."

"I can believe it," Charlene said. "Your professor had an ex-wife and a horde of angry ex-girlfriends."

There was a crash from the kitchen, and I winced, rising from my barstool.

Charlene grasped my arm. "Don't do it. Hunter will take care of the mess."

With Hunter in the kitchen, none of us doubted there *was* a mess.

"He wasn't like that," Abril insisted. "Professor Starke, I mean. But . . ."

"But what?" I asked, frowning at the glass display case. It was low on pies and pies in a jar and hand pies, which was good for this time of day. But I needed to shove everything closer, fill in the gaps, so the display didn't look so empty.

"It's crazy, but I can't help thinking how ironic it was that he read that poem and then he was killed."

Charlene and I looked at each other.

"What poem?" I asked.

"You know, Val," Abril said, "the last one. That night was the launch of that poem—it wasn't published yet, and Professor Starke had never read it for anyone before."

"I didn't hear it," I said. "I was in the kitchen with Doran."

"But you must have heard it, Charlene," Abril said. "You were there."

"Mm . . ." She thumbed her ear. "Refresh my memory."

"You know, the poem about the murder. The dark parking lot. The wrong car in the spot."

Murder? My pulse accelerated.

"That was the poem?" Charlene made a face. "The meter's all wrong."

"No," Abril said. "That's what it was about. I didn't mean to rhyme."

Abril hadn't been rhyming or poeticizing for days now. The murder of her professor seemed to have knocked the poetry out of her. I hoped it didn't last.

"That's okay," Charlene said. "It wasn't a very good rhyme."

"Abril, do you have a copy of that poem?" I asked quickly.

"Who would want that?" Charlene asked. "No offense," she said to Abril. "But I prefer poems you can rap to. Like Poe."

"Well," I said, "it does seem weird that the first time he reads his new poem about a murder, he got killed."

"Oh, no," Abril said. "I didn't mean it that way. I just meant it was ironic. The poem was fiction."

"Still," I said. "I'm curious. Is there any way you can get that poem?"

She shook her head. "He didn't give away any handouts of his work."

"But he was reading off a paper," Charlene said.

"Which means Gordon might have it," I said.

The bell jangled over the front door, and I slid from the pink barstool.

Charlene grinned. "All you need to do is put on something low-cut and slinky—"

"I'm not going to Mata Hari that poem out of Gordon."

"Mata Hari?" he rumbled from behind me. "I wouldn't mind if you tried."

I lowered my head and sighed, turned, smiled. "Hi, Gordon."

Abril flushed. "Detective Carmichael."

"Thank you for your help yesterday, Abril," he said. "You cleared up a lot for us."

She smiled. "You're welcome."

A light wave of relief flowed through me. I'd hate it if things were awkward between the two of them after yesterday's questioning.

He kissed my cheek. "At least I'll never be bored with you," he murmured into my ear, and I shivered. He wore a neat blue suit and looked heavenly. "Nice to see you on terra firma," he said in a louder voice. "Now, what's this about a poem?"

"I didn't mention it at the station," Abril said, twisting her apron. "I didn't think of it then, but now it seems kind of weird."

"What was weird?" he asked sharply.

"The last poem he read that night," Abril explained to Gordon. "It's probably a coincidence, but it was about a murder."

"You must have read it," I said to Gordon. "Do you remember what it was about?"

He shook his head. "Why do you think I read it?"

"Because he had the poem on him the night he died," I said. "He read from it at Pie Town."

"There was no poem on him when we found him," Gordon said. "Maybe he threw it out after he was done?"

Charlene and I stared at each other.

Threw it out? In Pie Town?

"No," I said, horror dawning.

"Garbage comes on Monday," she said.

I shook my head. There were limits to being a Baker Street Baker. "No!"

"You're talking about the dumpster," Gordon said, "aren't you?"

"The dumpster filled with the detritus of days of rotting fruit," Abril said. It was almost poetic, and I almost smiled.

"But he was killed a week ago Friday," Gordon said. "Wouldn't the trash have already gone out?"

I shook my head. "No. We don't keep a waste basket at the front of the restaurant. Normally, napkins and things are collected by whoever's busing tables with the dirty dishes. But that night, there were some papers lying around after the reading. I tossed them into my office waste bin, which didn't get emptied until Wednesday."

"So . . . recycling?" he asked hopefully.

"San Nicholas doesn't have a recycling service for businesses yet, only residential," I said.

Grim-faced, Gordon pulled off his navy suit jacket and folded it neatly, setting it on the counter. He pulled two sets of gloves from the pockets and handed one to me. "Let's go."

"What? Me? Shouldn't only official police personnel search for evidence? What if I contaminate the chain of whatever?"

"You're a Baker Street Baker," he said, "aren't you?"

"Go on." Charlene nudged my shoulder. "It'll be fun."

"You'll help?" I asked her.

"Are you kidding? With these joints?"

I groaned. "Can you manage things here?" I asked Abril.

She nodded eagerly. And Abril usually hated working the front restaurant. But when dumpster diving was the alternative . . . well, it puts a lot of things in perspective.

Gordon and I trudged through the kitchen and into the alley.

"This one yours?" Gordon angled his head toward the closest dumpster and snapped on the gloves.

I nodded, unenthusiastic.

He lifted the lid and let it drop, clanging against the metal side and echoing down the narrow brick alley.

Noses wrinkling, we peered inside at the garbage bags.

"Any idea which are from your office trash?" He rolled up his sleeves.

"I combined it with the kitchen trash," I said, eyes watering. The slimy, smelly, rotting-in-the-late-summer-heat kitchen trash.

"Oh." He swallowed and grabbed a bag. "Let's get this over with."

An hour later, Pie Town garbage was spread across the alley, Gordon was inside the dumpster, and my gloves were sticky. Charlene sat on her wooden stool by the open kitchen door and made unhelpful comments.

I brushed sweat from my forehead with the back of my wrist. Even my wrist felt dirty.

"What about that bag?" Charlene asked, pointing.

"I already checked that bag." My gaze flicked skyward.

"Maybe you should check again."

I moved to jam my hands on my hips and thought better of it. "I'm checking this bag." I pulled it open and looked inside. Damp envelopes and a goldenrod flyer lay on top. My heart jumped. "I think I've found it!" I pawed through the papers, then grabbed them and spread them on the road.

"Anything?" Gordon asked.

"I'm not sure. This is definitely from my trash." I stared at the flyer. The tiny symbol in the corner kept drawing my eye.

"But we can't be certain Starke left his poem at Pie Town," Charlene said. "This whole affair could be a complete waste of time."

I glared at her, and she shrugged.

"Well," she said, "it *could* be."

Triumphant, I retrieved a sheet of laser paper with a double-spaced poem down the center. "This is it!"

Gordon sprang from the dumpster, which was super impressive (the leap, not the dumpster). He crowded behind me. "What's it say?"

I cleared my throat and read out loud.

Death in a Parking Lot
A woman taken,
Her ghost,
A silver shimmer on asphalt,
A gleam of the wrong fender,
In the wrong spot.

A woman found,
Upon the water,
But no one knows,
Her spirit wanders
The fateful lot.

I work my way through
And try to forget
But I stand, keys in hand
And wonder
What I am not.

There was a long silence.

A seagull landed on a bag of trash and cocked its head.

"I don't get it," Charlene said, scribbling in a notepad. "How can someone be found and no one knows?"

"You don't have to get it." Gordon plucked the page from my hand. "It's evidence."

"Of what?" Charlene asked.

"Nothing, probably," he said, "but I spent an hour digging for it in that dumpster, so it's damn well going in an evidence bag."

I winced. "I'm sorry, Gordon. I guess Abril heard something in it that we didn't."

"It's all right," he said. "Just don't tell anyone how we got it. If the guys at the station learn about this little adventure, I'll never hear the end of it."

I stooped, picking up the flyer from the reading, and pointed to its tiny symbol. "Have you seen this before?"

He squinted. "Nope."

"What?" Charlene asked, snatching the paper from his hands.

"In the lower-right corner," I said. "It's probably nothing."

She sucked in her breath. "An occult symbol."

"You know it?" Gordon asked.

"No," she said. "But look at it! If that's not occult, I don't know what is."

Lightly, he plucked the flyer from her grasp and slipped it into another evidence bag. "I'll do a reverse image search online."

Whoa. You could do that? Why hadn't I done that?

He tucked the page into another evidence bag, and helped me return the garbage to the dumpster. Unpeeling his gloves, he left.

I picked up Charlene's chair and lugged it into the kitchen. She closed the alley door behind us.

Abril poked her head through the order window. "Did you find the poem?"

"Yeah," I said, scrubbing my hands in the sink and scrubbing them again. "For all the good it did." Me and my dumb ideas. I pulled off my apron and exchanged it for a fresh one.

"Why?" Abril asked. "What's wrong?"

Charlene brandished her notebook. "This poem is useless. It's not even about a murder. A woman found, and no one knows? That doesn't even make sense!"

"Sure it does," Abril said. "Her body was found, but no one knows she was murdered. And I need a slice of blackberry pie."

"It doesn't say she was murdered," Charlene said, "just taken."

"Exactly," Abril said. "She didn't leave of her own accord. She was taken. She becomes a ghost. Something happened to her."

"It's a little, um, oblique," I said, plating the slice. Blackberries oozed from the crust, and my mouth watered. "But at least the police have the poem now."

"But they won't understand it," Abril said, "will they?"

"I'm not sure I do," I said, walking through the swinging door into the restaurant.

Charlene trailed after me.

"You just need to do a close reading." Abril gently detached the notepad from Charlene's hand. "Okay, a shimmer on asphalt. That implies night and dampness."

I glanced around the near-empty restaurant, saw a pieless diner in one of the booths, and brought him his dessert. I rejoined the two women.

"A dark and stormy night," Charlene was saying. "Gotcha."

"Her spirit's wandering the parking lot," Abril said. "Whatever happened to her, happened there."

"And the line about the water?" Charlene scratched her head with the eraser-end of her pencil.

"The author is in conflict about what happened. He may have killed the woman himself. Is he a killer or not?"

"So Professor Starke killed her?" Charlene asked.

"Well, of course not. He's no— He was no killer. He's imagining it from the killer's point of view. Don't you see?"

"All right," I said, "so it *is* fiction."

"Well," Abril said, "yeah, that's what I told you."

I lowered my head, my shoulders slumping. Had we been on the wrong track all along?

CHAPTER 12

Fortunately for we amateur detectives, Professor Jezek's Monday class schedule was posted online. Unfortunately, we were still suffering under Gordon's no-interviewing-outside-of-Pie-Town rule.

"It's not interviewing," Charlene said, stepping from the Jeep and stretching. The shadow of the sixties-era, concrete bell tower pointed across a short lawn and ended at her bumper. "It's dropping off an invitation." She walked to the rear of the yellow car and opened the door, pulling out a fishing pole.

"An invitation we could have emailed." I looked guiltily around the college's parking area.

Sun glittered off fenders in the packed lot. It had taken us way too long to find an empty visitor's spot, but we'd finally snagged one, right next to the dean's reserved space. Set high on a hill, the lot had an amazing view of the bay. The spires of San Francisco skyscrapers rose in the distance, and massive ships plied the far-off bay. I sighed. It was good to be dean.

"Any luck on that reverse-image search?" she asked.

"None." I'd tried my hand at it after Gordon had given me the idea. I'd found pieces of the symbol though. The five-spoked wheel could symbolize Vedic astrology, or Thespis, the Greek god of actors. And the snake could symbolize change, or the gods Mercury or Dionysus, or a hundred other things.

Frederick, draped around Charlene's neck, raised his head and sniffed.

"So," she said, "if its meaning is hidden, that means it's occult." She pumped her fists in the air. "Woo-hoo, we've got an occult mystery on our hands!"

"We don't know if it's occult. It could be anything. Or nothing."

"Keep on thinking that." She hooked her pie-plate UFO to the end of the fishing wire.

A breeze tossed my hair. I'd taken it out of its band because my head was starting to hurt. Though on reflection, that might not have been due to a too-tight hairdo.

"Do we have to take this pie-plate photo now?" I asked.

"No time like the present. And with this view, I can make the UFO attack San Francisco." She cackled. "When I get the perspective right, it'll look huge."

"Considering your interest in real UFOs, I'm a little surprised you're spoofing an old hoax."

A shadow crossed her wrinkled face. Charlene spun away, the UFO whizzing over my head, and I ducked.

"Aren't you over your fear of being kidnapped by aliens?" she asked. "I'm a little surprised by your own lack of enthusiasm."

I stiffened. "It has nothing to do with . . . I'm not afraid of UFOs." I'd gotten to the bottom of that phobia, rooted in an incident in my childhood when, thanks to my father, I really *had* been taken. Just not by aliens. Because they don't exist.

Probably.

"Whatever. Here. Hold this." She handed me the fishing

pole and directed me to a spot on a grassy mound overlooking the bay.

"A little to the left . . ." She peered through the camera on her phone. "A little to the right . . . There!"

After we got a photo that met Charlene's high hoaxing standards, we returned the equipment to her Jeep.

She looked up at the bell tower. "I wonder if—"

"No," I said sharply, determined to nip that bad idea in the bud.

"But—"

"I'm not dangling from a bell tower for a UFO selfie. Nearly breaking my neck on Father Serra was enough."

"Suit yourself."

We made our way to the English department.

"I do have a theory, you know," Charlene said.

"About the murder?"

"About your UFO phobia."

"I don't have one anymore." I raised my palms. "We know what caused it, and it's over." I held open a glass door, and she walked into the bleak hallway.

"Is it?" she asked.

"Sure it is."

"Because I think sometimes we hold on to things because subconsciously we get something from them."

"I get zero from a fear of UFOs." My voice echoed off the tile floor, and I snapped my mouth shut. "Which is why I'm no longer afraid."

"Your phobia doesn't remind you of anyone?"

"Who could the phobia I don't have possibly remind me of? That doesn't even make sense. There's the main office."

I strode inside a drab, seventies-era room with wood-paneled walls.

A receptionist peered up at us from behind the counter. "Can I help you?" she asked without much enthusiasm.

"Yes," I said. "Where—?"

Charlene whipped the pie-making invitation from the pocket of her pale green, knit tunic. "An invitation for Professor Jezek."

The receptionist glanced from the envelope in Charlene's hand to a row of cubbies ten feet behind her. Her expression suggested a horde of spiders might crawl from the wooden boxes.

"Professor Jezek should be in his office right now," the receptionist said.

"We'd rather not disturb him," I said.

The receptionist snorted. "Then you know Professor Jezek."

"Not that well," I said. "Is it true what they say . . . ?" Hopeful, I let that thought dangle.

"That he sacrifices co-eds and walled his mentor up in his basement?" The receptionist adjusted her glasses. "Probably not. He'd just like everyone to *think* that."

"I was thinking more about that business in the parking lot," I said.

"What business?"

"I guess I was wrong," I said. "Um, where's his office again?"

The receptionist pointed with a pen. "Number one-fifty-two. Down the hall, second right."

"Thanks." I glanced over my shoulder at the hallway behind us. "Er, have any tall, handsome men been asking about the professor recently?" Because I *really* didn't want to run into Gordon here again.

The receptionist snorted. "Why would they?"

"Great. Charlene—"

But Charlene had already disappeared from the office.

I trotted into the hallway and caught up with her outside the closed door to 152.

She rapped on the wooden door, and something crashed inside.

A curse, the sound of things being shifted. "Come in," a sepulchral voice intoned and hiccupped.

We glanced at each other, then opened the door and walked inside.

I stopped short. The walls were covered with prints of gilt icons. They glimmered, dazzling, beneath the fluorescent light. In the center of the prints was a framed, wooden icon— Saint George slaying the dragon. A black, square-shaped cross had been painted above the window.

"Suffering cats," Charlene said.

Professor Jezek looked up from his desk and tugged on his mustache. His lined face was haggard. "Can I help you?" His eyes sloped downward in his domed forehead. The professor's thick gray hair crawled over the collar of his black sports jacket.

The office smelled heavily of booze.

"Um . . . yeah," I stammered, dizzied by the shimmering walls. "I mean, no. We brought your invitation to the pie-making class."

"How kind of you to bring it personally." His gaze darted about the room as if seeking escape. "So few people understand the power of the personal touch. It's all texting these days."

Staring openmouthed at the array of big-eyed saints, Charlene pulled the invitation from her pocket. She extended it to the professor. "What's with the icons?"

His head twitched. "A tribute to my Georgian heritage, on my mother's side. Georgia the country, not the state." He plucked the envelope from Charlene's hand and opened it, pulling out the thick, paper invite. The professor scanned it. "Perfect. I shall be there. Will it be a very large class?"

"No, just you and Dorothy Hastings and Rudolph and maybe Aidan," Charlene said, gawking at the icons.

I closed my eyes briefly. *Charlene!*

He blanched. "I . . . see. These were your *randomly* drawn guests from the poetry reading?"

Whoops. I *had* told him that, hadn't I? And Dorothy hadn't been at the reading.

He steepled his fingers. His hands quivered slightly. "I suppose it was inevitable after the murder," he muttered.

"What was inevitable?" I asked.

"Everything is connected, is it not?" He frowned.

"I guess," I said, baffled. But it was as good a segue as any into a little light interrogation. "Did you know Professor Starke well?"

"As well as neighbors can, which here in California is not very well."

"You were neighbors?" I asked.

His head spasmed again. "Unfortunately, in life and in work. He had the office next door, one-fifty. Michael made the perfect murder victim. Arrogant, ignorant, and leaving a trail of destruction in his wake."

The saints stared down at me, and I shifted my weight. Was he confessing? "Who would have killed him?"

"Who was always a step behind him," he slurred, "never quite measuring up?"

"Measuring up?" I prompted.

"Professionally nor romantically," he said.

Charlene rubbed her chin. "Romantically, eh? I suppose you're talking about Professor Aidan McClary."

"Professor McClary accused Starke of plagiarism," I said. "Do you know anything about that?"

Another odd twitch of the head. "No," he said, "but it wouldn't surprise me."

"Why not?" I asked.

"Let us say that in meetings, Professor Starke had a habit of hearing other people's ideas and making them his own."

"Anyone else want him dead?" Charlene asked.

Hands trembling, he shuffled a stack of papers from one side of his desk to the other. A half-dozen pages whispered to the cheap linoleum floor. "There's always the ex-wife, Dorothy. No one knows our weaknesses as well as our exes, don't you think?"

"You think Dorothy and Aidan did it together?" Charlene asked.

"Are you aware that Aidan's visa is about to expire?" The professor hiccupped.

"So he needs tenure to stay?" I asked.

"Immigration officials don't care about tenure. But I imagine marrying an American would keep him in the country at this point."

"You mean, marry Dorothy?" I asked. "But what's stopping them? She's divorced."

"I think I'd prefer not to speculate further. Thank you for the invitation. I look forward to an . . . enlightening evening." He bent his head to the computer on his desk, his long fingers flying across the keyboard.

We edged from the room and shut the door behind us.

"For someone who'd prefer not to speculate," I muttered, "he was quick enough to throw Dorothy and Aidan under the bus."

"No wonder that receptionist thought he murdered coeds," Charlene said loudly. "Anyone who needs that many saints on his walls has got a guilty conscience. And he needs a haircut."

"Did you notice the crosses over the window and the door?" I asked, stopping in front of room 150.

"No. But we get the picture he's religious."

"That seemed like something more," I said. "I've got a friend from college who's Georgian. I'll ask her."

"You think he killed Aidan out of some religious mania?"

I studied a sheet of paper on the door. A tiny symbol had been drawn inside the O in OFFICE HOURS—a snake, caduceus, and wheel.

Uneasily, I frowned. "Here it is again." But what did it
mean?

Charlene hissed. "That symbol. It could be a warning
from a secret occult society. Maybe he was being targeted.
Maybe Starke and Jezek were occulting together, and Jezek
killed him?"

"Hm. Did you notice what Saint George was using to kill
that dragon?"

"Looked like a big spear." She snapped her fingers.
"Jezek thinks he's Saint George and Michael Starke was the
dragon. That explains the sword Starke was stuck with."

"The fact that the guy's creepy doesn't make him a murderer. I mean, even if he did have some Saint George com-
plex, what made Starke the dragon? There still needs to be
some kind of a motive."

"Crazy is a motive."

I shivered. "We don't know he's crazy."

"We don't know he's not."

CHAPTER 13

"Done!" Hunter whipped the Pie Town apron over his head, knocking his hairnet askew. He dropped the apron on the just-cleaned kitchen counter. "Can I go?"

I propped the mop against the wall and wiped my brow. After a murder-free Tuesday, I was feeling generous. "The dishes are all put away?"

He pointed to the racks, filled with steaming dishes.

"Good enough," I said. "Have a great—"

He fled out the alley door, and it banged behind him.

"—night," I finished. *Sheesh*. Was the job *that* bad?

The door to the dining area swung open, and Charlene poked her head inside the kitchen.

"What are you doing here this late?" I asked. "Did you learn something about Professor Starke?"

"No. Did you learn anything from that Georgian friend of yours?"

"I talked to her last night." I returned clean baking implements to their ceramic jars on the work island. "She said collecting lots of icons isn't uncommon. Some people do it out of a sense of Georgian pride. Others collect them because the icons are beautiful, and others because they're religious."

"Hmph. I need to use your office computer."

"Do I want to know why?"

"Probably not. Nothing to do with the murder."

"The password's *EATPIE*, all caps."

"Duh." She vanished through the swinging door.

I finished mopping and replaced the black fatigue mats, letting them fall to the floor and then nudging them into place with my feet. They were surprisingly heavy.

Grabbing my mop and bucket, I strode into the flour-work room. But I didn't start cleaning. Instead, I leaned against the central butcher-block worktable to enjoy the air-conditioning and the silence.

I flapped the collar of my *Pies Before Guys* t-shirt, trying to get some air circulating beneath the cotton. Who needed the gym next door? Lifting fifty-pound sacks of flour and shoving a mop around was plenty of exercise.

I sighed and got to work. Mopping was always the last thing I did. We worked from the top down when it came to cleaning. Having Hunter around had eased a lot of my workload in that regard, but I still didn't quite trust him to clean in the corners.

Outside, glass shattered, and my shoulders hunched. But whatever Charlene had broken, she'd deal with. Or, more likely, I'd deal with later.

I backed to the door and let myself into the kitchen. An acrid scent burned my nostrils. Startled, I turned. Smoke billowed from the restaurant through the order window to the kitchen.

Fear prickled my scalp. "Fire!"

I reached into my apron pocket for my cell phone, and then I remembered Charlene. My pulse rocketed. Was she still in my office?

"Charlene!" I plowed through the swinging door and into

a bank of gray smoke. Lungs searing, I fumbled, blind, for the office door.

I found the knob and stumbled inside, gasping.

"What'd you break?" She glared up from my desktop computer, and her eyes widened. "What—? That's smoke!"

"Fire in the restaurant. Come on."

She leapt to her feet and handed me the base of the computer, wrenched its cable from the wall.

I hurried to the door.

"Wait," she said. "Frederick!"

I turned, computer under my arm, one hand on the knob. Frederick was, as usual, draped around her neck.

"He won't know to hold his breath," she wailed. "He's just a cat!"

"He'll figure it out." I laid my hand on the door. It was cool, which meant there were probably no flames behind it.

"How? How will he figure it out?"

I grabbed a discarded silky scarf from the bookshelf and draped it over his head. "There. Take a breath!" I opened the door and grasped her hand.

We plunged into the hallway, dark as tornado weather. Panic, hot and jagged and choking, lurched in my throat. Charlene and I stumbled through the swinging door and into the kitchen. It was easier to see here, the smoke lighter. Coughing, we made our way to the alley door and stumbled outside and into the cool air.

Charlene wheezed and bent, hands on her knees. "Frederick," she croaked.

My eyes streamed as I carefully pulled the scarf from his head.

He was purring.

Setting the computer against the tire of my pie van, I called 911. I spoke in ragged, hysterical bites, frantic with worry. Now that I knew Charlene and Frederick were safe, my fear turned to the pie shop.

My bakery. I'd put everything into Pie Town. It was my life, my livelihood. Would I be able to salvage anything besides the hard drive Charlene had grabbed? And all that was good for was telling me exactly how much I'd just lost.

Drained, I slithered down the brick wall. My t-shirt bunched against my back, my phone loose in my hand.

Sirens wailed.

"It'll be all right." Charlene coughed, her face blackened by soot. "You've got insurance."

My stomach butter-churned. But would insurance cover the loss? I hadn't splurged for business-interruption insurance. Sure, fire insurance would replace what was damaged. But Pie Town would be closed during that time. My staff wouldn't be paid, and so they'd move on. Meanwhile, I'd have to keep paying rent while I wasn't earning any money. . . . I moaned.

The sirens grew louder.

"No one was hurt," Charlene said, stroking Frederick's fur. "That's what matters. We're alive to fight another day."

I forced myself to smile. "You're right."

Gordon raced down the alley, the tails of his suit jacket flapping. "Val!"

I clambered to my feet.

He pulled me into a hug. "Are you all right? What happened?"

I clung to him, and now the tears in my eyes were not because of the smoke. A despairing ache swelled behind my ribs. I shook my head and tried not to cough into his muscular chest. "I was in the flour-work room, and when I came out, there was smoke pouring from the dining area." I stepped away and grimaced. I'd left soot on his white dress shirt.

His brow creased. "The dining area? Not the kitchen?"

That . . . *was* strange. There was nothing to burn in the

restaurant itself. Unless there'd been an electrical fire. "There was a crash," I said.

"I heard it too," Charlene said. "I was editing my picture of the UFO over San Francisco, and then I heard Val break something in the kitchen."

"I thought you'd broken something in my office," I said.

"All right," Gordon said. "Wait here. I'll see what's happening with the fire department."

He strode down the alley.

Charlene and I looked at each other. I set the computer on the floor of the van. Wordlessly, we followed him around the corner and to Main Street.

A police officer stopped us outside the comic shop. "Sorry, you'll have to wait here."

Two ladder trucks blocked Main Street. Their lights cascaded across the darkened storefronts. People in workout clothes clustered outside Heidi's gym and gawked. Two uniformed policemen ordered them away.

I pressed a hand to my mouth and forced myself not to cry. Glass glittered on the sidewalk outside Pie Town. Had the firemen had to break a window? And then I remembered the crash I'd heard, and my gaze clouded.

My nemesis, Heidi, stormed down the street, her blond ponytail bouncing. She shook her finger at me. Even her knuckles looked fit. "This is just typical. Is there anything you won't do to disrupt my business?"

"Oh, put a sock in it," Charlene growled, and began hacking. She bent, hands on her knees, her body racked by rough coughs.

Heidi stepped back, eyes widening.

A chill tightened my gut. My lungs were rough after the smoke I'd inhaled, but Charlene was somewhere north of seventy. In the amber light from the street lamps, she looked greenish.

I looked around for help and spotted a paramedic truck parked slightly down the road.

"Wait here." I ran to the two paramedics, a man and woman. "My friend was in there. She's elderly and is coughing badly."

They straightened off the red truck's bumper. "Where is she?"

"This way." I raced back to Charlene, and the EMTs followed.

I fretted, and Charlene snapped, while the paramedics peered into her eyes and put an oxygen mask on her face.

"She'll be okay," the man told me. "But we're taking her to the hospital for observation."

"The hospital?" Charlene wheezed beneath her mask.

A firefighter emerged from the restaurant carrying a cannister. He conferred with Gordon and pointed to the sidewalk.

I moved toward them.

A police officer, hands raised, intercepted me.

"You'll have to stay back, ma'am."

"It's my restaurant!"

"Oh, sorry, Val." Officer Sanders grimaced. "I didn't recognize you under all the soot. But you'll still have to wait here until the fire department gives us the all clear."

Expression stony, Gordon strode to us. "It's all right," he said to the uniformed officer.

Sanders nodded and walked away.

"Is the fire out?" I asked, hopeful. *Say it's not bad. Say it's not bad.*

"There was no fire," he said.

"But— The smoke!"

"A smoke bomb. Someone kicked in your front door and tossed it inside. That must have been the crash you heard."

I went limp with relief. "Oh, thank God. I mean—that's terrible, but at least it wasn't a fire. I can fix the door."

"Yeah." His gaze didn't quite meet mine.

Something dark and cold slithered inside my gut. "Why are you not looking at me like that? What's wrong?"

"The smoke made a real mess in there."

My breath caught. "How big of a mess?"

"The fire department is checking for more incendiary devices. I'll let you know when it's safe to go inside."

I shook my head, my lips clamped together. If he wasn't telling me how bad it was, it was bad.

"I'm sure it will be okay." Gordon rested his hand on my shoulder. "There are specialists for this sort of damage."

Which wasn't in my budget to pay for. But there was insurance. I smiled tightly and brushed off some of the soot I'd deposited on his button-up shirt. "It will be fine." At least, I hoped it would be fine. "I've got to check on Charlene."

"I'll come with you."

We walked to the spot where I'd left my piecrust maker. The paramedics were loading a struggling Charlene into the ambulance.

She wrenched the oxygen mask from her face. "They won't let me bring Frederick! I can't go without him."

An exasperated EMT shook his head. "Honestly, Mrs. McCree—"

"Where is he?" I asked.

She pointed to her yellow Jeep, parked in front of the comic shop.

The white cat sat on the hood grooming himself.

"I'll take care of Frederick," I said.

"You'd better."

They pushed her gurney all the way inside the ambulance. An EMT hopped inside and shut the doors.

Gordon pulled me into a one-armed hug. "She'll be all right. Charlene's a tough old bird."

I nodded, because I was having a hard time speaking. "I'd better get Frederick."

I made my way to the Jeep.

Frederick regarded me warily, pink tongue out, one leg raised.

"Okay," I told the cat. "Charlene's going to be fine, but you and I are stuck together. So don't try anything."

He laid his head on his paws and closed his eyes.

Taking that for assent, I picked him up and, not knowing what else to do with him, laid him over one shoulder. His weight and warmth were weirdly comforting, even if he did weigh a ton.

I paced outside my pie shop. *A smoke bomb.* Who would have done this and why?

The obvious answer was that it had something to do with our investigation. Was the killer trying to scare us off? Anger replaced my anxiety, and I forced myself to think calmly.

But why kick in the door when you can just break a window? And whoever'd done it had been taking a chance with a frontal attack on a Tuesday night.

Or maybe they hadn't been. There wasn't a lot of activity on Main Street at this hour. In San Nicholas, the sidewalks tended to roll up early. The restaurant across the street was closed on Mondays and Tuesdays. There was the gym, but that was twenty-four hours, so there was no avoiding that.

It was all . . . weird.

An hour later, the fire department finally let Frederick and me inside Pie Town.

My white ceiling was dark gray. Smoke smeared the walls and left an oily film on the pink booths and tables and glass counters. Near the broken door, shards of glass littered the checkerboard floor.

I clawed my hands through my hair.

Frederick's tail curled, tickling my chin.

Gordon came to stand beside me. He set several pieces of plywood against a grimy table. "I'll take care of the glass in the door, but the lock was damaged. You'll need a locksmith. I know a guy, if you need one."

Gratitude surged through me with such force that tears sprang to my eyes. I blinked rapidly. "That would be great. Thank you."

"I'll call the locksmith." He pulled out his phone.

"Val!" Gamer Ray crunched across the broken glass and stopped short, staring. "Are you okay?"

"I'm . . . fine. How—? What are you doing here?"

"Charlene's been tweeting," he said. "She said she saved your life. How can we help?"

I ignored the lifesaving comment and focused on the last bit. "We?"

His girlfriend, Henrietta, and three other gamers piled behind him in the open door.

"Damn," she said. "Is this only a cleanup job, or do we need to repaint?"

"I'm not sure," I said, my voice wobbly.

"One way to find out," she said. "Buckets in the kitchen?"

Gordon pocketed his phone. "The locksmith will be here in an hour."

I stopped blamestorming and started cleaning. We didn't miraculously clean Pie Town overnight. The oily schmutz on the booths, tables, and counters wiped off fairly easily. The damage in the kitchen was minimal and cleanable. But the ceiling and walls in the restaurant needed repainting, and the smell . . .

I swallowed back tears. Pie Town wouldn't be opening tomorrow.

CHAPTER 14

Pie Town's front door shuddered beneath someone's fist. I took the mop I'd been using to clean the ceiling and balanced it in the bucket. Tiptoeing to the door, I peered out the bottom glass pane, since the top was covered in plywood. Two pairs of dingy male trousers stood on the sidewalk.

I unlocked the door and opened it to Tally Wally and Graham. "Hi, guys."

Outside, the fog hadn't lifted, the dour skies matching my mood.

"What's going on?" Graham demanded.

"Why aren't you open?" Tally Wally said. "It's six o'clock."

The blinds in the front windows rattled with the breeze. I'd opened all the windows in the hope the acrid smell would fade.

It hadn't.

"Someone threw a smoke bomb through the door last night." I motioned to the plywood. "We're closed today and probably tomorrow morning as well." At least it was midweek, when sales weren't at their Sunday best. If we'd had to close Pie Town on a beach weekend, I would have lost my mind. As it was, I was still stress-eating from the trauma.

Charlene waved from the bar. "Hello, boys. Come in and take a load off."

"You got coffee?" Graham asked.

She motioned to the urn. "For you, we've always got java."

They ambled past me and seized their regular seats at the counter.

"So what's the word?" Tally Wally looked around. The counters, pink booths, and tables were shipshape, thanks to Gordon and Ray and his friends.

I dunked the mop and took another swipe at the ceiling, leaving a long streak of pale gray.

"Val's got to repaint the entire ceiling again, except for the office," Charlene said. "She'll need to redo the walls in the dining area too. Fortunately, I know a guy. His team is coming this afternoon."

And the rush job was costing me a mint. But I'd rather pay extra for a speedy paint job than have Pie Town closed the rest of the week. The ceiling issue was cosmetic, but in food service, appearances counted.

I kept mopping, ignoring the ribald comments from the oldsters at the counter.

What worried me was the smell. Even though the grime had seemingly come off the furniture, the restaurant reeked. The pie oven was running this morning for our wholesale orders, but the scent of baking pies did not cover up the smoke-bomb's stench.

Depending on how quickly the paint dried, we might be open tomorrow for lunch. But paint came with its own chemical smell, and I suspected we'd have to wait to open until Friday.

Abril stacked pink boxes of pies for delivery on one of the tables. She shot me a worried glance.

Charlene and I had decided to plow ahead with the pie-making class on Thursday night. Except for some staining near the order window, the kitchen was in good shape. My jaw clenched. Which one of my pie-making students was responsible for the smoke bomb? Or was there an X factor? Someone involved we still hadn't pegged?

Graham and Tally Wally helped me carry pies to my van. I delivered them to our clients, who were still blissfully unaware of our little tragedy.

I pulled up beside a newspaper kiosk and crossed my fingers. Would the smoke bomb be small enough news to escape notice by our local paper?

Avoiding the gum stuck to the kiosk's handle, I grabbed a paper, still warm from the presses. "Oh, come on," I whined. We were front-page news.

I stormed inside Pie Town and brandished the paper. "Have you seen this?"

Charlene blew on her coffee. "Sure. They called me for an interview."

Graham and Tally Wally swiveled on their barstools.

I sputtered. "That's— This—"

"If people show up and see we're closed," she said, "they'll get angry or worried we're shut for good. This way, we get sympathy and community support. Any business on this street could have been vandalized."

"But that's the thing," I said. "It wasn't any business. It was Pie Town. What are the odds it was a prank?"

"You think this has to do with the murder?" Graham asked.

"Pie Town's always connected to murder," Tally Wally said.

"It is not! And what are you two still doing here?" Usually by this hour, he and Tally Wally were long gone. I wasn't sure if they were staying to see what happened next or if they just liked having Pie Town to themselves.

"We're here to support you," Graham said, slurping coffee. But his eyes twinkled.

"I just keep wondering why the vandal broke the door instead of the window," I said to Charlene.

"Because the door was easier to break?" she asked.

"Maybe because he or she wanted to get inside," I said. "Maybe the smoke bomb was a distraction to get us *out* of Pie Town."

Tally Wally pulled a face. "That seems like a stretch."

"Wally's right," Charlene said. "The smoke bomb didn't give them much time to themselves, if that's what they wanted." Charlene sipped from her white mug. "The fire department was here in five minutes."

We'd been lucky. The fire department was at the south end of Main Street, seven short blocks away.

"I didn't say it was a smart vandal," I grumped.

The door rattled, and I bent to see a pair of black-clad male legs. *Doran.*

My half brother never stopped by this early. Had he read the newspaper article and come to see how we were managing? I unlocked and opened the door. "Doran!"

He brushed past me. "Is Abril okay?"

Seriously? My shoulders slumped. What was I? Chopped liver? "Thanks, I'm fine," I said, my voice clipped.

His skin darkened. "I can see you're all right."

"Nice save. And I am all right, and so is Abril. She wasn't here last night, and she's in the kitchen."

"Do you mind . . . ?"

"Go ahead," I said, resigned.

He strode behind the counter and through the swinging door to the kitchen.

"There you go." Charlene raised her mug in a toast. "My plan is working."

"What plan?" Tally Wally asked.

"Operation Young Love."

"Operation Make Me Sick is more like it," I said.

"Someone's jealous," Charlene said in a singsong voice.

"I am not."

In her elegant trench coat, Marla strode inside, diamonds flashing and a Gucci purse slung over one arm. "Hm." She scanned the room, her lips pressed into a line. "It's not a *total* disaster."

"Why do you sound disappointed?" Charlene asked.

"Well, a place like this"—she motioned languidly—"the materials are all plastic and chemicals, aren't they? I expected the furniture would either melt into a puddle or be utterly indestructible. Clearly, the latter is the case. Oh, is that coffee?" She beelined for the urn.

I sighed. At least she'd finally figured out we were self-serve.

While Charlene and Marla bickered, I returned to my ceiling cleanup. If I could get the roof cleaned properly, it would save the painters time and me money. But it was slow going, and ashy water kept dripping into my face.

The bell over the door jangled.

Exasperated, I turned. "We're closed."

Brittany, the teaching-assistant-turned-engineer, hesitated, one denim-clad leg raised over the threshold. Slowly, she placed it on the checkerboard floor. "Um, have you got a minute?" She tugged on the collar of her green turtleneck sweater.

"Oh. Right! Sorry." I put the mop in the bucket and locked the front door behind her. "I thought you were a customer. You're not a customer, are you?"

"No." Her voice dropped. "I mean, I love pie, but that's not why I'm here."

"Why *are* you here?" Tally Wally shouted.

"Speak up," Graham said. "I forgot my hearing aid."

My gaze flicked to the dingy ceiling. "Come into my office."

I led Brittany past the old-folks society and into my Spartan office, shutting the door behind us. "Sorry about them," I said. "Watching the world from Pie Town is their jam."

Her gaze traversed the metal bookshelves, the dented metal desk. It stopped on the poster of the Acropolis. Charlene had taped it up last week for reasons known only to herself. "I don't mind. I'm sorry we left you high and dry at Father Serra. Did you get away?"

"In a manner of speaking."

She covered her mouth with her hand, and her brown eyes sparkled. "Oh no. You got caught."

"The police let us off with a warning due to Charlene's advanced age."

"I feel terrible."

"You getting caught too wouldn't have done us any good, so don't worry about it."

Her gaze landed on the veterans' charity calendar on the back of the door. She tapped the photo of ocean cliffs. "Acadia National Park. It's right by where I used to live."

"In Maine? When did you move to California?"

"Three years ago. Look, I'm really sorry about the thing with Father Serra."

"It's okay." I cleared my throat. "Er, is that why you came? To apologize?"

Her back straightened. "I came to hold up our end of the deal. You wanted to know about Professor Starke."

"Yes. Yes! Sit down." I motioned to the rickety chair in front of the desk. Walking to the opposite side, I sat in the rolling "executive" chair. "What can you tell me? Anything, and I mean anything, will help."

She sat and drew in a deep breath. "Okay. Well. You know we dated?"

"You and Professor Starke? Um, no. But I heard . . ." I

trailed off. Never mind what I'd heard. "So, it didn't end well?"

She sighed and clasped her hands between her knees. "It was amazing." Her brown eyes glowed.

"It was?" I asked, disbelieving.

"Michael was wonderful," she enthused. "He made me feel magical, like anything was possible. He believed in me, and then *I* started to believe in me."

"But it ended."

Her gaze shifted away, and for a moment I thought I caught something hard and angry in her eyes. In an instant, it was gone.

Brittany shrugged. "I realized English wasn't for me. I was an engineer at heart, and when I changed majors, I had to quit working for Michael. We just drifted apart. I think it really hurt him."

I shook my head. "I'm a little surprised. When we first met, I got the impression you didn't want to talk about Professor Starke, and I assumed—"

"I was a jilted lover." Her lips compressed, one corner angling upward. "I didn't want to talk about him because he'd just died. We were over, but I don't like to gossip. He really was a good guy."

"Okay. The night he was killed, at the poetry reading, he read a poem called 'Death in a Parking Lot.'"

She smiled. "Yes, he finally did it."

"Did what? Read the poem?"

"Write about it. He'd been talking about it for ages. That story got under his skin."

"What story?" Edging closer, I braced my elbows on the desk.

"Sorry—I assumed . . . Let me back up. So 'Death in a Parking Lot' is based on a true story."

Whoa. My pulse beat a little faster. "What story?"

"I don't know exactly, but Michael said it was true. It became his."

"*Became* his? What do you mean?"

"I mean he'd become obsessed with it and made it his own." Brittany leaned forward, her brows furrowed, expression intent. She tapped her finger on the metal desk, making her point. "Writers do that. He said the death happened in the college's parking lot."

Uneasy, I angled lower in my chair, and it edged backward. "The college he worked at? The college you attend?" *Was* there a connection between the poem and Starke's death?

"Right. He was planning on writing a play about the death."

"Who died in the parking lot?"

"No one. I checked."

"You checked," I repeated flatly. *Why?*

She sucked in her cheeks. "I was curious. But see for yourself. If someone died in that parking lot, it didn't make the news. And you *know* it would have made the news. Nothing ever happens around there, so when someone dies, it's a big story."

"Then it wasn't true?"

She shook her head. "No, it's like I said. He'd made it his own. That's what all great artists do."

"You mean he'd embellished." But how much?

"Art represents life, but it isn't life. If he'd just taken something that was real and repeated it, it wouldn't be art."

I fiddled with a stray pencil. In other words, the poem probably didn't have anything to do with his death. Gordon and I had gone dumpster diving for nothing. "Do you have any idea who might have wanted to kill Professor Starke?"

She blinked rapidly and studied a metal storage shelf loaded with boxes of paper napkins. "No. He was a wonderful man. A bit of a dreamer." She smiled. "I guess he didn't really see me as clearly as I liked to believe."

"What do you mean?"

She shrugged. "I wasn't exactly English professor material."

"What about his relationship with his ex-wife, Professor Hastings?"

She met my gaze, and her eyes now were damp. "They weren't like exes. They weren't bitter, I mean. They had a great relationship. He followed her to this college after they'd divorced. Dorothy wouldn't have killed him. Anyway, his relationship with Dorothy was one of the things that made him so attractive. You can tell a lot about a guy by the way he acts with his ex."

I thought of my own ex, Mark, who'd broken off our engagement. Though it had hurt like crazy then, now I was glad he'd ended things. But we still tended to avoid each other.

"Michael didn't even complain about the alimony," she continued, "and I guess it was pretty generous."

Alimony? I perked up. I hadn't even considered that. Now that Starke was dead, would Dorothy lose her alimony payments?

"Do you . . . Do you know who killed him?" she asked.

"Me? No. If I did, I'd tell the police."

Her shoulders dropped. "Oh."

I asked her a few more questions. When I got nothing useful in answer, I thanked her.

She scrawled a number on a notepad and ripped out the paper, handing it to me. "If you need anything else, call me. I'll do anything to help."

"Thanks." I showed her out, locking Pie Town's damaged front door behind her.

"Get anything good?" Charlene asked from the counter.

Marla, Wally, and Graham looked up, interested.

"I'm not sure." I trotted back to my office and woke up

my laptop, searching for a death at the college. There was nothing.

I tried other word combos but came up empty. A female professor from the college *had* died five years ago in an accident. Her car had gone over the cliffs on a bad stretch of road in San Nicholas. But nothing on campus. And if Starke's TA was right, that accident had been before Professor Starke's time anyway.

Uncertain, I rubbed the back of my neck. Was there something to Starke's poem or not?

CHAPTER 15

As I'd feared, we were closed again on Thursday. But I'd called our pie-making class "winners" to assure them class was on that night. They all arrived on time.

Our suspects stood assembled in the sparkling Pie Town kitchen. They wore our pink aprons and hairnets and eyed each other with mutual suspicion. To my relief, Dorothy had brought Aidan, so all my suspects were here.

"So." Rudolph rubbed his beefy hands together. "Your winners all work at the college. Should I be suspicious?"

I took a step backward, my body heating. "Your English department was the backbone of the poetry reading. And I had two extra spaces for tonight's class. I thought it would be more fun for you to have a class with people you knew, like Professor Jezek and Professor Hastings." I nodded toward Jezek, standing to one side, near the kitchen knives hanging from a wall magnet. He looked haggard in his tweed coat, his dark eyes sunken, his domed head covered by a hairnet.

FYI, no one really looks good in hairnets.

"It's team building," Charlene chirped from her perch near the door to the flour-work room. Tonight, she was sporting a sea-green tunic and brown leggings.

Aidan's intense gaze narrowed. "Dorothy wasn't at the reading," he said in his Irish lilt. Aidan somehow managed to look dashing, in his black button-up shirt and apron. So, okay, maybe some people *did* look good in hairnets.

"No," I said, "but I ran into Dorothy at the White Lady, and we got to talking."

Aidan whirled on her. "When were you at the White Lady?"

Dorothy tossed her golden curls, an effect ruined by the hairnet. But her seventies-era beaded earrings swung daringly in compensation. "I do have a life, you know." *Outside of you*, was the unspoken end to that sentence.

Aidan's sensual expression grew pained.

I launched into my lecture before the couple's crackling-ice tension could shatter. "The history of pie stretches back to the ancient Egyptians, who baked the filling in reeds as containers. But the first pie recipe, for a rye-crusted goat-cheese-and-honey pie, was published by the ancient Romans. By the fourteenth century, *pie* was a popular English word."

Narrow shoulders hunched, Professor Jezek took notes in a small black leather notebook. His gaze darted nervously between Rudolph, Dorothy, and Aidan.

The latter looked slightly bored and kept one hand on the small of Dorothy's back.

"These early pies were made of meat and foul," I continued, "with the birds' legs hanging over the filling as handles. The crust was known as a coffyn, with a *y*, probably because these early pies were baked in long, narrow tins, reminiscent of coffins."

"This is truly fascinating." Rudolph folded his arms over

his stomach, bulging beneath a Pie Town apron, and grinned. "I'd no idea the humble pie, pun intended, had such an intriguing history."

"It really is." I smiled at the jolly dean. "Most of these early pies were more crust than filling, but the crust wasn't eaten. It was just there to hold the filling."

"Worthless." Charlene sniffed. "The crust is the best part."

"And that leads us to our flour-work room." I strode to the metal door and opened it, motioning our guests inside. Charlene came last, shutting the door behind her.

On the long butcher-block table in the center of the room, I'd arranged place settings. Measuring cups on the right and small bowls of flour, water, and butter along the top.

"A piecrust at heart is only three ingredients," I said, "flour, water, and some type of fat."

Aidan stepped in front of the place setting beside Dorothy. Professor Jezek and the portly dean stood on the opposite side of the table, and I stood at its head.

"Flour, water, and butter, plus my secret ingredient." Charlene brandished a plastic bottle marked *SECRET INGREDIENT*.

"What's your secret ingredient?" Dorothy asked, and shivered in the cool room.

"It's secret," Charlene said, smug in her comfy knit top.

The ingredient was apple cider vinegar. Though Charlene swore to me that she added *another* secret ingredient that did not go on our recipe cards.

Dorothy raised a blond brow and opened her mouth to speak.

"It's all on your recipe card," I said hurriedly. "But the key to a good piecrust is balance and temperature. Piecrust recipes usually have several chilling periods. At Pie Town, we use this temperature-controlled flour-work room to make sure our butter doesn't get too warm. If the butter melts, the water in it will react badly with the gluten in the flour, and your dough will be more bready than flaky."

Aidan sniffed a plastic bottle of "secret ingredient," winced, and extended it to Dorothy.

"What's the ideal temperature?" she asked, ignoring him.

Aidan's forehead wrinkled, his teeth chattering.

"We like to keep the dough between sixty-five and seventy degrees Fahrenheit." I glanced uneasily at Aidan. What was bugging him? It wasn't *that* cold. "And we keep this room at sixty-five degrees, because we use butter in our piecrusts. It melts more easily than other fats, and that makes it harder to work with. But it just tastes and browns better. When you're working at home, you're making one pie at a time, so it's fairly easy to maintain a consistent temperature. But in a bakery, with ovens heating the kitchen, we need a separate space for our dough—this flour-work room."

"I'd no idea there was so much science behind baking," Rudolph said.

I beamed at the dean. "Few people do. But don't worry, all this information will be on the recipe cards I'll give you later."

Aidan grunted. "I don't know why I bother. Trying to teach me to bake is biscuits to a bear."

"This is his Irish way of saying it's a waste of time," Dorothy explained, and smiled.

The air conditioner kicked in, humming.

"Not when you know the tricks," I said. "And by the end of the night, you'll know them all. There's a reason we have the saying 'Easy as pie.' Pies are simpler than they may look."

I led them through measuring out their ingredients.

Charlene demonstrated the proper technique for rubbing in butter and flour with their fingers.

Dorothy playfully flicked a pinch of flour at Aidan's nose.

His handsome face creased in a lightning smile.

We wrapped their balls of dough in plastic and set them in the refrigerator. Because cleanup is what turns so many people off baking, I showed them how to use a plastic scraper to clean the bits of dough off the table. We followed with a wipe across the table with a clean dishcloth.

"I'll bet you wish you could clean up problems at the college this easily," Aidan said to Rudolph.

The dean stiffened. "What's that supposed to mean?"

"Alas poor Michael," Aidan misquoted, "I knew him well. And we all knew his story *too* well, boyo."

"By which you mean . . . ?" Rudolph asked.

"The plagiarism," Aidan said. "It should have disqualified him for tenure."

"Aidan," Dorothy murmured.

"Not that again," Rudolph said.

"It's rather an issue for an English professor, don't you think?" Aidan asked.

"Yes, it would be if it were true," Rudolph said. "There was no evidence—"

"My evidence!"

"Wasn't evidence," the dean finished.

"There is evil at that college," Professor Jezek intoned, his thick gray mustache quivering.

Dorothy rolled her eyes. "Boys, boys . . ."

The older man pointed a quivering finger at her. "You mock, Dorothy Hastings, but you of all people have felt this evil. You've been touched by the darkness."

"And you're a lunatic," she said.

"Because I see something is very wrong with this department?" His bushy gray brows lifted.

"Because of you and your damn trees." Dorothy slapped her dishcloth on the table.

I started. Hold up. Professor Jezek and Starke had been

neighbors. Had it been *Starke's* trees Jezek had complained about when he wrote those letters to the online paper?

"So much loss." Professor Jezek shook his graying head. "First Theresa, then Michael."

My breath caught. *Theresa?* I edged closer. Who was Theresa?

"And the last with Dorothy's own sword," the dean said, lowering his voice.

"I didn't kill him," she flared.

"Of course you didn't," Aidan said. "Obviously, someone was trying to implicate you."

"Or they grabbed what was handy," Dorothy said. "It was a mugging. Michael was at his car, someone saw him, he looked well-off—"

"But did he?" Professor Jezek asked.

"None of this is helping anyone." The dean's round face creased. "Perhaps we should return our attention to our hostess."

I cleared my throat. *"Anyway*, since apples are in season, I thought we'd bake salted-caramel apple pies tonight."

I led them through making the salted-caramel apple sauce. Then I let them take turns using the apple peeler and corer.

"The best apples for pies are Granny Smiths," I said. "Combined with the sugar, they give the perfect balance of crisp and juicy."

At their kitchen workstations, they mixed sugar and spices into their ceramic bowls of sliced apples. "Now here's another secret to perfect apple pies," I said. "We're not going to use the mixture you just created."

"What?" Dorothy jammed her hands on the hips of her loaner apron. "Then what was the point?"

"For the perfect apple pies," I said, "you should let your apple mixture sit overnight. The sugar will draw the liquid from the apples. That way, when you bake them the next day, you won't get a soggy filling."

"So what do we do with the juice?" Dorothy asked. "Just throw it away?"

"No, no, no," I said. "That juice is gold." I pulled bowls of apples I'd mixed that morning from the refrigerator, and swapped them for the bowls in front of my students. "I made these last night. Now, you're going to pour off the juice into the sauce pans at your workstations."

I worked with my students as they reduced the juices to a thick syrup and poured it back into their bowls.

I returned to the flour-work room for their wrapped and labeled rounds of dough. So no one accidentally got their fingers mashed, I ran the dough through the flattening machine myself.

Looking wary, they spread their dough in the pie tins. My students mounded the tins with apples, then poured salted-caramel sauce over the fruit mixture. I showed them how to lay a second sheet of dough on top without breaking it.

"Crimping the crusts is just a matter of tearing off any extra dough along the edge." I demonstrated. "Now, fold the bottom crust over the top. Then, using both hands, take your thumbs and index fingers and pinch the dough together."

"Mine's in tatters," Aidan said, frowning.

"Don't worry," I said. "No one will care when they try your pie. Now comes the part where we get to show off." I handed out extra sheets of dough and plastic cookie cutters shaped like apples and cornucopias and leaves.

Charlene led them in cutting out pieces of dough and decorating their pies, then brushing them with egg whites.

Since we were baking only four pies, we weren't using the big oven today. I slid the pies into one of our smaller ovens.

"And now, while we wait for those to bake," I said, "we'll make a no-bake chocolate cream pie."

I had them whipping up cream pies in no time.

"Yes, that's perfect," I said to Professor Jezek.

"Thank you."

Catching a whiff of vodka on his breath, I smoothed my apron and frowned. Did he have a secret flask in the pocket of his rumpled blazer? Was he drinking and blending? The older man whipped the chocolate cream with furrowed brow. The roar of his machine muted the conversation nearby.

Aidan left his mixing bowl to glare at Rudolph. "I was passed over for tenure because of that plagiarist."

Casually, I edged closer to Aidan.

The dean grimaced. "You were passed over for tenure, because it's unclear if you even plan to stay with the college."

"Of course I plan to stay with the college!" The Irishman reached up as if to claw back his wavy black hair and remembered at the last moment it was in a net. His hand dropped to his side. "Is this about my immigration status?"

"No, it's not," Rudolph said. "That would be against college policy."

"Aidan." Dorothy came to him and put a hand on his arm. "Now isn't the time."

Aidan stabbed a long finger at the dean's chest. "You and your damned policies. They always managed to work in Starke's favor."

"That's not true," the dean said.

Dorothy laughed. "Of course it was, and it made you crazy, Rudolph. I know you tried to cut funding for Michael's teaching assistants. But he always tied you up in policy knots."

The dean removed his round glasses and polished them on the shirt beneath his pink apron. "I don't know where you heard that—"

"From Michael," she said. "He told me you were furious and that he laughed in your face."

Rudolph replaced his wire-frame glasses. "I assure you, Michael was exaggerating."

"That I can believe," Aidan muttered.

"Just because I can't give you the extra hours you want," Rudolph said, "is no reason to attack me, Dorothy."

Dorothy needed extra hours?

"You can't bring in an outsider to take Michael's classes," she hissed. "It isn't fair to me or Aidan."

"And this isn't the time," Rudolph said.

Dorothy must have lost her alimony when Starke died. That meant Dorothy had a strong motive to keep her ex-husband alive. But if she wanted him alive for the alimony, then that could also explain her unwillingness to marry Aidan. If she re-married, she'd probably lose the alimony, which Brittany had said was "generous."

The other two seemed to notice me. One corner of Aidan's mouth quirked upward, and my face warmed.

"Best keep an eye on Jezek," Aidan said as he passed me. "He looks ossified."

Dorothy shot me a look sharp enough to cut an overdone steak. The two ambled back to their workstation.

"How's the pie coming?" I asked the dean brightly.

Rudolph sighed. "I suppose you heard all that?"

"I did," Charlene said, appearing suddenly at my elbow.

I started, pressing a hand to my heart. "I guess we kind of did. Sorry."

"You have nothing to apologize for," he said. "You have no idea what it's like on campus. The smaller the stakes, the bigger the infighting. But in the end, it's much ado about nothing."

"Not nothing if it got someone killed," Charlene said.

"Er, yes," the dean said, "but as Dorothy said, Michael's death was most likely a mugging."

I forced a smile. "I'm sure it was." *Not.* "Let me help you with that pastry tube."

"What," he said, "the squeezy thing for making dollops?"

"Yeah." Charlene rolled her eyes. "The squeezy thing."

The lesson went downhill from there. Jezek and Dorothy argued about whether women were oppressed in the humanities department. Aidan stormed off for a reason I wasn't able to discern, leaving his apple pie behind.

Charlene and I shuffled the remaining students out the door with their pink boxes of pies and locked up.

She rubbed her hands together. "I'd call that a success."

"You're right. Everyone came, no one got killed, and just think of all the petty rivalries that we uncovered for Gordon. We learned a lot tonight."

"Damn skippy," Charlene said, plucking a mallet from its hook on the tile wall. "Even better, we've learned Aidan's a vampire."

CHAPTER 16

"A vampire? Really?" I eyed the mallet swinging in Charlene's hand. She wasn't thinking of staking him, was she?

Just in case, I gently plucked the potential weapon from her grasp and slid it into a drawer. At least Charlene didn't think Aidan was Bigfoot.

"Think about it." She boxed Aidan's salted-caramel apple pie. "That weirdly smooth, white skin! It's like a twenty-year-old's!"

I leaned against a metal counter and folded my arms over my apron. "So Aidan uses sunscreen."

"He's hypnotized Dorothy with his vampire eyes. Why else would someone like her put up with his jealousy?"

"Because love is strange?"

She shrugged into her brown, hip-length knit jacket. "And killing someone with a sword. That's old-school, vampire-style."

"Okay, I admit I wondered if Aidan killed Starke. They were arguing right before Starke died. Aidan was dating Starke's ex, so there's probably some jealousy there. And

with Starke out of the picture, Dorothy might be more willing to marry Aidan and keep him in the country. But there
are so many things we still don't know. We haven't verified
that she's getting enough alimony to make staying single
worthwhile—"

"Staying single can be worthwhile for the right person.
But I'll never regret getting married." She sighed. "Those
were happy days."

"And we have only Professor Jezek's word that Aidan
was on the verge of getting kicked out of the country—"

"I knew vampires would come to San Nicholas eventually. It's the fog. It blocks the sun."

Right. Logic. Who cared?

While she scrawled notes in her casebook, I finished wiping the metal counter and cast my gaze around the kitchen.
We'd confined the pie-making class to a small area, and the
cleanup went quickly. Even better, you couldn't smell the
new paint. The scent of our students' freshly baked pies
hung heavy in the air, smothering any fumes.

I jammed my hands on my hips and grinned. Pie Town
would be open for business again tomorrow.

I tugged my apron over my head and hung it on the hook
behind the kitchen door. "But if Aidan is the killer, does that
mean that business with the downed wire in his yard was
just an accident?"

"I've seen this before."

"You've seen downed power lines before?"

"Vampires!"

"Hm." I shrugged into my Pie Town hoodie. I loved
Charlene, and I could take her supernatural sensibilities in
stride. They made life more interesting for us both. But I
didn't like where this was headed. "And when Aidan's not
biting people on the neck, what? He's teaching classes at the
local college?"

"Vampires use regular human jobs as cover." She taped

the edges of the pink box. "That's why he left his pie be-hind."

"Because he has to work as a college professor?"

"Because he can't eat normal human food. Only blood. Have you ever seen him in the sunlight?"

"No, but—"

"Little wonder someone tried to electrocute him. Not that electrocution would have done any good. Everybody knows only sunlight, fire, beheading, or a stake through the heart can kill a vampire." Charlene tugged down her knit jacket. "The jury's out on silver."

She grabbed the pink box off the counter and walked to the alleyway door. "Well?" she asked over her shoulder. "Are you coming?"

"You want to take Aidan his pie," I said, realization kicking in along with a side helping of dread.

"He paid for this pie, and your classes are expensive. The vampire's earned this pie."

"We gave them the class for free." I crossed my arms. "And my class prices are in line with courses at comparable restaurants."

"We failed at delivering a pie to Aidan last time. So try, try again, I say. It still makes a good excuse to detect." She sailed out the alley door.

I hurried after her and locked the heavy door behind me. The alley smelled vaguely of dumpster, and the light above the door flickered and buzzed.

I was curious about Aidan too—not because of Charlene's vampire theory. That was nuts. But he'd been tense and angry. And that made for a bad combination when Charlene was on a mission. She was so going to get herself into trouble.

She started her yellow Jeep, her headlights flooding the alley with a sulfuric glow.

There was no way I was going to stop Charlene when she

was hell-bent on doing something. The best I could hope for was containment. I trotted to her Jeep and swung into the passenger side.

Charlene pointed at the passenger seat. "Watch out for the pie!"

I froze, my butt suspended over the pink box. Leaning awkwardly against the back of the seat, I slid the pie from beneath me and set it on my lap.

The Jeep lurched forward. I made a frantic grab for the seatbelt.

We barreled down the alley and went onto two wheels making the turn.

"This is a twenty-five zone," I creaked out.

"Eh. No one's out at this hour. And we've got to get to Aidan's before it becomes too late for pie deliveries."

We bounced across Highway One and into a residential area. Charlene slowed a block from Aidan's house and turned off her lights, gliding to a halt across the street. Lights shone from the two brown Victorians opposite. Both Aidan and Graham were in their matchy-matchy homes tonight.

"If he's a vampire," I said, "it won't matter if your lights are off. Don't they have super hearing?"

She patted my knee. "I'm glad to see you can finally admit the possibility of a supernatural element to this case. There are flashlights in the glove compartment. If worst comes to worst, we can blind him with their combined beams."

I opened the door, climbed out, and grabbed the pie and flashlight. "I'll be right back." I jogged across the street to Aidan's. Grabbing and going was a little mean of me, because I could move faster than Charlene, but who knew what she'd do?

"Good idea!" she called after me.

That should have made me suspicious, but I ignored the twitch between my shoulder blades and trotted onward.

The pond that had covered Aidan's front yard had vanished, leaving a soggy lawn in its place.

Diverting from the Victorian's concrete path, I sloshed across the spongelike ground to the plum tree. I shined my light at the broken branch. A thin sliver of wood, raw on top but with bark on the bottom, stuck from the tree. The break looked like it was vertical. As if someone had yanked downward to snap the branch?

I looked closer. The inside of the branch was green. Would a live, thinnish branch like that have snapped *downward* in the wind?

I returned to the path, scraping the bottoms of my muddy shoes on a rock before climbing Aidan's porch steps. A bicycle leaned against the front window beside a wilting Boston fern.

I knocked on the front door. Waited.

Knocked again.

Waited again.

I knocked harder.

Was our pie delivery scheme going to be thwarted? Twice? I didn't want to leave the pie on the porch. Raccoons would probably get it and leave a ginormous mess.

"You keep him busy," Charlene called from somewhere in the darkness. "I'll go around back."

"What?" I spun.

The light from her flashlight bobbed low and to the right of the porch.

"Charlene," I whispered. "Wait!"

I hesitated, turning to the door and back to the steps, torn between waiting for Aidan and stopping Charlene.

Setting the pie on a carved and paint-flaking banister, I trotted down the stairs and around the corner. There was no high fence to hide us from view, just the strip of ivy that Graham had claimed was rat-infested.

Rats. I shivered.

Charlene's flashlight bobbed ahead of me.

"Charlene!" I whisper-shouted. "We can't be here. It's trespassing!"

She rounded the corner.

"Come back! Charlene! Urgh." I hurried down the concrete path.

Charlene yelped.

Something metallic clanked.

Her flashlight rolled around the corner of the house and rattled to a stop at my feet.

My heart stopped. "Charlene?" I croaked, frozen in place. Oh, God. What had happened?

My heart made up for its earlier lapse and banged erratically against my ribs. I scooped up her flashlight, my palms sweaty on the cool metal, and crept forward. "Charlene?" I called, hoarse.

I rounded the corner.

Charlene stood with her hands on her hips. "Take a look at this."

My shoulders slumped, and I breathed normally again. "Charlene! We can't—" The beam of my flashlights illuminated a sparkle of glass on pavement. I followed the trail of broken glass to a shattered glass door with a picnic bench halfway through.

"Vampires," Charlene said. "It's their work all right. They've got super strength."

"I could have thrown—" I shook my head. Was I really going to argue about vampires? I crunched through the glass. "Hello . . . ? Aidan . . . ? Is anyone in there?"

"We've got pie," Charlene bellowed.

A window scraped up in the house next door. "Did someone say pie?" Graham's voice floated through the darkness. His bulky silhouette leaned from an upstairs window.

"Yes! Hi, Graham," I said, thinking fast. "We brought you a pie. But there seems to have been a break-in at your neighbor's."

"Damn kids! I'll call the cops."

"Thanks, we'll—" I looked around.

Charlene had vanished from the yard.

I closed my eyes. *No, no, no. Not at a crime scene!* I turned and shined my flashlight into what appeared to be Aidan's living room.

My elderly piecrust maker stood beside a couch and stared down at the carpet.

"Charlene! Get out of there before you—we get arrested."

"I was wrong," she said in a small voice.

"It's okay," I hissed, motioning frantically. "Just get out of there before the cops arrive."

"Aidan wasn't a vampire."

"He wasn't . . ." Lead weighted my stomach. I moved forward, unthinking. Unthinking, I walked up the concrete step. Unthinking, I stepped over the fallen bench. Unthinking, I joined Charlene by the corpse of Professor Aidan McClary.

CHAPTER 17

I spent the next morning trying not to think about Aidan, dead. So of course, that was all I could think about. Not even serving pie helped. The sight of Doran through the order window, walking into the restaurant, didn't even lift my spirits.

My brother passed the rapidly filling tables and pushed through the Dutch door. I extracted my head from the order window and turned toward the kitchen door.

"I've got someone." A black-clad Doran strode past Charlene, sitting on a barstool that braced open the door.

Trailing behind him was a young African American woman with cheekbones to die for and an impressive Afro.

"Oh," I said. "Oh, wait!"

The young woman froze, her eyes widening. What looked like a vintage sixties scarf was knotted around her neck, and she wore an army-green safari jacket.

"Sorry," I said, pointing to my own hairnet. "It's just, the both of you, we're a commercial kitchen."

I scowled at the hairnet-free Charlene, Frederick draped

over one shoulder. The white cat was banned from the kitchen, but Charlene's toes were just outside the door.

"But Angie used to work for Starke," Doran said.

I frowned harder. If anything, Aidan's murder last night had made me both more determined to investigate and to keep my little brother out of it.

Gordon hadn't been thrilled to find us at another crime scene last night. Fortunately, Graham had heard the crash of the glass door breaking. He'd confirmed that Charlene and I had arrived well after that. Not that Gordon would consider us suspects, but he had to report to Chief Shaw.

Charlene angled her head toward the hallway. "Let's go into my office."

My office, but I didn't argue, shepherding Doran and the newcomer toward my inner sanctum. I paused in the short hall to peek into the dining area. It was a sunny Friday afternoon, and the restaurant was getting crowded. I followed them into my office.

Angie's gaze traversed the office. Metal shelves. Uninspired linoleum. A slightly tilting chair in front of the battered metal desk. Charlene and Frederick. The corners of Angie's mouth turned down. "Should a cat be in a commercial kitchen?"

"He wasn't in it," Charlene said loftily. "He was outside it."

I peeled off my disposable gloves and stuck out my hand. "Frederick's got narcolepsy and needs special care. I'm Val."

Warily, she shook it, her grip firm. "Angie."

"She was Professor Starke's first teaching assistant." Doran sat against the desk. "Four years ago."

"We're investigating his death," Charlene said.

"No," I said quickly. "Not investigating. That would be illegal without a private investigator's license."

"Then what?" Angie asked.

Doran snorted. "They're just nosy."

"You weren't so fussy earlier, kid." Charlene slammed the door behind her, and the veterans calendar fluttered to the floor.

Frederick looked up, his white ears flicking, then settled his head back on her shoulder.

My piecrust specialist's nostrils flared. "We've solved multiple homicides."

"Multiple?" Angie asked skeptically. "How many is multiple?"

Charlene touched her gnarled fingers together, her lips moving silently. "Does it count if it's the same killer?"

"Yes," Angie said.

"Let's stay on Starke," I said. "You say you worked for him four years ago?"

Angie nodded, her hoop earrings swinging. "He'd come from a college on the East Coast."

"Do you know why?" I asked.

She lifted one shoulder. "He said he wanted a change. I think he was following Dorothy."

"His ex-wife?" I motioned to the chair, and she shook her head. It did tend to rock a bit, because one leg was shorter than the others, but it only *looked* dangerous. "I heard they were on good terms after their divorce," I said.

"Too good," she said, "if you ask me."

Charlene balanced on the tips of her high-tops. "What do you mean?"

Angie's expression turned wry. "Michael was a hopeless romantic, by which I mean he hopelessly romanticized the women in his life. Every woman was a mysterious goddess." She cocked her head, her gaze losing focus. "It was incredibly empowering." She straightened, her lips flattening. "Until it was over."

I stuck my hands in my apron pockets and frowned. Gordon and I were in that honeymoon phase of our relationship.

Everything he did was adorable—even the things that would normally irritate me. I hoped we weren't headed for a hard fall. But we were adults, and not delusional fantasists.

"In other words," Charlene said, "you fell off the pedestal."

Frederick's whiskers twitched.

Angie nodded. "Guilty. No woman could live up to Michael's fantasy. I mean, at first, I felt like I *was* the woman he envisioned. But then it got frustrating living up to his standards. And then he realized I wasn't who he'd thought, and bye-bye."

"And you were his teaching assistant?" I asked.

She nodded. "It was a new program for the college, sort of a training for teaching assistants. The assumption was we'd go on to universities and grad schools and could become teaching assistants there."

"And the administration didn't mind Starke poaching students for his personal life?" Charlene asked.

"They didn't know," she said, "and I was over eighteen."

There was still a big power imbalance—teacher/student, older man/younger woman, employer/employee. But I said nothing. It had happened, and Starke was dead.

"Any reason one of his girlfriends would want to kill him?" I asked.

Doran shifted against the desk.

"Well, I didn't," she said. "I mean, the breakup was painful, but aren't they always? And it was years ago."

"Someone accused Starke of plagiarism," I said. "Did you see any indications of that when you worked for him?"

"Plagiarism?" Angie's eyebrows shot skyward. "No way." She tugged on her plump bottom lip. "But . . ."

"But what?" I asked.

"Well, you know, *ideas* aren't copyrighted."

"He took other people's ideas?"

"No, not exactly. He kept an idea file of news stories and such, and then he'd mix and match ideas to create something original. That's often how creativity works. You take two or three ideas and mash them together to get something new."

"So 'Death in a Parking Lot' might not have even happened in a parking lot," Charlene said.

"What?" Angie asked.

"It's a poem Professor Starke read the night he died," I said. "Someone suggested he'd plagiarized the story. Someone else told us it might have been based on a true story."

"Well, if it was true, his poem wouldn't have been plagiarism," Angie said. "It's not unusual or necessarily unethical to dramatize a true story. I mean, there are some ethical gray areas, but it's done all the time."

"Especially if he had direct knowledge of the event," I said, leaning one hip against the desk. "His poem was written in the first person."

"There you go," she said. "Not plagiarism."

Frederick sneezed.

"Did you know Professor Aidan McClary?" I asked.

She rolled her eyes. "Oh my God. He was crazy! I mean, that Irish accent is amazing, but he played the impassioned Irishman cliché to the hilt."

"So no rumors of anything odd or unusual about him?"

She shook her head. "He gave me an A. That was all I cared about."

"Thanks." Charlene reached into the pocket of her knit tunic and handed Angie a card. "If you think of anything else, call us."

She flushed. "Doran said something about a pot pie . . . ?"

"After taking up her time," Doran said, "I figured a free pie was the least we could do."

"Sure," I said. I led Angie into the restaurant, and she selected a chicken curry pot pie. Under the interested gazes of Tally Wally, Graham, and Marla, I boxed the pie and saw her to the door.

Its bell jingled lightly.

"Where'd you find her?" I asked Doran, who'd trailed us into the dining area.

He made a face. "I've been building contacts on college campuses, and they put out feelers for me. I often work with copywriters, and that means English departments."

"Nicely done." Bracing one hand on the cash register, I glanced at the avid faces of my regulars at the counter.

My brother shrugged, his motorcycle jacket creaking. "I don't think it helped much."

I bit my bottom lip. Should I tell him it wasn't helpful, to discourage him from investigating? Or should I make him feel better? "I don't see where any of this is going either," I said in a low voice, "but we're at the information-gathering stages. When we know more, we'll be able to take everything and piece it together. It's like a puzzle."

"Ever get stuck with leftover pieces?" he asked.

I changed the subject. "Did you hear about Professor McClary's death last night?" I asked more quietly, edging from the eavesdroppers at the counter.

He straightened. "What? No! Does Abril know?"

In a whisper, I told him about how Charlene and I had found the professor.

He pulled his phone from his jacket pocket. "This is bad. Abril could be in danger."

"How do you figure that?" I asked.

Charlene strode behind the counter, narrowed her eyes at Marla, and pushed through the Dutch door. Finding an empty stool between the register and her fremesis, she sat. Charlene planted her elbow on the counter, blocking Marla's view of Doran and me. "Figure what?"

Doran's head bent toward his phone, his thumbs flying across the keypad. "The murders have to be connected to the college," he said in his outside voice, "and she was working for Starke."

I glanced at the counter regulars, who'd stopped pretending to drink coffee and stared avidly.

"Abril hadn't started working for him yet," I whispered, hoping he'd take the hint and lower the volume.

He blew out his breath. "She's on her way here," he said loudly, not taking the hint at all.

"Now?" I asked, surprised. "Abril worked a morning shift. She's not due back until tomo— Oh. You mean to meet you." My brother and Abril seemed to have bonded quickly if she was dropping everything to meet him. Or maybe she just wanted to learn more about our interview with Angie. Or maybe their budding relationship hadn't been so quick, and I just hadn't noticed.

I studied Doran's pensive face, and my chest squeezed. Abril was a good person, and I knew she wouldn't lead him on. But that didn't mean he wouldn't get hurt.

The bell over the door jingled.

Gordon strode into the restaurant holding a massive bouquet of daisies. He met my gaze and smiled, the corners of his emerald eyes crinkling.

My heart jumped. He'd been freakishly Zen after catching me at another crime scene last night. I hadn't quite trusted his reaction and had been waiting for the other cast-iron pan to drop.

Tally Wally whistled. "Flowers? For me? You shouldn't have."

"I didn't." Gordon leaned across the counter and kissed me. "Hey."

"Hey back," I said. "What's with the flowers?"

He handed me the bouquet—gerbera daisies in a rainbow of colors. "They're for you."

"They're beautiful," I said, smiling uncontrollably. "Thank you."

"Hi, Doran," Gordon said.

My brother muttered something and slunk to the other side of the counter, next to Graham.

"I don't think your brother likes me," Gordon murmured.

I sighed. "I don't know him well enough to say."

"That was a heavy sigh." Gordon massaged my shoulder, and I leaned closer. "What's going on?"

I steered him into the hall and to a spot outside the kitchen door, where I could keep an eye on Charlene. "Doran told me he was leaving San Nicholas, but about two minutes after he said that, he saw Abril and got all googly-eyed. Now he's convinced she's in danger."

"I guess I can see that," he said, "after what happened to Professor McClary."

My mouth went dry. I stepped away to get a better look at him. "Wait. You think Abril's in danger too?"

"No, but I can see why Doran would worry. I worry about you too."

"Gordon, about last night—"

He raised his palm. "Don't say it. I know who you are, and I knew what I was getting. But it's a good thing Chief Shaw was out of town last night. Otherwise, you'd probably be sitting in the pokey charged with interfering in an investigation."

The pokey? "We called 911 right away—"

He lowered his head and gave me a look. "After you'd invited all the suspects to Pie Town for an Agatha Christie–style interrogation. Yes, I told you listening for gossip in Pie Town wasn't out of bounds. But that doesn't mean you can lure suspects into your kitchen for the third degree."

I swallowed. "I know. I stepped over the line. I should probably be the one bringing *you* flowers. So what gives?" I angled my head toward the daisies, their stems damp in my hand.

"There was a break-in at the nursery. The daisies reminded me of you."

"Aw . . ." I warmed. Even when he was annoyed with me, he was still thinking nice things. And—oh my God—we were totally honeymoon-phase fantasists!

"What's wrong?" he asked.

"It's just . . . I mean, aren't you even a little mad?"

"Do you want me to be?"

"No, of course not, but . . ."

Marla leaned closer on her barstool.

"But what?" he asked.

I swallowed. "I know we've had this conversation before, about boundaries between your job and my, um, the Baker Street Bakers."

His lips quirked. "Go on."

I opened my mouth and closed it, because I wasn't sure where I was going with this. Why was my stomach knotting, my hands clammy on the flowers?

"Charlene told me she went to Professor McClary's house and you were pretty much forced to follow," he said.

"She did?"

"Well, not in so many words, but I got the gist."

"But you said that wasn't what was bothering you," I said. "It was us inviting the suspects to Pie Town."

"Nothing is bothering me today. My father does not have bladder cancer."

I blinked. "Does not—" Wait. Bladder cancer? "That's wonderful, but you mean you thought he had?" And he hadn't said anything about it to me. My mother had died from breast cancer. I knew that dread fear. Why hadn't he said anything?

"The doctor wasn't sure, so I didn't want to say anything."

"But you know you could have, right?" I asked, worried.

"I know." He kissed me again. "Listen, I'm on duty, so I've got to go. But I'll call you tonight."

"Great. And thanks again for the flowers. They've really brightened my day."

I watched him walk out the door, a sinking feeling in my gut. He hadn't told me something important, and he hadn't blown up when I'd clearly crossed a line. I wanted to think it was nothing. He'd brought me flowers, after all. But I couldn't shake the feeling that something was very, very wrong.

CHAPTER 18

Marla swiveled her barstool to face Pie Town's front door. She braced her elbows on the counter. "Ah, young love." The older woman eyed me. "Well, in your case, not *that* young."

Oh, please. Marla was a well-preserved seventy if she was a day. She and Charlene had gone to school together.

"Put a cork in it, Marla," Charlene growled. Limp on her shoulder, Frederick rumbled a warning.

The cheerful voices of customers filled the restaurant. The gamers were in their usual corner booth. Afternoon sun slanted through the mini blinds and across the black-and-white-tiled floor. The front door had been repaired, crystal clear glass filling the top and bottom panes.

"Why, it's obvious something's wrong." Marla tapped a bejeweled finger on her chin. "Just look at Val's face. It's the face of someone about to get dumped. At least you're not at the altar this time."

"I wasn't at the altar the first time," I said calmly. "The breakup was mutual and pre-wedding." Even if I'd already bought the rotten dress.

Graham and Tally Wally pretended not to listen and blew on their coffees.

Marla pressed her hands to her chest, framing her gold anchor pendant. "So brave. So very, very brave."

"Can I get you a slice of pie?" I asked pointedly.

A half-dozen tourists walked through the door, looked around, and ambled to the counter.

"Oh, no." She smoothed her hands over her blue-and-white-striped knit shirt. "I'm sticking with coffee. I need to watch my girlish figure."

"You haven't been a girl since the Japanese bombed Pearl Harbor," Charlene snapped.

I could see there would be no winners in this argument. So I took orders from the new arrivals. Then I returned to the kitchen and sent Hunter into the dining area to bus tables and Petronella to man the register. The ovens were off at this hour, the pies baked for the day, and I wanted to think. Pie Town was oddly crowded with tourists, even for a September Friday afternoon. After our closure due to the smoke bomb, we could use the business, so I wasn't sure why I was looking this gift horse in the mouth. Natural suspicion, I guess.

Plus, I had the gnawing feeling Angie had said something important, but I couldn't figure out what it was. Busying myself placing orders for tomorrow's deliveries didn't clarify matters. Neither did figuring out tomorrow's specials, or plating customer orders spun through the kitchen window.

Petronella whirled the ticket wheel, and six new orders for pie appeared. Giddily, I plated the pies and shoved them through the order window. Woot! That was a pleasantly big sale. "Order up!"

And more orders kept coming. This was the time for people to stop by to take pies home, not to order pies by the slice. I adjusted my apron strap and shoved another order through the window. Not that I minded the boom, but what was going on?

An hour later, Charlene strolled through the swinging kitchen door. "You've got a visitor in your office."

I wiped my hands on my apron. "In my office? Who is it?"

"Professor Hastings, Dorothy Hastings. And since Marla's still loitering at the counter—"

"Say no more." I raised a hand, palm out. "The office it is."

I hurried through the door and paused behind the counter. Petronella leaned one elbow on the register and stared, eyes narrowed, at the full tables.

Was a convention in town?

"Petronella, I've got to talk to someone." I motioned down the hall. "Are you okay here for a few minutes?"

"Yeah, yeah." She waved me off.

Charlene followed me into my office, which was getting more of a workout than usual on a Friday afternoon.

Arms crossed, Professor Hastings paced in front of my desk, her Shirley Temple curls bouncing.

"Professor Hastings," I said, "I'm—"

"This is your fault!" Her eyes were red-rimmed, and she'd missed a button on her long white blouse.

Charlene quietly shut the door behind her and leaned against it.

"I'm so sorry for your loss," I finished, my shoulders curling forward.

"Are you? Michael comes to Pie Town and dies that night. Aidan comes to Pie Town, and he dies! Do you detect a pattern?"

When she put it that way, it did look a little odd. I swallowed, my throat thick, not knowing what to say.

"Why did you really invite us here last night?" Her arms dropped to her sides.

My cheeks heated. In the face of her grief, I couldn't bring myself to lie. "Because I thought one of you had killed Professor Starke, and I wanted to know why."

She gaped. "Are you kidding me?"

"Now, now," Charlene said, leading her to the wobbly chair. "Why don't you sit down, and I'll get you a cup of coffee. Or would you prefer tea?"

"Tea."

"I'll be right back." Charlene bustled from the room.

The professor and I stared at each other, the silence stretching and thickening.

When Charlene returned with the tea and a saucer filled with sweetener packets, I blew out my breath.

"Take your time." Charlene handed Professor Hastings the mug and saucer.

"If what you say is true, if you really believed one of us killed Michael, then you put Aidan in a room with a killer," the professor said.

"If you believe that's true," Charlene said, "then we didn't put them together. The pack of you work together on a regular basis."

Guilt curdled my insides. Had the pie-making class precipitated another murder? But no, I didn't think so, because someone had tried to electrocute Aidan McClary earlier.

"That night of the storm," I said, "Charlene and I went to the home of Aidan's neighbor. There was a downed power line in Aidan's flooded yard."

"I told Aidan to get that fixed." Dorothy's voice hitched. "He had it wrapped around a tree branch."

"I looked at the branch later," I said. "It looked like it had broken downward."

Professor Hastings looked at me blankly.

"The wind wouldn't have broken it that way," Charlene said. "It looked like someone broke that branch by hanging on it."

"Intentionally?" Dorothy lowered the saucer to her lap. "But— Because of the live wire? But that's crazy."

"Why would someone want Professor McClary dead?" I asked.

Her shoulders slumped. "Not someone. Piotr. Piotr Jezek. I saw him slash the tires of Michael's car." She gulped. "He must have come back, and . . ."

"Come back?" I asked.

She shook her head. "His car was parked across the street from Michael's the night of the reading. I saw him drive away after he cut the tires."

Charlene jolted forward, and the calendar slipped to the linoleum floor. "But what—?"

I shook my head. I didn't want to interrupt Dorothy's flow. "Tell us exactly what you saw."

"I saw Piotr get something out of the passenger side of his own car. He crossed the street and bent down by Michael's tires. Then he got into his car and drove off. I didn't realize what had happened until I learned much later Michael's tires had been slashed."

I nodded to Charlene.

"And what were you doing there?" she asked. "You said you were home that night."

"Aidan and I'd had an argument. I didn't want to go to the reading. I knew it would just turn into a pissing contest between Aidan and Michael, and it would be even worse if I was there. But I felt awful. So I came late and was driving around, looking for parking, when I saw Piotr."

"And then what?" I asked.

"Then I realized I'd been right, all the men in the English department are insane, and I really did drive home."

"Why did you lie?" I asked.

The professor colored.

"Because the wife, or in this case, ex-wife, always is the most likely suspect," Charlene said. "Dorothy's behavior was suspicious. She never came inside Pie Town the night of the poetry reading, even though she was here, in San Nicholas."

"It's ridiculous," the professor sputtered. "I'm not a suspect. I lose by Michael's death."

"How so?" I asked.

"The alimony I received from Michael was substantial. Now that he's dead, it's gone. I'm on my own."

But she had the same type of job her husband had had. Their income shouldn't be that different. Was losing the alimony a hardship or an inconvenience? Something must have shown on my face, because she continued.

"Michael had family wealth." Dorothy looked toward the metal shelves, lined with supplies, and blinked rapidly. "When we were married, I lived quite well. And when we divorced, Michael agreed I should continue living in the manner to which I'd been accustomed. He was . . . good that way. But that's over now."

It was also probably why she hadn't wanted to marry Aidan. As I'd suspected, the new marriage would have ended the alimony.

"The question," Charlene said, "is what do Aidan and Starke have in common, besides you?"

"A question I'm sure the police will be asking," she said bitterly.

"What do you know about Michael's poem 'Death in a Parking Lot'?" I asked.

"Nothing. Why?"

"Aidan seemed to think it was plagiarized," I said. "Did he say anything about it to you?"

"N-no. But he wouldn't. He knew I hated the conflict between him and Michael. It was like two dogs fighting over a bone, and I was the bone."

"Michael told some people that the story about the death was true," I said, "that he planned on writing a play about it."

"That explains why he didn't say anything to me. He always kept his work from me until it was done. He never spoke about works in progress, not to me."

"Professional jealousy?" Charlene asked.

Dorothy's mouth twisted. "Not exactly. He just . . ." Her

hands fluttered, and the teacup in her lap rattled. Hastily, she set it on the metal desk. "He didn't want me to see his work until he was satisfied with it."

"Have you told the police about Professor Jezek?" I asked.

"Not yet." She looked away. "I suppose I need to."

"Tell us about this business with the trees," Charlene said.

"Piotr and Michael are—were neighbors. Piotr complained that Michael's trees were blocking his ocean view and wanted to cut the tops. But Michael wouldn't have it. He loved the shape of the trees and felt lopping off the tops would ruin them."

"And you think Professor Jezek might have killed over it?" I asked, dubious.

"Piotr claimed the trees reduced his property value by several hundred thousands of dollars." The professor stood, scraping back the chair. "And he's crazy. Have you seen his office?" She shuddered. "I'd say crazy makes a good motive." She looked as if she wanted to say something more, but she strode to the door.

Beside Charlene, Dorothy turned. "Aidan just wanted things so damned badly, you know? Tenure, respect . . . me."

Charlene edged aside, and Dorothy Hastings left.

"Are you thinking what I'm thinking?" Charlene asked.

I rubbed my palm with my opposite thumb. "That Dorothy lied about that poem?" But why would she?

"That, and I'm wondering how a professor at a community college can afford an ocean view. Michael Starke had family money, but what's Jezek's story?"

The door edged wider, and Doran sidled into the office. "Learn anything?" His motorcycle jacket dangled from one finger.

Charlene shot me a look.

"Maybe," I said, noncommittal. "Is Abril here?"

His face fell. "Not yet. But I think I'm barking up the wrong tree." He jammed a hand in the front pocket of his black jeans. "She's obviously got a thing for your busboy."

"Hunter?" I said. "No way." Sure, he was cute, but Abril was about a zillion times smarter than him.

"I don't know if I'm helping anything by staying here," he continued.

My heart crashed to my soft-soled shoes. "Don't tell me you're thinking of leaving San Nicholas now?"

"I told you I was going."

"Yes, but . . ." But what? But a part of me had hoped that Charlene's dastardly honey trap would work? I'd rather he stuck around because of me.

Charlene folded her arms over her knit tunic. "So you're bugging out, just like your old man."

His blue eyes flashed. "I am not."

"You just said you were."

"I didn't say I was leaving. I said I wasn't sure I was helping."

She sniffed. "Sounds like an excuse to me. Are you saying that Abril deserves your help only if she's in love with you?"

"No, of course not—"

"Because that's pretty crummy."

I cleared my throat. "Charlene, that's not fair."

"Isn't it?"

He shook his head. "She's right. I don't know what I was talking about. I was in a bad mood and shooting off my mouth, but I'll stick this through. What do you want me to do next?"

And that was the problem. After the near electrocution and two murders, I wanted to keep him out of it. But he was a grown man.

"Research," Charlene said. "One of the professors at the

college was killed in a car accident five years ago. We need to know everything there is to know about it."

He nodded. "I'm on it." He strode from the office.

I sagged against the desk and blew out my breath. I really needed to get over my abandonment issues. Just because Doran and I were related didn't mean we were going to be best friends. He'd had a life before me, and he'd have a life after. And so would I.

Charlene drew her phone from her tunic pocket. "So that's that. Doran will be out of our way and happy, and maybe he'll turn something up."

"Yeah. That was a good idea. Thanks."

She glanced up from her phone. "What's wrong?"

"What? Nothing," I lied. "I was just thinking—Starke read more than one poem at Pie Town. What if we're looking at the wrong poem?"

CHAPTER 19

"The wrong..." Leaning against my office door, Charlene absently petted Frederick. "Oh, for Pete's sake. That other poem was all about death and destruction too, wasn't it?"

I stared at the metal supply shelves opposite and tried to remember. But the only thing that came to mind was I needed to buy more toilet paper.

"I think so." I winced and levered myself off the desk. "But I can only remember the last line. *Die, die, die.*"

"I thought he said *pie, pie, pie.*"

"What do pies have to do with death and destruction?"

"Have you seen the state of our dishes when Hunter takes them to the washer? Talk about destruction!" She brightened. "Does this mean you're going dumpster diving again? I forgot to get pictures the last time."

"No. It means we talk to Abril." I called her, and a phone rang outside the office door.

Charlene jerked it open.

Abril stood in sweatpants and a gray hoodie that looked a lot cuter on her than it would have on me. "Oh. Hi." She tucked the phone into her pocket and wiped her palms on her thighs. "You wanted to talk to me?"

I peered behind her but didn't see my brother. Maybe he was giving her some space. Or maybe he'd left.

"Yeah," I said. "We were thinking that we should take a look at Starke's first poem."

Her face cleared. "Oh, I've got that one. We workshopped it in his class. It's at home."

"Great!"

She shuffled her feet. "Um, do you need some help here? It's getting kind of crowded out there." She pointed with her thumb over one shoulder.

"Is it?" I hurried from the office and into the restaurant.

Every table was filled. Ten customers queued at the register. Petronella raced from the kitchen carrying two slices of choco-peanut-butter pie and deposited them at a four-top.

"Oh, boy," I said. "Yes, we need help. Thanks for offering. Abril, you can take the kitchen." She wasn't dressed to work the counter, and she hated working up front anyway.

I studied the chalkboard menu. Half the pies had been crossed out—we were running low but didn't have time to bake whole pies. I glanced at the near-empty glass shelves beneath the counter and at the tables. The single-serving pies in mason jars were popular and assembled more quickly. We had time to bake more.

"I'll work the register," I said. "Charlene . . . You do you." As she lived to remind me, she was piecrust only, and that duty ended in the morning. Besides, she couldn't go inside the kitchen with the cat.

She saluted with one finger and ambled into the dining area. "Gotcha."

Blood pumping, I took orders and made change, whirling from the counter to the order window. My fingers whizzed across the register.

A tall, gray-haired man stepped to the counter. "I'd like a choco-peanut-butter pie in a jar."

"Excellent choice!" I preferred fruit to cream pies, but chocolate plus peanut butter was hard to beat. I whipped to the glass display case, slid back the glass door, and grabbed a mason jar. Ringing it up, I handed him the jar.

He leaned over the register. "It's all right," he said. "We're here to help."

"Here to—?" Something thunked against a front window, and I looked up, alarmed. People milled on the sidewalk outside.

I turned to the gray-haired man, but he was gone.

"What's going on?" I asked a white-haired gentleman queuing in his place. "Is there a festival I don't know about?"

"It's for the UFOs," he said, blue eyes watery. "They're on their way. And I'll have a slice of chocolate cream pie."

"UF—" My jaw hardened. "Charlene!"

She squeezed from her spot at the counter and blinked innocently. "Yes?" On her shoulder, Frederick yawned.

I rang up the customer, handed him a numbered tent card, and clipped the order onto the window rack, spinning it to face the kitchen. "Charlene, why do you think all these people are here?"

"Top-notch marketing, I reckon. You're really doing a bang-up job."

My insides seemed to caramelize, and not in a good way. "UFO marketing?"

She stroked Frederick's white fur. "I told you the pie-plate UFOs would attract attention."

I ground my teeth. "Charlene, what exactly did you tell these people?"

"These people? Twitter doesn't work that way. I don't know who sees what I post."

The bell over the door jangled, and more people squeezed

into the restaurant. Sweat dampened my forehead. Soon we'd be over the fire code, if we weren't already.

"I'd like a slice of raspberry pie," the woman on the other side of the register said.

"Sure. Just one moment, please." I grabbed my cell phone from my apron pocket, started to open my Twitter app, then thought better of it. I called Gordon.

"Miss me?" his voice rumbled.

"Yes." I tucked the phone between ear and shoulder and rang up the customer. "But that's not why I'm calling. I've got a mob scene at Pie Town. I love the business, but it's more than a little unnerving."

Brittany squeezed through the door, and I frowned. What was the ex-TA doing here?

"I was just going to call you about that," Gordon said.

"You know?" I straightened, nearly dropping my phone.

"One of your neighbors complained."

I shut my eyes. I could guess which neighbor—Horrible Heidi. "I've never had to deal with a crowd like this before."

I made change for the customer, gave her a numbered tent card, and put the ticket in the wheel, spinning it toward the kitchen. "What do I do? Close up shop?" *Please don't make me close up shop.* A hard bite of guilt followed on the heels of that thought. Public safety came before profits.

"Is it really that bad?"

I looked around the packed restaurant. The line went to the door. People stood in the aisles and ate pie from mason jars. "It's incredible. I mean bad. It's really bad."

"Okay, I'll be there in five. In the meantime, close up if you think you need to and start getting people out."

"Can I have one of those cherry jar pies?" a rotund, red-faced man asked.

"Absolutely. I'll be right back." I wove through the crowd and flipped the sign in the glass door to CLOSED. A lady mashed against the other side of the door made a despairing face, and I started.

"Sorry," I mouthed. I hurried to the corner booth, where my regular gamers were hard at a match involving dungeons and damsels in distress. "Guys, I've got a problem."

Red-headed Ray looked up, and his broad face creased with concern. "What's up?"

"Charlene told people that aliens were coming to Pie Town, and now this place is dangerously crowded. Can you—?"

"Help move people outside?" Ray asked. "Sure."

I'd been about to ask them to give up their table, but that worked too. "Great. Thanks! Start with the people eating from mason jars. They've been served and can eat outside. Just tell them we're over the fire code, and it's a safety issue."

"Are we?" Ray asked, motioning toward his girlfriend, Henrietta. She began scooting from the booth.

"Possibly," I said. "Probably. Thanks!" Making apologies, I pushed through the crowd to the counter.

At the register, the red-faced man's brow furrowed with impatience. "My cherry pie—"

"Here you go." I grabbed a mason jar from the glass display case and handed it and a plastic fork to the man. "On the house. Thanks for waiting. And we've just closed due to the extreme crowd, so I'm afraid you'll have to take it outside."

"Outside, inside, I don't care. It's pie." He waddled into the crowd.

The sweat had migrated from my forehead to the skin above my lips. It was okay. It was going to be okay. But a million awful scenarios raced through my mind.

I smiled at the next customer in line. "What can I get you?"

I worked my way through the line. Thankfully, none of the customers objected when I asked them to eat outside.

There was nowhere to sit inside anyway—the gamers' corner booth had quickly been claimed.

Ray and Henrietta shuffled people onto the sidewalk. Some of the tightness between my shoulder blades eased.

I glanced out the window and whispered a curse. The crowd on the sidewalk had spilled onto the street. We were a traffic hazard.

A black-and-white police car stopped in the road. A grim-faced uniformed officer stepped from the car.

The front door opened, and Gordon walked inside, striding to the counter.

Heart lifting, I handed a jar of cherry pie to the last waiting customer. "Thank you. If you wouldn't mind—"

"Taking it outside," the blonde said. "I heard." She sniffed and walked to the door.

"It looks like you've got things under control in here," Gordon said.

"Thanks to Ray and his friends."

The student engineers escorted an elderly couple to the door.

"The crowd's focused on your restaurant," he said. "Your pie is fantastic, but what's going on?"

I winced. "Charlene might have led people to believe an alien invasion was taking place at Pie Town."

Gordon's mouth quivered with repressed laughter. "Of course she did. I've got to ask. How?"

Charlene popped up at his elbow. "Twitter! The power of social media."

Marla swiveled her barstool to face us. "False advertising is illegal."

"It's not false advertising." Charlene shook her fist. "It's a pie-tin UFO! Does no one in this town understand historical parody?"

"I do," Graham said beside her.

"Me too," Tally Wally said.

I gripped the top of the register. "I'm really sorry, Gordon. I had no idea."

"I know," he said, "but you need a license for an event like this, to pay for extra police services."

"If I'd known—"

"The mayor's office has gotten involved. I'm going to have to write you a citation."

A citation? *Charlene!* "I understand," I ground out, humiliated. It wasn't like Gordon could sweep this under the rug. Every merchant on Main Street could see something was going on at Pie Town.

"There will be a fine," he said. "Sorry."

"A fine?" I wailed. How much was that going to cost me?

"Now, Officer Carmichael," Charlene said. "Let's discuss this in my office."

"No!" I calmed my breathing. "No, Charlene. It's all right. We'll pay the fine."

Gordon drew me aside. "I won't say I told you so—"

"You just did."

"Look, I get it," he said in a low voice. "My parents are getting up there in age, and I want to take care of them without interfering in their lives. They're grown adults. But Charlene—"

"Has been a troublemaker her entire life. This stunt has nothing to do with her age."

"Are you sure about that?"

"She was in the roller derby."

Marla drifted past. "*I* was in the Ice Capades."

I rubbed my temple. "I'll have a talk with Charlene."

He grinned. "Better you than me."

"I'm sure she didn't mean for this to happen."

An elf-sized woman carrying a pink box above her head bobbed through the crowd.

"But it did," he said, "like you just happening to find Aidan's body, or inviting several persons of interest to Pie Town for a baking lesson/interrogation. Would you have done any of that without Charlene egging you on?"

"Yes." Meh, probably not. But I didn't regret it!

"I'm worried that she's going to push you too far."

"Come on," I said. "It's not like that. I'm not some high school victim of peer pressure. I do things because I want to do them."

"Like this near riot?"

"That was an accident." I hoped.

"Hm. You'll get your citation in the mail. I'll see what I can do to minimize the damage."

"Thanks," I said, glum.

He patted me on the shoulder and walked outside.

Charlene came to stand beside me. "Well, that went well."

"No, Charlene, it didn't. Someone could have gotten hurt." And I was feeling uncomfortably smushed between the rock of Gordon Carmichael and the hard place of Charlene Mc-Cree.

Her shoulders sagged. "I didn't think people would believe it was literally true. Who knew I had such a talent for hoaxes? Did you sweet-talk Gordon out of the citation?"

"No."

"Why not?"

"Because he can't give me special favors just because we're dating."

She lifted a single snowy eyebrow.

"At least not when the entire town knows about it," I amended. Gordon had been cutting us a lot of slack on our murder investigations.

Hunter edged from the kitchen. "Is it over?"

I looked around the restaurant. We were back to our regular Friday-afternoon capacity, my elderly regulars lined up at the counter and half the tables full. People still massed outside. But they roamed the sidewalk rather than flooding Main Street. "I think so."

"Cool. 'Cause we're on the news." He handed me his phone.

A news anchor filled the small screen. "Mass hysteria strikes a small town amid fears of . . ." She laughed, wind tossing her brown hair. "UFOs?"

I groaned. Not good. So not good.

CHAPTER 20

"You know," Charlene said, "there's only one thing left to do now." On her shoulder, Frederick snored.

I adjusted the CLOSED sign in Pie Town's glass front door. A few people milled on the darkening sidewalk outside Pie Town, but the crowd of UFOnauts had mostly disbursed.

"I'm not sure calling the TV station will help," I said, wringing my hands in my apron. "Explaining the situation to the press will only give them more to talk about." And this wasn't the sort of publicity I wanted for Pie Town. Though it might put people's minds at ease about the Invasion of San Nicholas. And yes, I'd begun to think about it in capital letters. I swallowed hard. Maybe calling the station *was* the right thing to do, even if we did look like greedy idiots.

Something clattered behind us, and I turned.

Hunter bent to retrieve the mop he'd dropped on the checkerboard floor. "I don't get it," the teenager said. "What do we need to do now?"

"I'm glad you asked." Charlene adjusted the cat around the collar of her yellow tunic. "Follow Dorothy."

He looked at her blankly. "Like in *The Wizard of Oz*?"

She shook her head sadly and patted his shoulder. "No, son, though I'm gratified you're familiar with the work."

"What work?" he asked. "I already finished loading the dishwasher and mopping the kitchen."

"Never mind," I said. "And thanks for staying late. You can take off now, if you're done."

"Cool." He dropped the mop again and jogged toward the kitchen. The teen slipped on the wet floor and caught himself by grabbing a pink barstool at the last minute.

"You do realize he tracked footprints across the floor he just mopped?" Charlene asked.

"And he's boxed us in." I might make it across the slippery black-and-white tiles, but I didn't want Charlene to risk her neck. "Come on." I unlocked the front door and followed Charlene onto the sidewalk.

"What about your purse?" she asked.

"I've given it up," I said, pleased with myself. "I've switched to a man's wallet, which fits inside my back pocket." I patted the rear of my jeans. My phone was in the other pocket, loose change in the front. My pants were hanging a little low, but it felt great not to lug a purse around.

"Forget your wallet. We need to stake out Dorothy."

I shivered in my thin *Pies Before Guys* tee. "I don't think that's such a good idea."

"All righty, then," she said. "*I'll* go to Dorothy's and let you know what I find."

Gordon's warning rang in my brain. "Charlene, we already started a near riot today. Maybe we should just call it a night and watch some *Stargate*." We were on the final season. Soon we'd have to switch to *Stargate Atlantis*.

A Prius glided past on the street.

She angled her head, considering the offer. "Nah. I'm going to Dorothy's."

Charlene and I walked past the comic shop, its windows filled with superheroes. We rounded the corner.

"We don't even know where Dorothy lives." I rubbed my arms. It wasn't exactly cold, but the evening wasn't warm either, a breeze nipping in from the Pacific.

"Sure I do. Doran got me the address."

Doran did what? "And what's with this *I* stuff?" I thought we'd gotten past this. "I apologized. We agreed we'd work together. We're a team, aren't we?"

"Well, since *someone's* letting her boyfriend tell her what to do when *someone's* not running around trying to make her brother happy, and *someone's* refusing to interrogate Dorothy, I figured I'd go by myself."

"Gordon's not telling me what to do." Okay, maybe he *had* on occasion. But he was a cop, and his requests hadn't exactly been out of bounds.

"And Doran?"

We turned the corner into the brick alley.

"Of course, I want to get along with him," I said, "and he's leaving soon."

"You can't make everyone happy," she said gently. "You're a kind woman, Val. But it's time to stand in your power." She punched her fist in the air.

"Stand in my power? Have you been watching those self-help videos on YouTube again? Charlene, we've talked about this. You just wind up watching Marla's channel—"

"She's starting a cooking show, Val. Next thing you know, she'll be giving away Pie Town secrets."

"She doesn't know any. You've kept the secret ingredient for your piecrust under lock and key."

"Well, I don't trust her. She's always lurking. And speaking of which, are you coming to Dorothy's or not?"

Since this was going to end in disaster with or without me, I agreed. And since Charlene wouldn't tell me Dorothy's address, she drove.

We roared through San Nicholas, depositing Frederick at Charlene's house, stopping at the mini-mart for snacks, and using the bathroom at the mini-mart. Finally, we crossed the One and hurtled west, toward the Pacific.

On two wheels, we screeched through a sleepy fishing village. Charlene slowed as we neared a collection of ramshackle townhomes near the private airport, tucked beneath a low hill. Fog crept beneath the golf-ball-shaped radar tower on its crest and blanketed the green hill.

A white cat darted in front of our bumper. Charlene slammed on her brakes, whipping me forward.

I flung up my right arm, and my elbow banged the windshield. "Ow."

The cat scampered over a collection of fishing nets draped across a faded wooden fence.

"Strange," she said. "That cat looked just like Frederick."

"Hm." I suspected Frederick led a secret, more exciting life when he wasn't pretending to be deaf and narcoleptic. But he'd have to have kitty superpowers to have beaten us here. "Which one is Dorothy's?"

"Number three, the one at the end, on the right."

I squinted at the two-story's peeling paint. "I thought Dorothy was set with her alimony, but this isn't super impressive." My tiny house was in better shape. But mine was smaller. Lots smaller. Though I had an ocean view.

"We're a block from the water," Charlene said. "These go for over a million. Who can afford paint after the mortgage and property taxes?"

"Dollars?" I squeaked. "A million dollars? For a town house?"

"It's Silicon Valley real estate. Everyone wants to live here. Few can afford the price tag."

Like Doran.

I slouched in my seat. If it hadn't been for Charlene's tiny house, I'd probably still be sleeping in my office.

"Stop pouting and take this." She reached behind her seat and handed me a scratchy, gray wool blanket. "Doran might be leaving the area, but he's not leaving your life. If he didn't want a relationship with you, he wouldn't have stuck around as long as he has."

I draped the blanket around my shoulders. "I know, you're right." But I was still disappointed he was going. Maybe I'd expected too much?

She leaned across me and pulled a bag of cheesy puffs from the glove compartment. "Your problem is you've got abandonment issues." A crumpled sheet of goldenrod paper fell from the glove compartment to my feet.

I bent to pick it up—the flyer from the poetry reading. The odd symbol seemed to wink at me from the corner of the page. "I do not."

She brandished a traffic-cone-orange puff. "Want one?"

"No, thanks." I stuffed the flyer in the rear pocket of my jeans. "I'm not hungry."

She crunched a puff, scattering orange dust. "It's understandable, what with your father taking off and that realtor leaving you at the altar."

I braced my elbow on the Jeep's open window, my head in my hand. "I wasn't left at the altar."

"Figure of speech. It was their loss, not yours. You own a pie shop. What man in his right mind wouldn't want that package?"

Their loss or not, I'd actually dodged a bullet with my ex-fiancé. Because we'd broken up, I'd found someone better. As to my father . . . I sighed. That was more complicated. But I believed he'd been trying to do the right thing, in his own wrongheaded way.

"Thanks," I said.

"Though you could stand to lose a pound or three."

"Then maybe you shouldn't be offering me late-night snacks. And my weight is perfectly healthy for my height." I blew out a breath. *Change the subject.* "Did you notice Brittany in Pie Town today?"

"The ex-TA? No. What was she doing there?"

"Not buying pie." I frowned. The restaurant had been a madhouse. But I was pretty sure I'd remember if she'd come to the register. Why *had* she come? To see the UFO chaos? Or for something else?

I sniffed. An acrid scent drifted on the cooling air. "Do you smell something?"

"All I smell is fish and cheesy puffs. They're one hundred percent chemical. It's what makes them taste so good."

My stomach twisted. "No, it smells like smoke." But not from a fireplace or barbecue.

A plume of smoke, gray against the black sky, rose from behind Dorothy's town house.

"There," I said, pointing. "Do you see it?" I scrambled from the Jeep.

"Let's find out what's what," Charlene said.

We jogged across the street, the blanket flapping around my knees. A low, gated fence blocked the side yard of Dorothy's townhome.

We hurried along it, toward the rear of the townhouse.

Dorothy stood over a firepit, the flames weirdly lighting her stony face. She tossed a file folder into the pit and poked it with a stick.

Charlene grabbed my shoulder and yanked me downward, behind the fence. She winced, her knees hitting the earth. "Oooh," she muttered, "that's going to hurt in the morning. What's she doing now?"

My insides like Jell-O, I peeked over the fence. "Same thing she was doing before, throwing papers into the fire."

"Suspicious."

I tugged the blanket tighter and leaned my back against the slatted fence. "There's nothing illegal about burning papers." Unless it was a Spare the Air day.

"We need to see those papers."

"Sure," I whispered, sarcastic. "You cause a diversion, and I'll go get them."

"I'm on it." She grunted, unmoving. "Well, help me up."

"I was joking about the diversion."

"A suspect in a murder investigation is burning documents. It's evidence."

"It's interfering in a police investigation," I said.

"What are you two doing?" Dorothy stared down at us, her elbows braced on the fence.

CHAPTER 21

I sprang to my feet and helped Charlene to stand. The blanket slithered off one shoulder. "Um, hi."

Moonlit tentacles of fog stretched down the hill toward the row of townhomes. I adjusted the itchy blanket.

"What are you supposed to be? Zorro?" Dorothy's eyes narrowed. "And are you going to answer me? What are you doing here?" A gust of wind tossed the professor's blond ringlets, coiling from beneath a navy knit cap.

"We were in the neighborhood and saw smoke coming from your yard," I said, sticking as close to the truth as possible. "We decided to see what was going on before calling the fire department."

"And that involved hiding behind my fence," she said flatly.

"What's in the firepit?" Charlene chirped.

Dorothy glanced over her shoulder at the rising flames. "Michael's works in progress. His wish was that they be burned after he died."

She had access to Starke's papers? So soon after his

death? *How?* My lips thinned. I struggled to think of a way to probe politely.

"Are you his executor?" Charlene turned up the collar of her yellow tunic.

"Yes," she said. "Are you satisfied?"

"Doesn't matter what I think." Charlene shrugged. "The cops aren't going to be happy you're burning the evidence."

"It's unfinished poetry," she said. "Not evidence."

"I don't suppose you have the poems he read on the night of his death?" I asked. "Or a play?"

Her brow wrinkled. "Why?"

"There's a theory that one of the poems might have a bearing on his death," I said, then winced. My response had popped out automatically. But that was probably more information than I should be giving a subject. Good thing I wasn't the police . . . who didn't believe that theory anyway. "Not because of plagiarism, but because it's about a true crime."

On the other side of the picket fence, Dorothy took a step back, and her ankle turned on a stone. The professor wobbled and straightened. "I . . ." She swallowed. "That's an interesting theory. But I wasn't there that night. I don't know what he read."

"The poem was called 'Death in a Parking Lot,'" I said. "And I can't remember the name of the other." I'd been daydreaming about pie. "But it ended with the words *die, die, die.*"

"Ah, yes." One corner of her mouth curled with derision. "The poem about driving with the farmworker. I don't see how that can have any bearing on his death."

"The farmworker?" I asked, excited. There were farmworkers in San Nicholas. Could it have happened here? "Then you have it?"

She looked toward the column of smoke rising above the firepit. "Not anymore."

"But you said you were burning only his works in progress," Charlene said.

"That *was* a work in progress. He liked reading them aloud to test them out, see what the audience's reaction was. The readings were a part of the process."

"What was it about?" I asked. "Can you remember?"

"Michael's car broke down, and he hitched a ride with a farmworker. It was a vignette of sorts, heavy with imagery about the starkness of the road and the brutality of life. But nothing happened that could possibly have . . . I mean, the ride took place last June in the Central Valley. It was nothing."

"What was he doing in farm country?" Charlene asked.

She shrugged. "How should I know? Wine tasting's my bet. That area might not have the glamour of Napa, but it's got excellent reds."

"If that were true," I said, "he wouldn't have gone alone, would he?"

"Probably not," she said. "Why?"

"Was there any mention in the poem of another passenger, like a date, hitching a ride too?"

She stiffened. "No, but he could have edited the other passenger out for effect. Poetry is a sort of heightened reality."

Nonchalantly, I tossed one end of the blanket over my shoulder. Why the reaction? Was she jealous? Or was it something else?

"Would he and a date have climbed into a stranger's car?" I asked.

"I don't know." Dorothy frowned. "I suppose it would depend on the stranger."

"Well," I said, "if you see any more copies of that poem—"

"I'll burn them," she said, "as Michael requested."

I sighed. Hopefully Abril would come through with the

missing poetry. "Right." And I would let Gordon know that Dorothy was having a bonfire. He might not be convinced of our half-baked poem theory, but who knew what was in the professor's firepit?

Dorothy folded her arms. "Is that all?"

"No." I pulled Abril's goldenrod flyer from the back pocket of my jeans. Unfolding it, I handed it to her and pointed to the symbol in the bottom corner. "What's this?"

One corner of her mouth lifted. "Ah. So that's how he filled the seats."

"He who?" I asked.

"Michael."

"I don't understand," I said. "What does the symbol mean?"

"Did you attend the college's production of *The Secret Society*?" Dorothy asked.

"I did," Charlene said. "It was pretty weird."

"It was meant to be unsettling," she said. "It was an interactive performance, with audience participation. The actors had to be prepared to use improvisation."

"What does that have to do with the symbol?" I asked, studying her closely.

"To prepare for their performance, the actors created and worked their own secret society. They held meetings, created passwords and secret handshakes, the works. You know."

I really didn't. "And this symbol is for the society?"

She handed me the flyer. "So secret, we didn't include the symbol on the program for our performance of *The Secret Society*. It was for cast members only."

Charlene gasped. "And the secret society is ongoing!"

"It would seem so." Dorothy braced her hands on the low, redwood fence.

A breeze slipped beneath the blanket, and I shivered. Professor Starke had used the symbol to call members to his performance at Pie Town. But why? Just to fill seats, as Dorothy had suggested?

I returned the flyer to my back pocket. "But Michael wasn't in theater. What does he have to do with this?"

"He was a playwright. He wrote *The Secret Society*. He must have stayed involved." Her eyes gleamed wickedly. "They used to meet on Sunday nights, in that cave in the cypress forest above Seal Cove."

Oh, that wasn't spooky. Not at all.

"In the haunted forest," Charlene whispered, her face wreathed in a delighted smile.

I blanched. *Uh-oh.* Secret societies were a little too on the nose when it came to Charlene's tastes.

"Wait here." Dorothy went inside her house, the rear door shutting firmly behind her.

Charlene rubbed her hands together. "I knew it. I knew there were secret societies operating in San Nicholas!"

"It's just a college society," I said, uneasy.

"Those are the worst. The Skull and Bones at Yale, The Flat Hat Club, Seven Society . . . Who knows what occult shenanigans those societies got up to? It's all about gaining power in the outside world. They sold their souls, most likely."

"This sounds more like a bunch of actors goofing around."

"And yet the symbol for this society is tied to murder."

"Not exactly," I said. "But I wouldn't mind talking to any society members who were at the reading. Maybe they saw something we didn't."

"We've got to infiltrate their next meeting." She rubbed her hands together. "Secret passwords and skullduggery!"

Dorothy emerged from the house with purple fabric draped over one arm. She handed us what turned out to be hooded satin robes. "This should help you get inside. I can't, of course, *tell* you the passwords. But . . ." She raised a piece of paper to my eye level. "The passcode to get into the meeting, and the password when you meet fellow members."

I read her brief notes and smothered a laugh. "Seriously?"

Dorothy walked to the firepit and tossed the paper into its flames. "Deadly serious."

"Why are you helping us?" I called over the fence.

Her smile turned ironic. "Are you sure I am?"

Was I? I stepped backward. "Well, thanks," I said, backing farther from the fence. "Sorry to have bothered you."

"I'm not sorry," Charlene grumbled as we returned to her Jeep. "She's behaving suspiciously."

I folded the lightweight robes on my lap. "Dorothy gave us an in to the next secret society meeting."

Charlene started the car. "We should return later and poke through the ashes."

I dialed Gordon and shook my head. "The police will want to do that." At least, I hoped they would. And I hoped Dorothy didn't tell Gordon about our planned secret society adventure on Sunday.

"Val." Gordon's voice crackled over the phone, and my body heated. "How are you?"

"I'm with Charlene."

"Oh?" he asked, more cautiously.

"We were driving past Dorothy Hastings's house and noticed smoke coming from her backyard."

He gusted a breath, and in it, I could hear his disappointment. "So you checked it out."

"It wasn't a fire, at least not an out-of-control fire. She's burning Professor Starke's papers."

He cursed. "How did she—? Thanks. Where are you now?"

"We're . . ." I scanned the dark road. We sped along an unfamiliar residential street—a mix of contemporary and Victorian homes surrounded by windswept cypresses. Where *were* we? I bounced one heel on the floor pad. Not headed home, that was for sure. "We left Dorothy's place. We're driving."

"All right. Stay out of trouble." He hung up.

"What did he say?" Charlene asked.

"He was interested. And annoyed." But I thought he was more irritated that Dorothy was burning potential evidence than that we'd been snooping. And that was a good thing. "Where are we going? To the White Lady?" I asked hopefully. I could use a drink to clean the smoke from my throat. *Smoke*. I fiddled with the seatbelt and wondered for the forty-second time about the smoke bomb.

"No White Lady for you," she said. "We're going to Piotr's house."

"Professor Jezek?"

"Don't tell me you object. You thought staking out Dorothy was a bad idea," she chided. "Look how much we learned."

"You are right," I said, "and I was wrong." We'd gotten lucky. But what were the odds we'd catch another college professor in a suspicious act? Still, it couldn't hurt to give Professor Jezek's house the eyeball. His house was near Starke's, and I was curious.

Professor Jezek lived in a gloomy, Hansel-and-Gretel cottage on a hill overlooking the ocean. Or at least, it would have overlooked the Pacific, were it not for the foreboding Monterey cypresses behind it.

We stood beside the entrance to his steep driveway and tried to peer over his six-foot fence.

"Yep," Charlene said. "That ocean view is blocked."

I consulted the map on my phone. "It looks like Starke lived right beneath him. Want to take a walk?"

We crept down the narrow, winding road. Five minutes later, we stood in front of an elegant Spanish-style home with a red-tile roof. Turning our backs on it, we crossed the road to a rope fence and peered over the cliff. The ocean crashed beneath us. In the darkness, we could make out lines of white foam. I wriggled my shoulders beneath the scratchy blanket.

"It's got to be worth at least eight million," Charlene said. "His family must have been loaded. But what's Jezek's excuse?"

I shook my head. "No idea. Professor Jezek's house is smaller though."

"In this location? It's still got to be worth a mint."

"Worth less than it was though, without a view." Was the view worth killing over, as Dorothy had claimed? And what would happen to Starke's house now?

I stared into the thick trees above the Spanish mansion. A light flickered between their branches, and my neck tensed.

"You have got to be kidding me," I said, pointing.

"Is that . . . fire? Woo-hoo!" She rubbed her hands together. "What did I tell you? It's a conspiracy."

I was pretty sure she hadn't mentioned a conspiracy. "Let's go see what Jezek's burning."

We trudged up the hill. The high fence encircling Professor Jezek's cottage made snooping more challenging. Or it would have, if Charlene hadn't just pushed the gate open and breezed on in.

"Charlene," I hissed. "Wait!" I trotted through the open gate, catching up with her as she reached the corner of the stone-and-wood house. "Wait," I mouthed, grasping her arm.

We peeked around the corner.

Professor Jezek stood on the opposite side of a firepit, nearly identical to Dorothy's. But unlike Dorothy, his eyes were closed, his hands raised in benediction. The fire cast demonic shadows across his sloping forehead and bushy mustache. A bucket of paint with a brush balanced on the lid sat on the ground to one side.

Hair prickled on my scalp. *What. The . . . ?*

His voice rang out beneath the branches of the Monterey

cypresses reaching over his fence. He spoke in a language I didn't recognize but guessed was something Eastern European.

The wind stirred the cypress branches, and the trees groaned.

He turned his head and spat three times over his left shoulder.

Gooseflesh prickled my arms.

His eyes opened, and his gaze locked on mine. The professor's face contorted. "What are you doing here?"

Crumb. "Ah . . . We saw the smoke, and—"

"Get out!"

Charlene stepped forward. "Are you—"

"Out!" he roared.

"We're leaving. Sorry." I turned.

The rear wall of his house was covered in painted black crosses, and a chill lifted the hairs on the nape of my neck.

I pushed and prodded Charlene down the path through the narrow side yard.

"If that wasn't an occult ceremony," she said, "I'll eat my roller skates."

"Did you see those crosses? He must have been painting all day."

"It reminds me of something I saw in Russia," she said. "My husband and I were visiting friends whose newborn had died. A local priest had painted crosses on the walls of their house to protect them from the evil eye. But not that many."

"And he did have all those icons—whatever he's doing could be religious."

I got her to the gate and slammed it behind us.

"Interesting that all those crosses faced Starke's house," she said. "And Michael Starke is dead."

"It is odd," I said, glancing over my shoulder at the gate. "But we won't figure this out in his driveway. Let's go."

Grumbling, Charlene stepped into the yellow Jeep, and we pulled from the curb.

I blew out my breath. "Wow." I looked again over my shoulder, but Professor Jezek hadn't followed us. And then we turned a corner and his cottage was gone.

"Dorothy burning evidence," she said, "and old Piotr covering his house in protective crosses. I'll bet he thought someone cursed Starke and he might be next."

"A curse didn't kill Professor Starke."

"You never know." Her knuckles whitened on the wheel. She cleared her throat. "I've heard stories."

"About Professor Jezek?"

"About curses."

Of *course* she had. But I couldn't muster my usual irritation with Charlene's crazy theories. Whatever Jezek had been doing, in the firelight, beneath the creaking cypresses, it had been seriously spooky.

Lights flared in the rearview mirror and vanished.

"You don't think he's following us, do you?" I asked, anxious.

She checked the mirror. "No one's following us."

"Right." *Right*. Unnerved, I kept checking behind us anyway.

When we arrived at Charlene's, we hustled up the porch steps and slammed shut her front door.

We looked at each other.

Charlene laughed weakly. "That was something for the books."

"Yeah. We're scaring ourselves over nothing."

"I'm not scared."

"Oh, me neither." But I pulled back the faded curtains and chanced a look into the front yard.

A dark figure crossed the street. Flames blossomed in his hand.

"Charlene—"

The figure cocked back one arm. The flame hurtled toward the house.

I shrieked. "Get down!"

The front window shattered. Fire exploded on Charlene's floral-patterned sofa.

"My couch!"

I raced for the fireplace, banged my leg on the coffee table, and grabbed the fire extinguisher. I sprayed the couch, white foam and smoke filling the living room.

Charlene flipped on the lights and coughed, waving her hand in front of her face. "My couch! My damn couch!"

I peered through the broken glass.

The person was gone.

Something sharp and hot pricked my palm. I jerked my hand from the windowpane I'd been gripping and rubbed away a smear of blood. My mouth went dry. He was gone. He'd done what he'd came for. He had to be gone.

Didn't he?

CHAPTER 22

I held a sheet of plywood in place while Gordon hammered it over Charlene's broken window. The living room smelled of burnt fabric, acrid and unpleasant.

"My damn couch!" Charlene's wail echoed from the kitchen.

"Haven't we done this before?" he asked me, and grinned. His suit jacket lay draped over a wing chair. The cuffs of his white shirt were rolled to his elbows.

"If you're trying to tell me that when Charlene and I investigate, mayhem follows, message received."

"Actually, I thought the déjà vu was romantic. You know, memories of before we were a couple."

My heart beat a little faster, and I smiled back at him.

Charlene howled. "I've had that couch for thirty years!"

He banged his thumb with the hammer. "Ow!" He cursed, shaking his hand.

I winced in sympathy and stepped from the window. Gordon's presence had driven away most of my freaked-outedness. But the overhead lamp didn't touch the shadows creeping in the corners. I switched on a lamp on a doily-covered table. And then another.

"You saw this guy," Gordon said, "even if it was only for a moment—are you sure you can't give me anything?"

I shook my head. "I couldn't even tell you if it was a man or a woman. It happened so fast, and . . ." Heat washed my face. How could I admit that I'd been so fixed on the fire, that it had seemed to bloom in the bomb thrower's hand as if by magic? Our attacker had looked like a vengeful wizard. Which just goes to show how much Professor Jezek's little ritual had gotten into my head.

"And what?" he asked.

"I can't help thinking that both Dorothy and Jezek had fires in their yard. Then someone threw a Molotov cocktail through our window." Earlier, Gordon's fellow police officers had taken away the fragments of the bottle—a cheap vodka. "Did you learn anything from Dorothy?" I asked.

"You know I can't talk about that."

After everything that had happened? I swallowed a hard lump of disappointment. "I know. But can you tell me if she was at home when you went to see her?"

Gordon had gone to visit Dorothy after I'd made the call. If she'd been busy with Gordon, she wouldn't have been able to firebomb Charlene's living room.

"She was home," he said slowly. "I was just leaving when you called about the attack."

"Then it couldn't have been Dorothy." I motioned toward the couch. "Not unless she had an accomplice."

"Thanks for letting me know about her backyard fire. It was helpful." He frowned. "I'm not sure what to make of Piotr Jezek though."

"I wonder if . . ." I hesitated. I didn't want Gordon to think I was pushing him for information.

"What?"

"It's just, his office walls were covered in icons. At first I thought Professor Jezek was super religious. But now I'm wondering if they weren't for protection."

He set the hammer on a doily-covered end table. "Go on."

Charlene stumped into the living room. "That man's afraid of something. The crosses over his office door and covering the back of his house are to ward off evil. The icons are probably just bonus help. I was sure Aidan was a vampire. But a vampire would never play with fire."

"Um, and Aidan's dead," I said, my chest tightening. Had Charlene forgotten? Was this old age taking its toll?

"I know he's dead," she snapped. "I'm just saying, if he was a vampire and faking his death, which he isn't, he wouldn't set something on fire. Fire is one of the things that can kill a vampire. Now what about my couch?"

Gordon shook his head. "I wouldn't bother trying to get it reupholstered. The stuffing's been burned as well. My mom got a decent couch at a nearby consignment store for not too much money. Maybe you can have some luck there?"

Charlene reached behind a blackened cushion and pulled out a shotgun.

Instinctively, Gordon and I ducked.

"Charlene," I said too loudly.

"Is that loaded?" he asked, straightening.

"Wouldn't do much good otherwise." She pointed it at the carpet. "Not that I was thinking on my feet when that bastard firebombed my home."

Gordon eyed it, a wary expression on his handsome face. "All right. There'll be a patrol car outside your house tonight, Charlene."

She snorted. "What about Val?"

"I'll follow her home. Val, where's your van?"

"At Pie Town."

We got Charlene settled, and Gordon drove me to collect my van.

His cop sedan trailed behind me as I wound up the road

to my tiny house. I crested the top of the drive. My headlights washed across the picnic table, the clearing, and the
tricked-out shipping container I called home.

No broken glass lay sprinkled in front of the picture windows. No smoke damage blackened the corrugated metal
walls. No necromancers with flaming hands lurked in the
yard, and the tension between my shoulder blades released.

Gordon insisted on poking into the bushes and eucalyptus trees that ringed three sides of my yard. He rattled all the
doors and windows. And then he came inside and drove the
rest of my fears away.

I poured sugared peaches into the waiting piecrusts. Sunlight streamed through the skylights—one of my favorite
features of the Pie Town kitchen.

I glanced toward the closed door to the flour-work room.

Charlene had been uncharacteristically quiet when she'd
arrived this morning. She put up a tough front, but I worried
the firebombing had shaken her more than she'd been willing to admit.

Abril cleared her throat. She laid a piecrust over a pie and
crimped its edges. "How's Doran?"

"He's good, I think."

"He's been so nice about everything," she said, her
cheeks pinking.

"He's a nice guy." I repressed a smile. Was Abril falling
for him?

"I'm sorry the poem wasn't helpful."

Abril had found the "die, die, die," poem. Though we'd
analyzed it backward and forward, it had contained nothing
remotely menacing.

"I'm ninety-nine percent sure the death of an avocado or-
chard is a metaphor for the death of farming in the Central
Valley," Abril said. "But I *could* be wrong."

"No poetry professors or anyone else were harmed in the making of that poem."

"Speak for yourself," Charlene shouted from the flour-work room. "It made my ears bleed."

Someone knocked on the kitchen's swinging door, and Abril and I raised our heads from our workstations. It was six thirty a.m. The only people here were our elderly regulars, serving themselves coffee and day-old pie.

"Yes?" I scrunched my forehead.

Tally Wally poked his head inside the kitchen. "There's a fellow out here who wants to see you. I told him it was all self-serve at this hour, but he's not getting with the program."

"Thanks." I wiped my hands in my apron. "I'll be right there."

He nodded and vanished through the swinging door.

I finished filling the pie and walked into the restaurant.

Professor Jezek stood on the other side of the cash register, his mustache quivering. "I have come to demand you stop harassing me," he said, exhaling stale alcohol fumes.

Looking interested, Marla swiveled her barstool to face the post-middle-aged professor. Her diamonds winked.

Charlene stormed from the kitchen in a floury apron. "What's happening?"

"This gentleman was about to file a restraining order against you," Marla drawled.

"You set my couch on fire," Charlene snarled, whipping the apron over her burnt-orange knit tunic. "You should be arrested."

Now Tally Wally and Graham turned to face us.

"That floral-print couch?" Graham asked.

"In your living room?" Tally Wally said.

"That's the one," Charlene growled.

"That was a good couch," Graham said.

"Good grief." Marla flicked her bejeweled hands, dismissive. "It was an outdated eyesore. This gentleman did you a favor."

"What couch?" Jezek scraped back his straggly gray hair.

"Don't *what couch* me." Charlene shook her finger at him. "If the police haven't interrogated you yet, they will."

His watery eyes blinked. "What are you talking about? What couch?"

Marla glided from her stool and extended a hand to the professor. "Marla. Marla Van Helsing. And you are . . . ?"

"Professor Jezek."

She arched a brow. "A professor?"

"Nearly half your age," Charlene said. "And a felon. He chucked a Molotov cocktail through my front window last night."

"I did not!"

"Maybe we should speak in private," I said. "My office is this way." I walked toward it, hoping they'd follow. To the groans of the regulars at the counter, Charlene and Jezek did.

I shut the door behind us, and the veterans calendar on its back rustled.

"What is this about a Molotov cocktail?" he asked in a low, intense voice.

"Where were you after we left your house last night?" I asked.

"At home. Why?"

"Because when we arrived at my house," Charlene said, "someone tried to set it on fire."

He ran shaking hands over his mustache. "So it continues. But why attack you?"

"What continues?" I asked.

He staggered, laying a hand on the metal supply shelf for balance. "The unclean force at the college. Rudolph has pushed someone too far."

I sat against my metal desk. "Rudolph? The dean?"

"The man puts too much pressure on everyone." His shoulders hunched. "He is fanatical. His expectations for staff behavior are unrealistically high."

"What's that supposed to mean?" Charlene folded her arms over her Pie Town apron.

"We are only a community college." Head twitching, he paced the small office. "But he insists his professors publish regularly, as if we were a four-year or graduate school. Dorothy came close to a breakdown last year because of his demands. Her strength is teaching. She spends most of her nonteaching hours working in the theater with the students. This is what she should be doing, not publishing. It's ridiculous. You saw how he acted at the pie-making class."

My mouth puckered. The dean had seemed pretty nice in a jolly, Santa sort of way.

"Dean Prophet's crusts *were* the most even," Charlene growled.

"Is that why the college has a TA program?" I asked. "Because he's trying to emulate universities?"

He shrugged. "No, these programs are becoming more common at community colleges. But I have no doubt Rudolph sees the program as another point of prestige for his department. The man is mad."

Mad? For having higher standards? "Is that who you're afraid of?" I asked. "The dean?"

He stopped beside a set of metal supply shelves. "Dean Prophet?" His eyes widened. "Haven't you been listening? He's too rule-obsessed to jaywalk, never mind commit murder."

"The crosses over the door," Charlene said. "The ritual we interrupted."

"It wasn't a—" He shook his head. "As you grow in the light, you attract unclean spirits. And such a spirit walks at that college. It's infested a human soul."

"But who's been infested, specifically?" I asked.

"If I knew, don't you think I'd tell the police? Two of my colleagues are dead, murdered. And now you say you have been attacked."

"We took a look at Starke's house," Charlene said. "Those trees really are blocking your view. Must be frustrating."

"Frustrating? I offered to pay to trim them myself. Michael refused. He enjoyed making others miserable."

"Others?" I asked. "Who else did he make miserable?"

"I meant in general."

"Where did you go after our pie-making class on Thursday?" I asked.

"To the British pub."

"Would anyone remember you were there?" Charlene asked.

His graying head reared backward. "Remember? You talk as if I need an alibi! Why would I kill Aidan?"

"I'm sure you wouldn't," I said smoothly. "So, about that alibi . . . ?"

"I was at the bar. I don't know if anyone would remember me or not."

"A witness saw you slash Professor Starke's tires," I said.

"It's a lie," he rasped. "Stay away from me. Stay away from the college, if you know what's good for you." He wobbled from the office.

The calendar slipped off its nail and to the linoleum floor.

"I'm not sure if that was a threat," I said, "or an honest warning."

"I don't trust him." Charlene jammed her hands in the pockets of her orange tunic.

"Me neither," I said, retrieving the calendar and returning it to its nail. I was going to need a better hook if I was going to keep inviting angry suspects into my office. "I wonder where Brittany was last night?"

"The TA?"

"I keep thinking of something Gordon told me when he

was trying to talk me into getting a PI license. Follow every lead. Is Brittany a suspect or a lead? She gave us useful information about Starke. But why did she return during the UFO, er, event? To give us more intel? Or is something else going on?"

"She did have an affair with Starke. There's bound to be some lingering emotions. It's probably exciting for her— knowing a murder victim. She's young. She can paint herself as a tragic heroine."

"Maybe that's all there is to it." I dug Brittany's phone number from my desk drawer and ran my thumb along one edge of the thin paper. "But I wonder where she was last night."

"If she was setting my couch on fire, she's not going to admit it."

"No, but let's see what she has to say."

I called her number, and she answered before the first ring had ended.

"Hello?"

"Brittany, this is Val Harris, from Pie Town."

"Oh, hi! Did you learn anything? What's going on?"

"I saw you in Pie Town the other day. It was so crazy, I didn't get a chance to talk to you. Did you have more information for us about Professor Starke?"

"I wasn't—" Her laugh was high and false. "No, I just saw all those people and was curious. What about you? Have you learned anything new?"

"Not really, but someone threw a Molotov cocktail through Charlene's window last night."

"Charlene? Who's that?"

I glanced at my piecrust maker. "You met her at the Father Serra statue."

"Oh, right! That's terrible! Is she okay?"

"We're fine. Look, we noticed your Mustang in the area earlier," I lied, "and wondered if you'd seen anything."

There was a long silence.

"I know it's a long shot," I said, "but we're asking anybody who was nearby. We didn't get a very good look at the person who did it."

"I . . . didn't. I'm sorry."

My jaw set. I hadn't told her Charlene lived in San Nicholas, but I had sort of implied it. "Too bad." I forced cheerfulness into my voice. "What were you doing in San Nicholas?"

"Just driving through. I was meeting someone at the British pub."

"Hey, who was playing there last night?"

"I don't remember. It was just noise."

"And Thursday night?"

"I don't remember. I guess I was at home."

"Well, thanks anyway." We said our goodbyes and hung up. "She was in San Nicholas," I told Charlene. "At the British pub. And she seemed uncomfortable."

"You weren't being exactly subtle. And the pub's always been popular. It's got a double-decker bus out front." She raised a foot and scratched the ankle of her orange-and-white-striped sock with her tennis shoe. "So what are we thinking? Starke broke her heart, so she killed him?"

"I guess it is a long shot. But there's someone else we haven't talked to."

"Dean Rudolph Prophet." Charlene nodded. "Make the call."

I dialed his office number.

"Dean Prophet."

"Hi, this is Val Harris."

"Ah, Ms. Harris. What can I do for you?"

I laughed and hoped he couldn't hear the false note in my voice. "Charlene and I are a little desperate. There was some vandalism at her house last night, and we're asking all our friends who were in the area if they saw anything."

"In the area? I'm not sure which area you mean."

"San Nicholas," I said.

"I'm sorry, I was home last night in San Mateo."

"Oh," I said, "I thought I saw your car."

"Mine's rather common, I'm afraid. You must have mistaken mine for someone else's."

Dishes crashed in the dining area, and I winced.

"Well," I said, "sorry to bother you."

"It's no bother," he said. "I'm sorry to hear about the vandalism. Nothing too dire, I hope."

"Nothing we couldn't deal with. It's just frustrating. And expensive."

"People have no respect for each other anymore," he said sadly. "We've lost our sense of community. Though I can see you haven't."

"What do you mean?"

"Your interest in justice for Professor Starke." He chuckled. "Are you any closer to unraveling the truth?"

"That's in the hands of the police," I said stiffly, because I knew when I was being made fun of. And I guess I couldn't blame him for doing it.

"I hope they can manage it," he said, "for all our sakes. The college has lost two good professors. The murders have devastated the students and staff."

I muttered condolences, and we hung up.

"Well?"

I shrugged. "He said he was at home. So he's got no alibi, but—"

"But we can't prove he was our firebomber."

"No." I shivered. We weren't any closer to understanding who had killed Aidan and Starke.

But the killer knew who *we* were, and I feared he wasn't done.

CHAPTER 23

Because pie waits for no man, I returned to the kitchen. Petronella wiped her brow. Beneath her hairnet, her black spikes looked a little wilted. It was warm in the kitchen, the scent of baking sugar flowing from the giant pie oven. "I can manage the orders," she said.

"I know, but things are getting busy out front," I said. "Why don't you help Abril?"

Hunter staggered into the kitchen carrying a plastic bin. Its black bottom was littered with broken plates.

My assistant manager eyed him. "Or I can do that." She wiped her hands on her apron and strode into the restaurant.

Figuring Hunter could deal with broken plates without my supervision, I whipped an order off the wheel. I plated a slice of pecan pie and shoved it through the order window.

Charlene trailed into the kitchen. "I almost wish that engineer was on the case with us again. Ray knew how to organize facts."

"We can organize facts," I said. "For example, Professor Jezek said he went to the British pub on Thursday night, when Aidan died. And Brittany said she was there last night, when your house was attacked. We should stop by there tonight."

"Sure, sure." Charlene plucked a fresh apron from a hook on the wall and wrapped it around her orange-y tunic. "But what we need are visual aids."

"Tonight—"

"Hold on." Charlene ambled to the industrial fridge, grabbed a metal tray, and loaded it with pies in mason jars.

Hunter shoved open the rear door and stomped into the alley. Plates crashed into the dumpster, and I briefly shut my eyes.

I plated a quiche Lorraine and added a side salad. "I thought you were boycotting our pies in a jar." She had issues with the low ratio of piecrust to filling.

"That's why they make good visual aids." She smacked a banana cream on the butcher-block work island. "Piotr Jezek's bananas."

"Is that a metaphor?"

Hunter returned to the kitchen and slammed the alley door shut.

"And Dorothy Hastings is cherry." She set a jar layered red and brown beside it. "Rudolph Prophet is pecan, and Brittany is olallieberry."

"Does she deserve olallieberry? She did leave me hanging from Father Serra." The olallieberry was a crossbreed between two crossbred berries. It was delicious, with hints of blackberry, dewberry, and raspberry.

Charlene straightened. "Brittany is olallieberry."

"I like pumpkin," Hunter said.

"Wrong season." She glared at him. "And Aidan's chocolate cream."

"We know Aidan was pushing Dorothy to get married," I said, "at least partly so he could stay in the US. She didn't want to, probably because she would have lost her alimony from Starke."

"But with Starke dead, that alimony was gone, which would have given Aidan a motive to kill Starke. But Aidan's dead."

"We don't know what's in Starke's will," I said. "Could Dorothy have benefited?"

Hunter sat on Charlene's stool near the flour-work room. His head swiveled back and forth, tracking us.

"I'll check the court records," Charlene said. "It's a little early, but maybe probate's been filed."

"All right." I picked up the olallieberry mason jar. "Brittany. Am I stretching for suspects? Odds are you're right, and she was just curious about the case and that's why she returned to Pie Town."

"Let's face it," Charlene said glumly, "there's still a lot we don't know about Starke. The killer could be someone else entirely, someone we haven't even met."

"Or someone you don't know," Hunter said.

"Thank you, Hunter," I said. "But I'm betting he or she was at that poetry reading." Another reason to track down that so-called secret society.

"Let's go back to the night of Professor Starke's death."

"Rudolph, Jezek, and Aidan were at the reading. Brittany was there too."

"I couldn't make it," Hunter said. "I had a date."

"Why don't you see if any tables need busing?" Charlene ground out.

He shrugged. "Nah. I was just out there."

The ticket wheel spun, and I grabbed the order form. A strawberry-rhubarb pie to go.

"But the ex-wife," Charlene said, "Dorothy, wasn't at the reading."

"*The Wizard of Oz* chick?" Hunter asked.

I grabbed a pie off the rolling rack and a flattened pink box from the shelf. "No, not that Dorothy. But that doesn't mean she wasn't lurking outside. She doesn't have an alibi for that night."

Charlene brushed flour off her apron. "But she couldn't have firebombed my house. She was busy with Gordon."

"You'll need to break her alibi." Hunter nodded.

We stared at him.

I unfolded the cardboard, locking the sides into place. "You're right. Unless we can break that alibi, we're wasting time."

"Cool." He rose and grabbed a plastic bin. "I'm glad I could help." Hunter ambled through the swinging door into the dining area.

"If you make him a Baker Street Baker," Charlene said, "I'm quitting."

"Never gonna happen." I grouped the pecan, banana cream, and olallieberry mason jars. "Rudolph, Jezek, and Brittany are alibi-free."

"At least we haven't turned up any good motives for the dean to have killed anyone. We may be able to count him out."

I boxed the pie, taped the ticket to the top, and shoved it through the order window. "But he was at the reading the night Starke died. We don't know where he was when Aidan died too, and they worked together." I sighed. "I don't suppose being irritated with his staff makes a good enough motive for murder."

"Of course not."

Dishes crashed in the dining area, and we flinched.

Hunter pushed through the swinging door, broken plates littering the bottom of the plastic bin he carried. "Sorry. But at least these are less dishes to wash," he said cheerfully. He dropped the container on top of the dishwasher, and the crockery crashed.

"Anyway." I forced the word through clenched teeth.

"Banana cream. Professor Jezek was seen slashing Starke's tires. He was really mad about those trees—"

"They *were* blocking his view."

"And if Aidan saw him attack Starke—"

"He could have tried to blackmail weird Professor Jezek."

"Or just let something slip," I said. "And what about that poem? Aidan accused Starke of stealing it. I don't suppose it matters now if he did, since they're both dead."

"Unless that poem was the reason they were killed," she said.

"We need to learn more about that professor who died in the car accident."

"Ask Gordon. He might know."

"It was before his time, but . . . all right. All he can say is no."

Abril pushed open the door and leaned in. "Val, there's a reporter here to see you."

My stomach tightened.

"I told you the UFO marketing would work." Charlene rubbed her hands together.

I blew out my breath. "Abril, can you take over in here while I talk to him?"

"Her," Abril said. "And sure."

"Thanks." I hurried into the pie shop.

The swinging door banged behind me, Charlene following.

The reporter, a twentysomething in jeans, looked up from her phone and turned away from Marla. *Uh-oh*. Had Marla been talking to her?

"Val Harris?"

I gulped. "Yes."

We shook hands.

"I'm Kada from the *San Francisco Times*. We wanted to do a follow-up on the little UFO scare your restaurant started."

The reporter held her phone closer to my mouth. "I'll be recording, if you don't mind."

Oh, goody. "We only intended to do something whimsical with pie plates. We had no idea people would take it seriously."

"Except, of course," Charlene said, "UFOs are real."

"But not pie-tin UFOs!" I laughed maniacally.

"Pie tins are real too," Charlene said.

"Real crazy," Marla muttered.

"Let's chat somewhere more private." I steered Charlene and the reporter behind the counter and into my uninspiring office. "So you had some questions?" I motioned her toward the chair in front of my desk.

"What gave you the idea of the hoax?" the reporter asked, eyeing the chair and staying standing.

Sweat dampened my forehead. "Again, it wasn't intended to be a hoax."

"It was an homage to a hoax," Charlene said. "The McMinnville pie-tin hoax."

"Sure," I said. "I mean, everyone knows those were faked."

"People still dispute that," the reporter said.

"Pie-tin UFOs are traditional," Charlene said. "For example, they were featured in the classic "The Night of the Flying Pie Plate," an episode of *The Wild Wild West* that aired in 1966."

"Right," I said, my voice rising. "I mean, it was totally obvious *that* wasn't real. In today's day and age, even amateurs can fake realistic pictures. Why would anyone take pie plates on a string as anything more than fun?"

Charlene smiled reminiscently. "Robert Conrad. He once attended one of my team's roller derbies. I fell right over the fence into his lap. Twice."

The reporter blinked.

For once, Charlene's bizarre ramblings seemed to be

working in my favor. If we could derail the reporter, maybe we'd come out of this okay. "And who doesn't love pie?" I asked.

"I don't," the reporter said.

What? "Not even quiche?" I asked.

She shook her head.

Seriously? Who doesn't love pie? The paper obviously had sent someone with an ax to grind.

"I understand a murder's been linked to Pie Town," the reporter said.

"No," I bleated. "That happened several blocks away."

"Maybe she mean's Joe's murder earlier this year?" Charlene leaned one shoulder against the closed door and rumpled the calendar.

I glared at her. "Which had nothing to do with Pie Town. The murderer was caught. And it had nothing to do with the pie-plate UFOs. We have our own custom-made pie tins, you know," I babbled. "So, if anyone looked closely, they could see the Pie Town name on the tins."

"Pie Town's been open only a year?" the reporter asked.

"Roughly. But as you can see, business is booming. We carry sweet and savory pies, as well as a selection of breakfast quiches. And you probably noticed our mini pies and pies in a jar. We also wholesale, and we've got a pie club, for those who want fresh pies delivered on a regular basis."

"Yes," she said. "I've reviewed your website." She pocketed her phone. "Well, that should do it. Thank you for your time."

I saw the reporter out of the office, then whirled on Charlene. "Honestly? Did you have to bring up the murders?"

"I didn't bring them up. She did."

"I just don't think death, pie, and UFOs make a good combo. Maybe we could *not* talk about these things around reporters?"

She sniffed. "At least I'm thinking of solutions."

"Yes. Thank you. As marketing ideas go, the pie-tin UFOs were clever."

"Clever! What about getting Doran to fall for Abril so he'll stick around?"

"That was—"

"What?" Doran asked from behind me.

"Really poorly timed," I muttered. I turned. "Hi, Doran. It's not—"

My brother folded his arms over his motorcycle jacket. "You two were trying to manipulate me so I'd stay in San Nicholas?"

"No! No," I said. "I mean, of course we noticed that you and Abril might have a connection and thought, wouldn't it be great if . . . ? But that was all."

He shook his head. "Unbelievable. I thought our dad was a master manipulator. He had nothing on you. Here." He thrust a USB stick into my hand. "It's what I could find on that professor who died. If you ever really wanted it." He turned on his heel and reached for the door.

"I did! We do! Doran—"

He slammed out of the office.

Charlene clapped her hand on my shoulder. "He'll get over it. What he needs is a visit from a pie-tin UFO."

Augh! "No Charlene. No, he doesn't."

"The great thing about family is they're stuck with you. He'll get over it." But her smile slipped, and I knew she was thinking about her own adult daughter, who still hadn't forgiven.

CHAPTER 24

Sickened, I fled to the kitchen and got busy whipping pies out of the massive oven and onto cooling racks. At the metal counter, Abril plated pies for customers.

This wasn't Charlene's fault. As much as I wanted to blame her, I'd gone along with her cockamamie scheme. Or at least, I'd let it unfold. But of all the stupid plans I'd let her talk me into, pushing Doran and Abril closer had been the worst.

I slid the humongous wooden paddle into the oven and lifted a blueberry pie off the rotating racks.

I hoped Doran could forgive me.

My lungs constricted. And that crack about me being like our father . . .

Our father might not technically be a criminal, but he was so close to the line the distinction was moot. And I *had* been acting a lot like him—playing fast and loose with the law, climbing on statues, manipulating my brother . . .

And all those little legal infractions . . . It disturbed me more than a little that Gordon didn't seem to mind. Was he seeing me for who I was? Or like Starke, was he projecting an unrealistic, idealized, non-pseudo-criminal version of Val?

Someone knocked on the kitchen's alley door, and Abril and I started. All our deliveries had already arrived.

"Do you want me to get it?" she asked, brown eyes wide.

"I will." I strode across the black fatigue mats to the door and yanked it open.

Two tattooed and middle-aged women scuttled past me and into the kitchen.

"Whoa," I said. "This is a private kitchen, and you're not wearing hairnets."

"This is bigger than hairnets," the taller of the two, with spiky violet hair, whispered.

I whipped two hairnets out of the box I kept on a nearby shelf and handed them over. "In a commercial kitchen, there's nothing bigger than hairnets. What can I do for you?"

"It's not the worst thing we've done." The shorter, more voluptuous woman snapped the net over her trim, graying hair.

The other shrugged and pulled hers on as well. "Whatever." She cut a glance at Abril and lowered her voice. "Look, we know they've got to you."

"They've . . . What?"

She narrowed her eyes at Abril. "Maybe we should speak alone."

I sighed. "Fine. My office is this way." I led them from the kitchen and glanced into the restaurant. Charlene sat at a counter stool, speaking earnestly to Tally Wally. This should have worried me, but I had bigger fish to fry.

I ushered them into my Spartan office and shut the door. "What's this about?"

"The government."

"Oh. You mean the pie-tin UFOs," I said. I'd gotten better at recognizing this brand of cray-cray. "Look, I helped

Charlene with that UFO photo above the Father Serra statue. They're fakes. She thought it would be a fun marketing gimmick, and I went along with it." Boy, had I been wrong.

The two women gave each other long looks.

"We knew you'd say that," the violet-haired woman said.

"Because it's true!" I breathed deeply, trying to calm myself. Maybe it was the breathing. Maybe I just snapped. But I had one of those horrifying brain-lightning moments, when life becomes brutally clear. "On second thought, that *wasn't* completely true."

The women started, leaning closer.

"I didn't just go along with it," I said slowly, dredging out the admission from a place I didn't much like. "I enjoyed it. I have fun with all Charlene's lunacy, even when she's dragging me through a muddy forest looking for Bigfoot."

The gray-haired woman folded her arms. "Everyone knows Bigfoot's not real."

"I know, right?" I reached to claw my hand through my hair and remembered the net. "The point is, everything that's happened has been *my* fault, not Charlene's." I felt ashamed I'd ever blamed her. Blaming Charlene for stirring up trouble was like blaming a dog for peeing on a tree. It was what they *did*. "As much as I love Pie Town, if it weren't for Charlene and our murder investigations—"

"Murder?" the violet-haired woman yelped.

"—or the pie-plate UFOs, which by the way, say Pie Town on them—you can see it in the photos—"

"Faked!" Gray Hair's eyes widened in consternation.

"It's me. I wouldn't have climbed that stupid statue if a part of me hadn't wanted to see if I could do it. I worry that Gordon doesn't see me for who I am, but I'm not even sure if I see me for who I am."

"Who's Gordon?" Violet asked.

"My boyfriend. He's a local detective, and he's wonderful. He's smart and tough and kind and honorable. And he's over six-feet tall and has that square-jawed cowboy look. I once saw him shoot a gun out of a man's hand."

"Seriously?" Gray asked. "I thought that only happened on TV."

"Anyway, I'm babbling. But this has helped me sort through some things." Though taking responsibility for one's poor choices doesn't feel as good as it should. "I know what I need to do now."

"What do you need to do?" Violet asked.

"I need to face up to my actions. I've been wishy-washy, complaining about doing things that I really wanted to do. I didn't want to take responsibility." My brother had held up a mirror to me, and I hadn't liked it. But I didn't have to be like my incorrigible father. Just look where that had got him!

"That isn't exactly what I got from your freaky monologue," Violet said.

"Thanks for listening anyway." I leaned against the desk. When I saw Gordon tonight, I'd put everything on the table. "Is there anything I can say to convince you that the UFO photos were all a big promotional joke?"

"You can show us proof of the UFOs," Violet said.

"Then I think we're done." I opened the office door and inclined my head toward it.

"We understand," the shorter, gray-haired woman said. "The pressure can be overwhelming."

"You can say that again," I muttered.

"But we're here to help." Violet put a business card on my battered desk, and, reluctantly, they shuffled out.

As bonkers as the UFO fans had been, they'd given me clarity.

It was time to procrastibake.

CHAPTER 25

I brandished a french fry. "And so, Doran's furious, and Charlene's unrepentant. But as much as I'd like to blame her, I realize it's on me."

Gordon nodded and sipped his beer.

The British-pub crowd swirled around us. A jukebox blared a Beatles tune, and people shouted over the noise in the cramped bar. Gordon and I sat at a damp corner table, our knees touching.

"And not only is it on me," I said, "but I *liked* it."

A smile tipped the corner of his mouth. "You really didn't know that?"

I tugged on the end of my ponytail. "What is wrong with me?"

His gaze roamed leisurely over my body. "Nothing that I can see."

"I've been telling myself I've been going along with Charlene's schemes to make sure *she* doesn't get into trouble. But I was deluding myself. I don't know what to do now. I mean, do I stop? How would I tell Charlene?" Acting like an adult and staying out of police business was the smart play. The safe play. So why was it so hard?

His mug froze at his lips. "You're actually considering quitting the Baker Street Bakers?" His handsome face clouded.

"I know Charlene lives for that sort of thing, but it's either quit or— Oh, by the way, Brittany says she was here at the pub when Charlene's house got firebombed. And Professor Jezek said he came here after our pie-making class, when Aidan was murdered."

"Yeah. I know."

I turned my beer glass on its coaster. "Sorry. Of course you do."

"I knew about Jezek, not Brittany." His emerald gaze never left mine. "I couldn't verify his alibi. He claimed he was here until closing at midnight the night Aidan was killed, but no one remembers him."

"So he lied?" I asked.

"Maybe. Or maybe he sat in the corner, and no one remembers him. Why do you consider Brittany a suspect?"

"Brittany was at the poetry reading." I shifted on the wooden chair. "And she said she was over Starke, but she didn't seem to be. She still idealizes him."

"I interviewed her, but I didn't get that at all."

"I'm sure it's nothing." I stared glumly out the steamy window. Outside, people huddled around barrels on the concrete patio.

He set down his mug. "It might not be. As much as it pains me to say this, you and Charlene have a strange knack for detecting." His mouth twitched. "It's unorthodox and random and based largely on luck—"

"Thanks," I said dryly.

"And you'll never get your private investigator's license with your haphazard techniques."

My face warmed. There was no way I was going to get

licensed *and* manage a pie shop. There wasn't enough time in the day.

The woman behind me pulled out her chair, jostling mine. We apologized to each other, and I turned back to Gordon.

"But," he said, "I can't argue with the results. Even if they have nearly gotten you and Charlene killed on more than one occasion." He rubbed his square jaw.

I goggled at him. "What are you saying? That you want the Baker Street Bakers to keep interfering with police investigations?"

"No, of course not." He rested his hand on mine, and his thumb caressed the inside of my wrist. "But you've been pretty good about staying on the right side of that line."

I straightened. "And that's the problem too. Doran sees that as well—my just skirting the law, I mean—and it reminds him of our father." Memories of my father's abandonment flowed back. They tasted like gall.

"You're not an enforcer for the mob." He squeezed my hand. "There's a difference a mile wide."

"But the reason my father hasn't been arrested is because his techniques are nonviolent. He still works for the bad guys. And gets paid by them."

His voice lowered to a rumble. "As I recall, he didn't have much choice going in. And it's not easy getting out."

"I can't believe you're defending him."

He exhaled heavily. "I'm not. I don't like what he did to your family. But sometimes we have to take people as they are, not as we'd like them to be. And your father's not all bad."

I shoved my plate aside. "He's not good."

"But you are." His brows drew together. "What I don't understand is where this is really coming from."

"I told you. Doran—"

"Is pissed because you and Charlene sat back and let him fall for Abril."

"You make it sound like he's being unreasonable."

He raised a brow.

"We did sort of encourage them for our own selfish purposes," I admitted.

He cleared his throat. "Doran's an interesting guy. But I don't think you need to turn your life upside-down for him," he said gently.

"I'm not!"

He canted his head and said nothing.

"How are your parents doing?" I asked in a lower voice. Gordon had returned to San Nicholas after an exciting career as a big-city cop to keep an eye on his aging parents. I could only imagine how the potential cancer diagnosis must have shaken him.

He released my hand, sliding back in his chair, and looked out the window. "Not too well. Bladder cancer scare aside, I'm going to have to take away my dad's driver's license."

My heartbeat seemed to slow. Poor Gordon. "Oh no." Would I have to have that talk with Charlene someday? As terrifying as her driving could occasionally be, I hated the thought of her losing her independence.

"I tried talking to him about it last night. He didn't react well."

"No, I guess he wouldn't."

"It's tough living on the coast. The bus service is terrible. There are some shuttle services for the elderly, but they're slow and he hates being dependent on anyone."

I laid my hand on his. "You'll get through this. And he'll understand, eventually. What does your mother say?"

"She doesn't like to drive anymore, so she's dependent on him. I think she realizes he needs to stop driving, but she doesn't want to seem like she's ganging up on him." He shook his head. "But about Charlene—"

"I kind of avoided her today. The thing is, I still don't know what I'm going to say to her. Yes, I love the Baker

Street Bakers too. No, I really don't want to stop investigating, I just think I *should* stop. And maybe I haven't been thinking straight with the whole new-brother situation. But Charlene and I recently did put a toe over the line when it came to interfering in your investigation. And—"

"She's behind you."

"I know she's behind me," I said. "She's been a rock. She's always supported me."

"I mean she's right behind you."

"Interfering?" Charlene asked, and my muscles jumped. "Don't tell me you're planning to arrest us?"

Gordon rose and motioned to his chair. "No. I'm going to have a talk with the bartender about a certain TA. That way, you won't have to interfere again tonight." He edged through the crowd to the bar.

Charlene seized his chair and dropped into it. "Interfering?"

"It's nothing. I was just hashing out whether we should keep investigating."

"And?"

"We've helped Gordon in the past." I hesitated, thinking. "We need to keep doing it. Pie Town doesn't need any more bad publicity, and . . ."

"What?"

"I need to get out of my head. As much as I go back and forth on if what we're doing is right or wrong, it *feels* right."

"Doing what we can to stop a killer *is* right. There's no feeling about it." She peeled off her white knit jacket and set it on the back of the chair. "I found the business card those UFO folks left on your desk. What did they want?"

"The usual. Proof of life on other planets. So of course they came to Pie Town." In spite of myself, I smiled. "I told them the truth, but they wouldn't believe me."

"Well, the evidence that this planet has been visited by

aliens is compelling." She dug her phone from the pocket of her orange tunic, tapped the screen, and handed it to me.

I studied the photo—an unaltered picture of Charlene dangling a pie-plate UFO off a fishing line.

"Is this the end of our pie-tin UFO promotion?" I asked.

She sighed, her shoulders folding inward. "It was time. Tally Wally convinced me people were starting to turn."

"So that's what you two were talking about."

"That, and . . ."

"And what?"

Her face crumpled. "It was stupid, really."

"What?"

"My husband. He loved the idea of UFOs and life in other worlds and flying to the stars. That's what gave me the idea for the pie tins. And I thought, if we made the international wire services, maybe my daughter would see . . ." She blinked rapidly. "Maybe I did take the pie-tin UFOs too far."

A lump hardened in my throat. She'd thought her daughter might see the article and make the connection between the pie-tin UFOs and her father.

"Well, it's too bad your promotion is ending." I wrinkled my brow, thinking of a way to salvage this without causing a bigger UFO panic. "Maybe, alongside your big-reveal photo, we could print instructions? A step-by-step guide to making a pie-tin UFO."

Her face lighted. "You think? Of course, any copycats would need two official Pie Town pie tins to make one, and the only way to get those is to buy two pies."

I nodded, somber. "There *is* that."

She thumped her fist on the wooden table, rattling my beer glass. "She's back! Now about Doran—"

"Doran will get over it," I said with more confidence than I felt. "We didn't actually do anything wrong, which he'll realize, if he bothers to think about it."

"That wasn't what I was going to say, but what you said isn't bad. Now, how much trouble are you in with the big guy?" She nodded toward Gordon at the bar.

"Not so much." I frowned. It was downright weird that he'd encourage us to investigate, even if he had warned us off interfering.

"What's wrong?"

"You know when you first start dating someone and you see them through rose-colored glasses? Everything seems perfect."

"That's the best part!"

"Yeah, but the glasses have to come off sooner or later." I paused, thinking of my ex-fiancé. I'd been burned so badly, but it hadn't all been Mark's fault. "Gordon and I are still in that glasses-on phase, and it feels great. But I guess I'm worried about what comes next."

"He's a copper. I think he sees people pretty clearly."

Gordon had said we needed to take people as they are. But he was a detective, and a good one who wouldn't want a case messed up. I glanced toward the bar. So why was he so easygoing about me and Charlene? "He encouraged us to keep investigating."

"How much did he have to drink?"

"Two beers." I gnawed my bottom lip. "He did tell us we needed to be more careful not to interfere with his investigation—"

"We're always careful!"

I shot her a look. "More careful."

"Fine, more careful. Whatever."

"But—"

"No luck on the alibi." Gordon rested one hand on my shoulder. "The bartender can't remember Brittany, and neither can the waitresses who were here that night. But that's not conclusive. It was a busy night, and they don't have photographic memories."

"I once knew a guy with a photographic memory," Charlene mused. "It came in real handy during that line-dance competition."

"How . . . ?" Gordon shook his head. "Never mind."

Creakily, Charlene lumbered from the chair. "I'll leave you two lovebirds. Word is there's been a Bigfoot sighting down behind the Circle K."

"Where the creek is?" I asked, alarmed. The bank there was steep and could get slippery. "Charlene . . ."

"Why don't we go with you?" Gordon looked down at me, his green eyes crinkling, and my heart lifted.

His hand lightly squeezed my shoulder. "I haven't been on a Bigfoot hunt in years."

CHAPTER 26

Outside, cars crawled along Main Street, their drivers searching for parking. Inside, the gamers huddled, dice rattling, in their regular corner booth. Families with sunburned noses slumped wearily at tables.

The coast was often deceptively warmer in early autumn than in summer. Today was one of those glorious September Sunday afternoons, and Pie Town was buzzing.

But my pulse skittered. Tonight, Charlene and I were infiltrating a secret society, even if it was only a bunch of college kids. And I couldn't tell if my jitters were worry or excitement. But I'd committed. We were doing this.

Petronella and I worked the front counter while Abril filled orders from the kitchen and Hunter bused tables.

Charlene sat at the counter, her face contorting. She made increasingly alarming noises, a newspaper clenched in her fists. Bigfoot had been a no-show last night. It looked like she was taking it hard.

I deposited plates of coconut cream, strawberry, and two pumpkin pies at a four-top and bustled behind the counter.

Charlene gave a strangled gasp.

The bell over the front door jangled. I ignored it.

"Charlene," I said, "what's wrong?"

"Marla," she croaked.

"You rang?" Marla asked, and glared at the full stools in front of the counter.

Charlene spun to face her. "You dare show your face here?"

"Oh, I see you read my article." She tried to pluck the paper from Charlene's grasp, but Charlene clung to it like baked fruit filling to the bottom of an oven.

"What article?" I asked, before one of the octogenarians could get into an actual brawl.

"Here you go." Tally Wally handed me an unrumpled copy of the paper, and my head rocked back in surprise.

"What are you still doing here?" I asked. "Don't you golf Sunday afternoons?"

He sipped his coffee. "I had a feeling things would be more interesting here."

His buddy Graham leaned forward on his stool and peered past Tally Wally. "And we were right."

Bemused, I scanned the page Tally Wally had neatly folded.

DID A PIE SHOP'S PROMO
GO TOO FAR?

A week ago, when photos of UFOs over San Nicholas began appearing on the Twitter account of a Pie Town employee, people took notice. Most believed the photos, clearly of two pie tins fastened together, were a marketing gag. But some took the pictures seriously.

"There was a near riot on Main Street," local resident Marla Van Helsing said. "I was there, in Pie Town, at the time. It was terrifying."

> *Pie Town's owner has confirmed that the photos were intended as a harmless joke.*
>
> *But were the photos harmless?*
>
> *"The police had to manage crowd control," Ms. Van Helsing said. "Someone could have been trampled. Did I mention it was terrifying?"*
>
> *"It was completely out of control," neighboring business owner Heidi Gladstone said. "My customers couldn't reach my gym, Heidi's Health and Fitness. The people who were trapped inside were afraid to leave and face that mob."*
>
> *In today's age of viral marketing, businesses are pushing the envelope in their attempts to get attention online. But when do publicity stunts go too far?*

I grimaced. It could have been worse. The article could have connected Pie Town with the recent murders. "It's fair," I said reluctantly. I was going to have to bake apology pies to my neighbors—except for Heidi. She was anti-pie.

"Fair?" Charlene glared at Marla. "Fair? Is it fair that this publicity hound plants her bottom at our counter for discount hand pies and cheap coffee, then turns on the hand that feeds her?"

Marla tossed her glamorously coiffed head. "You should be thanking me."

"Are you out of your mind?" Charlene's eyes bulged.

"Because of me, your little pie-plate stunt is in the news another day."

"I was going to post how-I-did-it photos," Charlene howled.

"No publicity is bad publicity," Marla said.

"Mm." That wasn't entirely true, but in the interests of keeping the peace, I didn't argue. "How have the old photos been doing online?" I asked Charlene. "Are people still sharing them?"

"That's not the point," she grumbled.

Marla arched a brow. "Isn't it? Isn't it, Charlene?"

A man vacated a stool at the far end of the counter, and Marla scuttled to seize it before someone else could.

"I could throttle her," Charlene muttered.

"But you won't," I said, "because we both know that even if her intentions were bad, the results were not. Doran gave me some files on that professor who died a few years back. I haven't had a chance to read through them yet—"

"Where are they?"

"My office."

Crumpling the paper into a ball, she stood and stalked into my office.

I followed, smothering a smile.

Charlene made herself comfortable in my executive chair. The purple satin robe I'd hung on its back this morning slithered sideways. I adjusted it and handed her the file folder.

"You heard from your brother?" she asked, scanning the first article printout.

"Not yet." And it was all I could do not to run to his rental to try to make him see things my way. But that would be wrong. I slipped my hands into my apron's pockets. "I'm giving him some space." Even if it was killing me.

"Professor Theresa Keller." Studying the article, she leaned back in my chair, and it creaked. "I remember this accident. Five years ago, one of those zippy sports cars took a curve too fast and went over the cliff out past that fancy hotel. The woman died. I didn't remember her name though, or that she was a professor at the local college. It happened late at night. No witnesses. Someone saw the car at the bottom of the cliffs the next morning and called it in."

"So, the question is, does this have anything to do with Starke's poem or with his death?"

"Starke wasn't here when it happened," she said. "He arrived four years ago, didn't he?"

"Then if there was something hinky about this accident, Starke couldn't have seen it. But Aidan might have."

"The plagiarism. If Starke stole Aidan's story—"

"It would be a motive to kill both Starke and Aidan," I said. "Assuming this has anything to do with the murders. And we still can't be sure it does. It's all kind of vague."

"We need to know where all our suspects were the night Theresa Keller died."

"If this is about Theresa Keller, then that lets out Brittany. She would have been, what? Fifteen? Sixteen?"

"You've never raised a teenager." Charlene's snowy brows pulled downward. "Don't count her out."

"But didn't she move here from Maine after Theresa's accident?"

"That's what she *says*."

"Okay, five years is a long time for a records check," I said. "We need help."

Charlene folded her arms over her fuchsia tunic. "Call your copper. I won't stop you."

I pulled my phone from my apron pocket and called Gordon.

"Dare I hope this is a personal call?" he asked.

My heart fluttered. "It's always personal. Except, no, we found some information that might be useful, but we aren't sure what to make of it." I explained about Theresa Keller.

"And you think she's connected to that poem? I thought the title was 'Death in a Parking Lot,' not 'Death on the Cliffs.' "

"She's the only professor there who's died in the last few years. Maybe Starke took some artistic liberties."

He sighed. "All right. I'll look into it, if only to justify digging through your dumpster for that poem. I'll get back to you."

We said our goodbyes, and he hung up.

"What did he say?" Charlene kicked her high-tops up on the metal desk.

"He's looking into it."

"Call Jezek. He's been around that college a while. Maybe he knows something."

"Maybe he did it." But I phoned Professor Jezek.

"Hello?" he asked cautiously.

"Professor Jezek, this is Val Harris, from Pie Town."

"Oh." His voice darkened.

"You were at the college five years ago, weren't you?"

"Yes . . . ?"

"Did you know Theresa Keller?"

There was a choking sound.

"Hello? Professor?"

He hung up.

"Well?" Charlene asked.

I stared at the phone. "Jezek hung up on me."

"Suspicious."

But was it? I wasn't sure I'd want to talk to me either.

I phoned Dorothy and the dean, but my calls went to voicemail.

"They're probably screening their calls." Charlene laced her hands behind her head. "That's what I do."

"Are we on the wrong track?" I asked. "I mean, it's kind of an out-there theory, isn't it?"

"That Aidan witnessed a five-year-old murder, told Starke, and Starke wrote a poem about it that got him killed? Then the murderer realized where the story had really come from and killed Aidan? Seems pretty straightforward to me."

"Uh, yeah. When you put it that way . . ." None of it quite fit. I shook my head. "Why do people commit murder?"

"Money, love, revenge, or to protect themselves. Oh, or craziness."

"All right, so why kill Theresa Keller?"

Charlene thumbed through the printed articles and shook her head. "This was reported as an accident. Most of the articles are about the dangers of that stretch of road and the need to improve it. Here's a quote from . . . Professor Piotr Jezek. *Theresa was an amazing woman and an asset to the department. She will be missed.*"

"Wait a minute," I said, excited. " 'To the department'? To the English department?"

She shook her head. "The article doesn't specify."

I scooted around the desk and grabbed for my computer keyboard. "There's got to be something online—"

Petronella opened the office door and stuck her head inside. "Hey, we're getting slammed out here."

My cheeks warmed. It wasn't fair to leave my staff in the lurch. Again. Pies before investigations. "Sorry. I'll be right out."

"Don't worry, Val," Charlene said. "I'm on the case."

That was exactly the sort of thing to make me worried. But hungry customers were calling, and I hurried into the dining area.

The crowd finally eased up around five. The tables were mostly clear, aside from the gamers in the corner. A handful of customers lined up at the register for pies to take home.

I handed a boxed chocolate-pecan pie to a round-faced man. "Here you go!"

"Thanks!" He bustled out the door.

I glanced at the corner booth. Charlene sat with the gamers, which either meant she'd taken up a new hobby or she was up to something. I ran my finger inside the collar of my Pie Town t-shirt.

The phone in my apron rang, and I checked the number. *Gordon*. My pulse gave a little jump. "Um, Petronella, would you mind taking over for a minute?"

She set a plastic bin beneath the counter and nodded. "Sure thing."

I stepped aside for her and answered the phone. "Hey, Gordon. What's going on?"

"I had an interesting conversation with the officer on the scene of that car accident you told me about."

"Oh?"

"He told me he was never satisfied Theresa's death was an accident."

"You mean, murder?" I whispered. OMG. We'd been right!

"No. Suicide. There were no skid marks, and she hadn't been drinking."

"Oh." That was disappointing. And did that thought make me a bad person? "Why suicide? Was she depressed?"

The owner of the comic shop next door poured herself coffee from the nearby urn. Joy somberly lifted her mug to me in a mock toast, and I smiled in response.

"Not as far as he could tell," Gordon said.

"But he didn't think foul play was involved?"

"The SNPD was understaffed at the time," he said carefully. "It's a small town."

Huh. If I was reading him right, Gordon thought the police officer had made the wrong call, but he couldn't say so.

"There's no real connection between that death and the recent murders," he said. "Not that I can see."

"But Theresa Keller was in the English department, wasn't she?"

"Yes. She was."

"I think Professor Jezek might know something."

His voice razored. "And why might you think that?"

"Um, no reason. I mean, he hasn't said anything about

Theresa to me. But he was at the college when she died, and I noticed he gave a nice quote in the paper about her after her, um, accident."

"Why don't I believe that's the entire story?" he asked.

But I thought I heard laughter in his voice.

"All right," he continued. "*I'll* talk to him."

We whispered a few non-Baker-Street-Bakers things to each other, and hung up.

I checked the line at the counter. There were only two people waiting, and Petronella seemed to be managing. So I hustled over to the gamers' pink corner booth.

I smiled at the group. "Hey, Charlene, have you got a minute?"

"Not right now," she said. "I'm ironing out some things with our friends."

"Gordon called," I said significantly.

"What did he say?"

"Maybe we should talk in my office."

"It's okay." Ray brushed his hand across the top of his red hair. "Charlene's told us all about the murders. We were wondering when you were going to bring us in."

I stared. "She . . . What?"

"Since your brother has deserted us," she said, "I thought it was time to bring in the big guns. Ray's team has not only infiltrated the college, but they also have access to its computers."

Henrietta's broad face creased. "I wouldn't say *infiltrated*. We're students."

"Same difference," Charlene said.

I studied the gamers. Ray and Henrietta had been auxiliary (honorary?) members of the Baker Street Bakers earlier this year. And it wasn't as if we'd been exactly quiet about the investigation. Tally Wally, Graham, Abril, and a host of other characters had all stuck their oars in.

I sighed. "Why not? Officially, Theresa Keller's death was accidental. But there were no skid marks at the scene, and there was no alcohol in her blood."

"Murder," Ray said.

"Or suicide," I said.

Charlene pointed at the gamers. "Your mission is to find out everything you can about Theresa Keller and our suspects who were at the college when she died."

"But only computer research," I said. "We can't seem to be interfering in a police investigation."

"Got it," Ray said. "Nothing IRL."

"That means *in real life*," Charlene said loftily. "You've got to stay on top of the modern lingo, Val."

Ray rubbed his pale hands together. "So, the usual compensation? We'll be paid in pie?"

"Pie left over at the end of the day," I countered.

"Deal." He stuck out his hand, and we shook. "By the way," he said. "I thought the pie-tin UFOs were cool."

"Thank you, Ray," Charlene said.

I smiled. As usual, everything was going to work out.

And then Ray spoke again, and my heart dropped to my soft-soled shoes.

I gaped, uncomprehending. "What?"

His freckled brow furrowed. "I said, is it true a group is protesting Pie Town?"

CHAPTER 27

Outside the window, a motorcycle buzzed down Main Street, its engine an angry wasp. My shoulders tightened at the noise. "Protest group? What group?"

Sunlight streamed through Pie Town's blinds and made prison-bar shadows across Ray's broad face. He tugged down the hem of his comic-hero tee. "I saw something online about the pie-tin UFOs."

"Where online? What was it?" I asked, frantic. We were being protested? This was *not* good publicity.

Ray looked toward the ceiling, and his broad face wrinkled in a frown. "It must have been on a message board, but maybe I was wrong about the consumer group. It would have been a UFO message board, though they can get pretty nutty."

Charlene rolled her eyes. "Tell me about it."

"Why would they—?" My nails bit into my palms. *No.* I couldn't panic over an unsubstantiated rumor. I had bigger fish to fry. In a few short hours, Charlene and I would be tracking a secret society through the creepiest cypress forest ever. True, the forest was small and on a super-charming ocean cliff, but it was still ooky.

His girlfriend, Henrietta, nudged him. "Freaking her out isn't very nice."

"But she should know," Ray said.

"But know what?" Henrietta said. "This is why we're only *associate* Baker Street Bakers. We need to get more specific with our data."

"Thanks for letting me know," I said, gulping. "Could you try to get more info and send it to my cell phone?"

"We will," Henrietta said.

"Right," he added hastily.

There was no use worrying over something I couldn't control and didn't have the facts on.

But I couldn't help worrying. I worried as I took the van out to deliver orders. I worried as I returned and closed the empty restaurant. I worried as I cleaned up, turned off the lights.

How could I stalk a secret society when I was in emotional tsunami mode? I took deep, cleansing breaths and grabbed the purple robe from the back of my office chair. Someone had printed on the inside collar in black felt-tip pen: PROPERTY OF THE DRAMA DEPT.

Okay then.

I draped it over my arm, walked to my van, and drove to Charlene's house.

She pirouetted in her living room, her purple robe billowing over her fuchsia tunic, hood pulled low over her eyes. "What do you think?"

Coiled in a fraying wing chair, Frederick buried his head in a cushion.

I thought her high-tops ruined the effect, and she really needed to take me up on dumping her burnt sofa. "Very secret society."

"Dorothy didn't give us the secret handshake."

"I'm sure we'll get by, with or without the capes."

"They're robes, not capes. Look, sleeves!" She flapped her arms. "You're not taking this seriously."

"Their entrance passcode is *Hello, Dolly!* I don't think they'll sacrifice intruders on a sacred stage. And I also don't think we should drive around San Nicholas in purple capes."

"Robes!"

"Robes," I said.

"But you're right. They'll get wrinkled. We should wait until we get to the haunted forest."

"It's not—" *Never mind.*

Robes folded over our arms, we climbed into Charlene's yellow Jeep. She thought my pink pie van was embarrassing, but she had no trouble traipsing around in purple satin. Go figure.

We whizzed down Highway One, screeching left in front of a line of cars to make our turn. Horns blaring behind us, we bumped down the road and along a cliff.

Charlene craned her neck and slowed in front of Marla's gate.

"The forest is a bit farther," I said.

"Yes, but we are so close . . ."

My eyes narrowed. "Close to what?"

She tugged on her ear and squinted. "I'm thinking." Charlene stepped on the gas, and we lurched forward, driving to the end of the road and a small, dirt parking lot.

I stepped outside. A wind blew off the ocean, and I shivered, zipping up my Pie Town hoodie.

Charlene's headlights went off, plunging us into autumnal gloom. I widened my eyes, trying to adjust to the lack of light.

The robes were roomy, and I slipped mine on over my hoodie. But they didn't provide much extra protection against the cold.

Robes flapping about our ankles, we walked through an arch of cypress trees, our footsteps quiet on the soft earth. The trees had obviously been planted, spaced evenly apart. A full, harvest moon glinted through the dark branches, groaning in the wind.

My jaw tightened. I'd been here in the daylight many times. But at night, this trail was creeptastic, and not in a spooky-Halloween-fun sort of way.

We moved along the broad path.

Out of the corner of my eyes, I caught movement in the nearby trees. I whipped my head toward the motion, my heart thudding. But in the darkness, all I could make out were the silhouettes of the broad and twisting cypresses.

It's just an animal. Like a raccoon. Or a coyote. Or a . . . Gulp *. . . mountain lion.*

Picking up a large stick, I tiptoed onward, my gaze darting around the miniature forest. What temporary insanity had convinced me this was a good idea?

A branch cracked, and I grasped Charlene's sleeve.

"Did you hear that?" I whispered.

She cocked her head. "Nope." Charlene hurried forward. "The cave's this way. Pull up your hood. We're getting close."

Something rustled in the trees. Nerves officially racked, I adjusted my hood, and we turned off the path and into the trees. Charlene and I hurried down a slope, branches crackling beneath our feet.

Near blind, I stumbled over a rock, my hands damp on the bark of the rough stick I carried.

"Shhh!" Charlene hissed. "A little farther. What secrets will be unveiled?"

My robe snagged on a branch. I tugged free. There was a faint ripping sound, and I winced.

"Shhh!"

"Sorry," I whispered.

We skidded down a steep slope, and Charlene stopped and grabbed my arm.

I froze.

Light flickered from a narrow, uneven entrance in a natural wall of jagged gray stone.

A still figure stood beside the entrance, not three feet

away. I smothered a gasp, forced myself to drop the stupid stick. Had it not been for the flutter of his robe, I wouldn't have noticed the person.

"Password," a man intoned.

I cleared my throat.

"*Hello, Dolly!*" Charlene boomed.

He nodded. "Enter and be silent."

She passed inside.

"*Hello, Dolly!*" I muttered, feeling foolish.

"Enter and be silent."

I scuttled past him and squeezed through the rocks.

The cave was bigger on the inside than its entrance suggested. At the far end, by a large, flat stone, people in hooded robes milled about. A card table laden with chips, brownies, and crudités stood on one side of the cave.

A purple-robed approached me. "*Hamilton*," she whispered.

"*Hamilton!*" I squeaked back.

"*Hamilton, Hamilton, Hamilton . . .*" The password echoed through the cave.

Someone clapped their hands. "Okay," a woman said. "It looks like everyone's here."

People shuffled into a circle. Charlene and I found spaces across from each other.

The woman raised a mask in each hand—tragedy and comedy. "Master of dialogue," she intoned.

"Master of dialogue," the others chanted.

She made a quarter turn, and the others did as well, facing in the same direction. Belatedly, Charlene and I turned.

"Mistress of representation," she said.

"Mistress of representation," they repeated.

Another smart quarter turn, and this time Charlene and I were quicker off the mark.

"Thespis," she said. "God of actors."

"Thespis, god of actors," they said, and we turned.

"Dionysus, great god of the theater," she said.

They echoed the chant and turned to face the center. The tiki torches lengthened our shadows, rippling on the gray stone walls.

Their so-called society was silly and harmless. So why were my palms damp, my pulse loud in my ears?

She raised the masks high. "And to the great in-between, the liminal space that represents the stage, we call you."

They repeated the words.

She dropped the masks to her side, and pulled back her hood, revealing a cheerful young blonde. "Hi, everyone. Thanks so much for coming tonight, after the tragic loss of Professor Starke."

People removed their hoods and spoke in low voices to each other.

My heart pounded. Oh, damn. It would look weird if we kept our hoods on. Across from me, Charlene stood, as indecisive as me.

Someone in a hood wandered into the cave. "You started without me?" he asked.

Everyone turned to him.

The blonde frowned. "I thought . . . I counted. Twice! Everyone was here."

Another robed person jogged in, panting. "Sorry I'm late."

"Hold on," the blonde said. "If you two weren't here, then—"

Charlene tugged down her purple hood. "You've been infiltrated."

The blonde colored. "You don't— How did you . . . ?"

"Don't get your occult knickers in a twist," Charlene said. "We're the Baker Street Bakers. We're here to investigate Michael Starke's murder, not expose whatever conspiracy you're running. Unless it connects to the murder."

I covered my face with my hands. *No one* took the BSB's name seriously.

"Where did you get those robes?" the blonde asked.

The volume in the cave rose.

Charlene whistled, a piercing shriek, and everyone winced.

"Now we can do this the easy way," Charlene said, "and you can tell us what you know, or we can reveal your little secret group to the world."

The blonde's lips flattened. "Fine. But we don't know anything."

"Which of you were at the poetry reading the night Professor Starke was killed?" I asked.

A half-dozen hands lifted into the air.

"All right," I said. "Could everyone who was at the reading please join me on that side of the cave?" I pointed. "We'll talk there."

Muttering, the group separated, one heading toward the food table. The other joined me on the far side of the cave.

"Okay," I said, looking around. But Charlene had migrated to the card table with the goodies. "First, the obvious question, did anyone see Professor Starke on the street, after the event?"

A tentative hand went up. A slender brunette. "I saw him walking away."

"Was he alone?" I asked.

She nodded.

"Did you notice anyone else?" I asked.

She shook her head. "I was going in the opposite direction."

"Okay, did anyone notice anything odd or unusual at the reading?"

People glanced at one another.

The blonde, who seemed to be the group's leader, cleared her throat. "Brittany was there."

"What was strange about that?" I asked.

Nervous laughter echoed off the stone walls.

"Well," the blonde said, "it was, like, *Brittany*."

"And?" I asked.

She tossed her head, her blond hair cascading over the satin robe. "Okay, I guess we were all weirded out, because she's, like, been totally stalking him, you know?"

"Stalking Professor Starke?" I asked, my scalp prickling.

"Everyone knew it," she said. "Professor Starke laughed it off, but it was just weird, you know? I mean, the real reason she switched to engineering was because she'd taken all the English classes the college had. The only way for her to stay at the college was to switch to a new program. She did it to stay close to Professor Starke."

The others nodded.

"Did you see Brittany leave?" I asked.

"I did," a slender young man with round glasses said. "She left just before Professor Starke."

So she could have been lying in wait. I shook myself. *Anyone* could have been lying in wait. "Anyone else?" I asked, brisk.

They shook their heads.

"Any other odd events?"

The young man pushed up his glasses. "I didn't expect to see Professor Jezek there."

"Why not?" I asked. "He's part of the English department."

"Yeah," he said, "but he hates going out at night. Everyone knows it."

"Why?" I asked.

The young man laughed. "Because he's nuts."

"I think something happened to him in Eastern Europe," a slender redhead said quietly. "He's not nuts. He's talked about it a little. When he was a child, the neighbors in their apartment building disappeared one night, taken by the secret police. The rest of the building pretended it hadn't happened. They were afraid they'd be next."

We fell silent. It was hard to believe a world like that had existed—still existed in some places. What had that childhood done to Piotr Jezek?

"Anything more?" I asked, subdued.

"Professor Starke and Professor McClary got into it," the young man said, as if trying to redeem himself. "But they were always at each other's throats."

"I thought it was kind of a joke," the blonde said. "Until Professor Starke and Professor McClary were killed. Now none of it seems funny."

"Anything else?" I asked.

They shook their heads. "Okay. Thanks." I walked to the snack table, where Charlene was in a heated discussion with a tall, sandy-haired youth.

"What do you *mean* you don't believe in the ghost light?" she asked.

He shrugged. "I'm not saying I don't believe theaters put them out onstage at night. I know they do. I'm just saying, it's got nothing to do with keeping the ghosts happy."

"But it doesn't make sense otherwise," she said, scowling.

"There are lots of practical reasons to put a light onstage overnight," he said. "That way, the last people out or first people in won't fall into the orchestra pit."

"But you're in a secret society! Passcodes! The occult!"

"Hey, I'm just here for the networking and the brownies." He stuffed one into his mouth and ambled away.

"Unbelievable," she said to me. "Not a single person here even believes in Bigfoot."

"But they were useful witnesses." I told her what I'd learned.

"You already suspected something was up with Brittany."

"I suspected, but I didn't know. This was confirmation."

"Are you going to tell your detective?" she asked.

"Of course." Just after I figured out how to explain why invading a secret society was totally not interfering with an investigation.

CHAPTER 28

It took me a good half hour to talk Charlene out of buzzing Marla's house with a faux UFO. Once that was settled to my satisfaction, if not Charlene's, we drove home.

Monday, I slept until the sun streamed through the blinds, which, for a baker, is positively hedonistic. We were closed Mondays. It was a win for me, because I had the day off. And it was a win for Pie Town, because if trouble was brewing thanks to the pie-tin UFOs, well, it was hard to make trouble at a closed pie shop.

I changed out of my pie pajamas and lounged, reading, on my futon. Outside, birds twittered a cheerful morning song.

A fist pounded on my door, and I jerked off the futon. Heart banging, I scrambled off the floor and pulled back the blinds.

Professor Jezek stood outside my door. His mustache drooped. Morning sunlight glistened off his domed head.

What was he doing at my house? I let the blinds drop, but not before he'd seen me.

"Come out!" he shouted.

"Keep your shirt on!" Wow. In moments of stress, I sounded like Charlene. Shelving that concern for a later day, I grabbed my baseball bat (a gift from Charlene and for self-defense purposes only). Hiding it behind my thigh with one hand, I cracked open the door. "It's a little early."

"You and your friend have come to my house and harassed me." He quivered with anger and perhaps fear? Alcohol fumes wafted from his rumpled brown suit. "I thought turnabout was fair play."

I couldn't really argue that. "Fine, but I can't talk long. My boyfriend, *Detective* Carmichael, is coming over to take me to the beach," I lied. "But give me a minute to put on my shoes, and I'll come outside."

He nodded and stepped away from the door.

My shoulders unknotted. He was backing off. I stepped inside, shut the door, and slipped into my tennies. I regarded the baseball bat, then set it on the kitchen counter. The nice thing about a tiny house? Everything's pretty much in arm's reach.

I opened the door and stepped outside.

Jezek sat at the picnic table, a move I suspected he'd regret since it was covered in dew. His fingers laced and unlaced. Behind him, beyond the edge of the cliff, sea and sky met in a wash of blue.

Keeping a cautious distance between us, I stood at the opposite side of the wooden table. "Was there something you wanted to discuss?"

His sloping face seemed to sharpen, grow more intense. He exhaled a shaky breath. "What do you know about Theresa Keller?"

So *that's* what this was about. "Only that she died in a car accident five years ago."

"Then why were you asking about her?"

"Professor Starke read a poem called 'Death in a Parking

Lot' the night he died," I said, "and it seemed to hint at a murder. And then he was killed."

"What does that have to do with Theresa?" he asked sharply. If he'd been drinking, he seemed sober enough now.

"There are some similarities between the poem and her death," I said.

"But she died on a cliff—"

"I know. It's a long shot, and the poem probably doesn't have anything to do with Starke and Professor McClary."

He stood and paced, and I tried not to look at the damp splotch on his baggy trousers. He cleared his throat. "Theresa was a wonderful woman, a true free spirit." His voice trembled. "Everybody loved her." He rubbed his glistening eyes with his thumb and middle finger.

"Everybody?" I pursed my lips. Not even the Dalai Lama is universally loved.

"Perhaps not Rudolph." He lowered his head. "Theresa was not one for following the dean's rules."

"What rules did she break?" I asked.

He scowled. "It was a tragedy when she died. I won't have you dragging her name through the mud."

Interesting. "What mud?"

"Leave the dead in peace," he said, shrill. He spun on his heel and stormed across my lawn and down my dirt driveway. A few minutes later, an engine revved, and the sound of a car's motor faded into the distance.

Professor Jezek had been afraid. And yet he'd stormed my ramparts to quiz me about Theresa Keller? He'd told me everybody loved her. I wondered if his feelings for her had run as deep.

Shaking my head, I walked inside. I wasn't going to puzzle this out on my own. I phoned Charlene.

"What?" she asked.

"Professor Jezek just came by my house."

"Did you use that baseball bat I gave you?"

"No, I didn't need it."

"Every woman needs a baseball bat," she said. "And to know to swing low. What did he want?"

I told her about our conversation.

"Huh," she said. "Listen, I'm at the courthouse, trying to turn up anything on Starke's will. On Aidan's too, since I'm here. I'll stop by your place when I'm done."

"See you then."

We hung up, and I started my Monday-morning house-cleaning. It didn't take much for my tiny house to get cluttered, so I had to stay on top of things. I went through my usual cleaning routine, working from top to bottom. By the time I'd finished, Charlene's yellow Jeep was pulling up to my picnic table.

I walked outside, and Charlene clambered from the Jeep. Frederick lay, depositing white hairs, on her red knit tunic.

"I've got motive," she crowed.

"You found something?" I eyed Frederick. How had she gotten him inside the courthouse?

"Dorothy may lose out on her alimony," she said, "but guess who gets Starke's beachfront house?"

"Dorothy?"

"Exactamundo! It's worth millions."

I sat on the picnic bench, remembering too late about that dew. Springing to my feet, I brushed off the seat of my jeans. "But Dorothy couldn't have firebombed your house. She was talking to Gordon about all the papers she was burning."

"And we'll never know what those papers were," Charlene said in a dire tone. "What if she had an accomplice?"

"Not Aidan. Someone killed him first."

"Well, maybe Starke wasn't the only professor with a thing for students?"

"I dunno. I didn't get that vibe from her."

"What sort of a vibe does a woman with a thing for younger men put out? Scratch that. A Marla vibe. I'm going to get that woman to print a retraction about my pie-tin UFOs."

Charlene and I blamestormed some more but couldn't come up with any better ideas. And since I was sure Gordon already knew who'd benefited from Starke's death, I didn't call him to report in.

"What about Aidan?" I asked. "You said you were going to check out his will."

"Couldn't find one. He either didn't have a will, or it's registered somewhere else, like in Merry Olde England."

"Ireland," I corrected.

"Whatever. I'll bet his accent was a put-on."

I paced in the shade of my tiny home's awning. "But he needed to marry Dorothy so he could stay in the country, re-member?"

"Maybe. What if it was all an excuse for Aidan to pres-sure her to say yes?"

"It didn't seem to be working," I said dryly.

"According to Patel." She perked up. "I know what we need. We need to pay another visit to the White Lady."

"Do you think Patel will have more information?"

"I think it's a beautiful day for mimosas, and their patio won't be crowded on a Monday."

As I had no better ideas, we hopped in Charlene's Jeep and drove to the White Lady.

The ocean crashed below the patio. As Charlene had pre-dicted, it was empty of all but a couple and their Irish setter.

Tail wagging, the dog strained against his leash toward us.

"Now, settle down, Frederick," she said, stroking the obliv-ious and limp cat. "I know how you love chasing dogs, but we don't want to be thrown out of our favorite watering hole."

The white cat yawned.

"Er," I said, "how did you get him inside the courthouse?"

"I didn't." She lifted her chin. "Bringing a cat to court

wouldn't be proper. I'm not one of those fakers who pretend their Fluffy is a service animal to take him into the grocery store. I left Frederick at home and collected him afterward."

I'd seen Charlene take Frederick into all sorts of places he didn't belong, but I didn't argue. It was too beautiful a day. It was September, and I was in a t-shirt at the beach, the sun warm on my arms. You can't beat California weather.

We sipped mimosas from a swinging bench and watched lines of waves surge and crash against the cliffs beneath us. The sun sparkled off the Pacific, and I felt my worries melting away. It's hard to be stressed out in the face of all that natural beauty.

A shadow fell across our bench. "Hey, guys, does this place serve beer in the morning?" Ray asked.

I squinted up at him and Henrietta. "What are you two doing here?" They were almost matching, in baggy cargo pants and oversized comic t-shirts.

"Charlene invited us," he said. "We got that information you wanted."

"Beers on me," Charlene said. "But you'll have to come with me to the bar upstairs."

Ray gallantly helped her up, and the two meandered inside.

Henrietta pushed back her sandy hair and sat on the edge of the unlit firepit. "So. Pretty crazy stuff. Huh?"

"You should probably wait until Charlene gets back, or you'll just have to tell your story all over again."

She glanced at the couple with the Irish setter. "Oh," she said in a low voice, "Charlene already knows we hacked into the college's system."

I coughed up mimosa.

Alarmed, Henrietta leapt to her feet and smacked me on the back.

"You did *what*?" I gasped, eyes watering.

"That sort of information isn't public," she explained.

I groaned and set my glass on the nearby end table. It was also the sort of information I could never share with Gordon, since it would land two of my favorite customers in trouble. "Tell me you didn't get caught."

"We didn't get caught."

"Really? Or are you just saying that to make me feel better?"

She laughed. "The college's security system is a joke. We could have broken in with a hacksaw, and no one would have noticed."

"But you're *engineers*," I said.

"Software engineers. Are you sure you don't want to know what we found?"

"Of course I do. But keep your voice down."

"All right—"

The glass door to the restaurant slid open, and Ray and Charlene emerged. Ray carried two beers. He handed one to Henrietta and sat beside her on the brick firepit.

Charlene settled in beside me. "Tell us everything."

Ray leaned forward, his brown eyes gleaming. "This is juicy. I think we've blown this case wide open."

"Enough with the dramatic suspense," Charlene grumped. "What did you learn?"

"It was buried pretty deep in the HR files."

"HR?" Charlene asked.

"Human resources," I said. "What did you find?"

"A complaint from a parent." Ray looked about expectantly.

"Well?" Charlene asked. "Complaint about what?"

"About an affair with a student," Ray said.

I slumped on the bench, and it swayed beneath me. "We already knew Starke was having affairs with his TAs."

"Not Professor Starke," Henrietta whispered. "Professor Keller."

Charlene jolted forward, and my feet skidded from beneath the swinging bench. "*Theresa* Keller?" she asked.

"When was this complaint lodged?" I asked.

"Three days before her death," Henrietta said.

I rubbed the back of my neck. That might explain Professor Jezek's remark about dragging Theresa's name through the mud. "Then the accident *could* have been suicide."

"Suicide?" Ray crossed his arms, resting them on the shelf of his rounded stomach. "I thought it was either an accident or murder. You didn't say anything about suicide."

"I wasn't supposed to know," I said. "Gordon told me, confidentially, that the officer in charge suspected suicide. But he couldn't find any reason for it. Now we have a potential reason."

Henrietta's broad face twisted in a scowl. "Sleeping with students didn't seem to do Professor Starke much harm."

"Did you find any complaints from parents in his HR files?" I asked.

"No," Ray said.

"Maybe that's why," I said.

"Was it a boy student or a girl student?" Charlene asked.

"What does it matter?" My mouth flattened. "It's an abuse of power in any case. Starke shouldn't have gotten away with it, and neither should have Professor Keller." But killing herself did seem extreme.

"It was a guy," Henrietta said. "And he was over eighteen."

"Val's right," Charlene said. "It was still wrong. Not that Marla would care," she muttered.

"What?" Ray asked.

"Nothing," I said quickly. "Did you find anything else?"

He handed me a thumb drive. "Just more HR stuff. Dates of hire, salaries, personnel evaluations, that sort of thing. I'm glad Dean Prophet isn't evaluating me. That guy is a real hard ass. Oh, and this will self-destruct after you open it."

I fumbled the drive, nearly dropping it on the flagstones.

Ray laughed. "Just kidding. But seriously, you should delete everything and get rid of it when you're done. It's not the sort of thing you want to get caught holding."

Because then we'd have to explain how we got it. "Gotcha." I tucked it into the front pocket of my jeans. "And thanks, this has been helpful. But no more crime solving through crime, okay?"

The others groaned.

"I mean it," I said.

"Killjoy," Charlene said.

The glass door slid open and closed behind us, and I glanced over my shoulder toward the source of the sound. A silver-haired couple claimed a table and angled their chairs to face the Pacific.

"Oh, there's one more thing," Ray said. "I took a peek in the files of that UFO group that's been on your case."

I glared.

"It wasn't hacking," he said, looking shifty. "I joined the group and gained access to their online discussions. It was quicker."

Charlene shook her head. "Should have hacked 'em. You're never getting off that group's email list, son."

He cleared his throat. "Anyway, the good news is they believe you, and they're not mad about being punked. They think you've brought new attention to old UFO cases. The pie tins also make people aware that not every light in the sky is a flying saucer."

"And the bad news?" I held my breath.

He tugged on the collar of his t-shirt. "After that sort of negative newspaper article, they're planning a rally of support tomorrow. At least, that's what they're calling it. But it seems like they're really rallying on their own behalf."

Charlene clapped me on the shoulder. "That's not so bad. Tuesday's a slow day. Think of all the extra customers."

"How big a rally?" I asked, wary.

He gulped. "Um. That's the bad news. They're expecting well over a thousand people. I've been tracking the group's social media, and I think they might be underestimating."

"Well over!" I couldn't manage a thousand people! The max occupancy in Pie Town was 125.

He winced. "And based on usual Main Street traffic flows on Tuesday afternoons—"

I sank my head in my hands. "My neighbors are going to kill me."

CHAPTER 29

"Blech. Modern poetry." Charlene shifted on her burnt couch, the plastic beneath her making crinkling sounds. "It's just lazy. There's no rhyme. No meter."

"But it might be a clue," I said, stopping in front of her boarded-up window. A chill night breeze slithered through the gaps and fluttered the curtains. "Er, what do you plan to do with that couch?"

Frederick raised his head from a nearby wing chair.

"Why?" she asked. "Do you want it?"

The cat's ears swiveled toward me. I thought I glinted hope in his blue eyes.

"I don't think it would fit in my tiny house," I said diplomatically. Also, it stank of burnt synthetics.

Frederick sank his head on his paws and sighed.

"I can take it to the dump for you though," I said. "If I remove the racks from the van, it should fit inside."

She shook her head. "Never mind about the couch. I've got a new one on order, and the deliverymen have promised to take this one off my hands." She patted the plastic and sighed. "It doesn't seem right to throw it out. We've got history, this couch and I. Bringing it home from the store when it was fresh and filled with possibility. Huddling together when it was storming outside. Making love—"

I cleared my throat. *TMI!* "But back to the poem!"

"Right," she said. "Clues."

I began to read out loud:

> *Death in a Parking Lot*
> *A woman taken,*
> *Her ghost,*
> *A silver shimmer on asphalt,*
> *A gleam of the wrong fender,*
> *In the wrong spot.*

Frederick growled.

"It's all right," Charlene said, "this horror won't last much longer."

I continued.

> *A woman found,*
> *Upon the water,*
> *But no one knows,*
> *Her spirit wanders*
> *The fateful lot.*
>
> *I work my way through*
> *And try to forget*
> *But I stand, keys in hand*
> *And wonder*
> *What I am not.*

Frederick rolled over and tried to wedge his head between the orange and brown seat cushion and the back of the wing chair.

" 'Wonder what I am not,' " I repeated. "Abril thought the author was conflicted about witnessing a murder. But what if he's conflicted about stealing the story?"

"He ought to be conflicted about writing that piece of garbage."

"And 'work my way through'—through the pain? Through trying to forget? Through college, like Abril suggested?"

"Worked his way through this literary desecration? What a slog."

I paced in front of her chipped coffee table. "The subject of the poem is standing, keys in hand. So, he's probably *in* the parking lot, right? Whoa. What if Theresa Keller was killed in the college's parking lot, and then her car and body dumped over the cliff? It would fit. It's all here!"

"That's a jump." She shifted on the couch, and the plastic beneath her crinkled. "But she worked at the college. If one of her colleagues saw her die, the odds are good she was killed in the college parking lot."

"But what's this line about a car being in the wrong spot? Her car? Someone else's car? The killer's?"

"All right. Let's imagine I kill you behind Pie Town."

"I'm not liking where you're going with this," I said, "but okay."

"And then I've got to get your ugly pink van over the cliff. I've got to drive it, because you're already dead."

"My delivery van is not ugly."

"So," she continued, "where's my Jeep?"

"Where you left it, back at Pie Town?"

"Exactly."

"But why's that the wrong spot?" I asked. "You have the right to park your Jeep near Pie Town, just like the professors have the right to park in the college lot."

She slumped on the couch, and it exhaled burnt-fabric smell. "Someone who wasn't from the college? They have parking permits in their windows, don't they?"

"But all our suspects are from the college," I said. "Are we on the wrong track?"

"Not necessarily," Charlene said. "Assuming Starke did steal this story, he might have been free with the details."

"It seems like a weird detail to add if it doesn't mean anything," I grumbled.

"That poem is so bad, it makes me want to bleach my eardrums. And you're worried about consistency?"

"Well, yes. Maybe if we do another close reading—"

She stood. "No. *¡Nada más!* No more, no closer. Let's take another look at those files Ray and Henrietta stole. My laptop's in the kitchen."

We shifted to Charlene's modern kitchen. Wide, black granite counters. A butcher-block work island. An expanse of white cabinets. If I didn't have a massive kitchen of my own at Pie Town, I'd be super jealous. The kitchen in my tiny home couldn't compare.

She shifted a coconut from the work island to the counter and opened her laptop.

I pulled up a barstool and sat beside her, then inserted Ray's USB drive.

We studied the complaint about Theresa Keller but learned nothing new. A coy administrator hadn't included the name of the complaining parent or the student in the file.

"That's weird, isn't it?" I drummed my fingers on the butcher-block island. "I mean, if they wanted to keep a record, shouldn't they have listed who complained?"

"They were probably trying to preserve the privacy of a minor."

"But the student wasn't a minor. He was over eighteen."

We kept reading, until we got to the personnel evaluations of our suspects by Dean Prophet.

Charlene whistled. "Jezek was right. Prophet *is* a royal pain. Look at this. 'The professor is too well-liked by her students. The professor went fifteen dollars over budget on her student anthology. The professor kept poor notes of student meetings. These should include the time of meeting, main topic, next steps, and any further appointments set.' "

"It does seem a little picky."

"A little? That's just for Professor Keller. Here's what he said about Starke. 'Incorrectly filled out form F-592 three times. Does not organize time for maximum impact. Disorganized office.' All the professors have disorganized office spaces according to this. 'Unprofessional appearance.' What's unprofessional in California? Naked?"

I smothered a yawn. "Fascinating."

"There's not a single good word in these evaluations."

"But if that was a motive for murder, Dean Prophet would have killed off his entire staff."

She cackled, reading further. "Professor Jezek 'has not grown as a team member'? What does that even mean? Good thing you don't waste time at Pie Town with this evaluation nonsense."

She picked up her phone and tapped the screen.

"What are you doing?" I asked.

"Posting to my followers about our investigation."

My eyes bulged. "You've been—" Why, oh why, didn't I follow Charlene's social media accounts? "You can't tell anyone about these evaluations. Ray and Henrietta could go to jail."

"I'm just letting them know we're close to cracking the case."

"Are we?" Had I missed something?

"No, but social media is about entertainment. You've got to give your followers what they want, and what they want is action." She made punching motions. "Suspense!"

"You posted online about a case we're not supposed to be investigating. I'm pretty sure that could be construed as interfering in a police investigation."

"It's not interfering. Your detective encouraged me to post online."

I gaped, disbelieving. "Gordon did what?"

"Said it made things easier for him."

I fumed. *Easier for him to keep track of what we were up to.*

"I don't post any actual clues," she said. "Except for the poem. I'm crowdsourcing."

"You're what?"

The refrigerator hummed, coming to life, and I started.

"It's when you consult the wisdom of the mob on a question," she said.

"I know what crowdsourcing is. I just didn't know you'd posted that poem online."

She clutched the phone to her chest. "Want to know what the mob thinks?"

Did I? "All right," I said, reluctant. "What?"

"This stinks—@Sadsquatch21. Makes me want to puke—@FoxMuldersaPutz42."

"All right. I get it."

"Soon it will be trending. I could use a drink. How would you like a piña colada with fresh coconut?"

I took a long, slow breath. Exhaled. "Charlene, what if the killer is following your account?"

"I'm not posting anything important. Only the weird and interesting clues, like that dog's breakfast of a poem."

I scrunched the hair close to my scalp. *Are you kidding me?* "That poem may have been the trigger for two murders!"

"It's in the public domain. So, what about that drink? Fresh coconut makes all the difference."

"Excuse me." I strode into her living room and called Gordon.

"Val. It's good to hear from you."

My insides turned liquid at the sound of his voice. Then I

remembered I was angry. "Did you tell Charlene to post the clues from our investigation online?"

"No. I told her not to post anything important on the Internet."

I rubbed my temple. "That's like giving her a green light."

"She's going to do what she's going to do. I can either toss her in jail or try to direct her forces for good."

"Are you crazy? This is the honeymoon-phase thing again, isn't it?"

"The what?"

"The honeymoon phase of our relationship," I said. "Nothing I do seems wrong, and you're not seeing me or us clearly. Worse, you're letting Charlene get away with interfering in an investigation."

"Uh . . . I've been watching her social media accounts. We're not at the interfering-with-an-investigation stage."

"In your opinion." I dropped into the wing chair, and there was a wild yowl. I leapt to my feet.

White tail low, Frederick streaked from the chair and out of the living room.

"What was that?" he asked.

"Frederick. And it's not just about Charlene's online activity. It's about everything. I mean, I don't want to push this whole Baker Street Bakers thing, you being the investigating officer and all."

"Yeah, I don't want that either."

"But you've been very . . . easygoing on the whole investigation issue. You haven't told me to get a PI's license once since this started."

"Do you want me to be a nag?" he asked.

"Of course not. It's just . . ." I heaved a breath. "It reminds me of what happened with Mark."

"Your old boyfriend?"

"I mean, you're not him. You're nothing like him. But

Mark and I were crazy about each other. I thought it was real and he was awesome, and then we got engaged, and so I moved to San Nicholas to be with him and started Pie Town. And then the blinders fell off, and he saw me for who I really was and dump— And we broke up."

"You think I don't see you for who you really are?"

I glanced toward the kitchen door and lowered my voice. "You practically encouraged Charlene to interfere in your investigation. And for me to do the same. You're a cop! And I think a pretty good one."

"Thanks," he said dryly. "Are you saying you think you're not seeing *me* clearly?"

"I didn't—" Was I? "I guess that sort of follows," I admitted. "It's a natural stage in the dating process."

"That's disappointing." There was a long silence.

My stomach twisted. "Gordon?"

"Sorry, I've got to go," he said, his voice hard and flat. "Let's talk later." He hung up.

Feeling sick, I stared at the phone. *Let's talk later?* I clutched it tightly in my hand.

But I was right, wasn't I? We did need to see each other clearly. And I didn't want to go through another Mark Jeffreys situation. Mark and I had both gotten swept up in the moment and made dumb decisions. I didn't want to do that with Gordon.

I cared about him too much.

Charlene emerged from the kitchen brandishing a machete. Its flat blade glinted, menacing. "Do I need to have a word with that boyfriend of yours?"

The phone slipped from my nerveless fingers. "No! Whoa! Whoa! Where'd you get a machete?"

"From the garage."

I eyed the weapon. "You don't need to threaten Gordon with a machete."

"Threaten Gordon?" She examined the blade. "This is for my coconut. How else am I supposed to crack it open? Now, if you'll just hold the coconut—"

"No, Charlene. I prefer to keep my arms and hands attached."

"Fine. Be that way. I'll find a clamp in the garage. Where's Frederick?"

"Um." I ducked and scooped up my phone. "I accidentally almost sat on him, and he left."

"Again? He'll never warm up to you that way. What did Gordon say?"

"He kind of hung up on me," I said.

"Hung up on you? Gordon Carmichael? That doesn't sound like him. Maybe he had a police emergency."

"I told him I thought we weren't seeing each other clearly."

"Oh," she said.

"Oh, what? What does *oh* mean?"

She scratched her head with the tip of the machete. "Well, it's the sort of thing one says when you're trying to break up with someone."

"I didn't suggest breaking up," I said, my voice rising.

"You want him to break up with you?"

"No!" My stomach burned. "That wasn't what I implied at all!"

But had I?

CHAPTER 30

Bushy brows furrowed, my regulars grumpily eyed Tuesday morning's full tables from their counter seats.

"I told you no publicity is bad publicity," Marla purred, sipping her coffee. The diamonds on her fingers glittered beneath the hanging lamps.

"I don't like it," Tally Wally said. "There are too many people. At this hour, it's not natural."

Carrying four slices of breakfast pie (a.k.a. quiche) and salads, I hustled from behind the counter. "It won't last." Though I wouldn't entirely mind if it did.

I dropped off the food, collected the plastic number tent, and raced back to the counter.

"Where's Charlene?" Marla asked.

"In the flour-work room," I said, "and no, you can't go back there to gloat. Not without a hairnet."

She pouted, but I knew she wouldn't try anything. Marla Van Helsing wouldn't be caught dead in a hairnet.

Outside the front window, a handful of demonstrators marched, brandishing picket signs. UFO AWARENESS! ALIENS ARE PEOPLE 2! THEY'RE HEEEERE!

I wasn't sure if they were upset about Charlene's hoax or if they were part of the promised support team. But I didn't have time to care. I was too busy racing from counter to tables, delivering food.

Charlene burst from the kitchen waving her cell phone. "We made the AP!"

"Advanced pie-making?" Marla gave Charlene's outfit the up-and-down look. Her lips curled at the sight of the purple-and-black-striped leggings. "Nice tights."

In fairness, they did match Charlene's purple tunic.

"Leggings! And it's the Associated Press." Charlene scowled. "My pie-tin UFOs are national news."

But not international, where Charlene's daughter might see the article.

"In the Weird News section, no doubt," Marla said.

Charlene's wrinkled cheeks pinked, and I knew it was true.

"Congratulations, Charlene." I made change for a customer and handed him a plastic number tent and a Pie Town t-shirt. "Your pie-tin promotion was a stroke of genius."

"Hers?" Marla asked. "If it wasn't for me, no one would know about your little promotion."

"People knew about it," Charlene said. "I posted on Twitter."

"And speaking of strokes," Marla said, "you're looking flushed, Charlene. Have you been taking your fiber, like the doctor ordered?"

"I go for a walk every day," Charlene said. "At least my only exercise isn't on a mattress, like *some* people."

"Jealous?" One corner of Marla's mouth tilted upward.

Charlene growled. "When the Baker Street Bakers solve these murders, I'll be in the news, and you'll be sucking eggs."

I changed the subject. "Have you seen any police?" Charlene had called the SNPD to warn them about the protest. I just hoped we weren't going to get hit with another fine. I still hadn't received my ticket for the first one.

"They're not rioting," Charlene said. "No cops are necessary. They're simply exercising their First Amendment rights to raise awareness about alien visitation."

"So—"

"Those demonstrators are free-riding on our publicity," my piecrust specialist said, indignant. And in a lower voice, "And no, the cops haven't interfered. But I don't think we should rile any of them."

"Gotcha." I whirled to the order window and snapped a ticket in the wheel, spun it to face the kitchen.

On the other side of the window, Abril snatched the receipt from the wheel and vanished.

Gordon strolled into Pie Town in his work uniform—a blue suit—and I straightened behind the register.

Charlene whistled. "Time to kiss and make up?"

Catcalls sounded down the length of the counter.

"Oh, grow up," I said pleasantly, not meaning a word of it.

Petronella burst from the kitchen. "I heard whistling. What's going on?"

"Take the counter, will you?" Chest tight, I hustled through the Dutch door to the detective. "Gordon, we called the police station when we heard demonstrators might show up. I had no idea—"

He raised his hand. "That Pie Town would make the national news? Congratulations." He bent to kiss my cheek and pull me into a hug.

"But the crowd—"

"Is under control," he said. "I spoke with the mayor. She's sent out a press statement."

Aghast, I pressed my hand to my mouth. "The mayor? She's going to bill me for the extra police, isn't she?"

"I don't think so. She's set up information booths at both ends of Main Street. Her staff is handing out business maps and brochures for next month's pumpkin festival. I think they've already sold some t-shirts."

"But last time—"

"Last time we got caught flat-footed. Today we had a warning, and the mayor was able to take advantage."

"Thanks to my article." Marla waved at him. "You're welcome, San Nicholas!" She patted her platinum hair. "I suppose I should go speak to the mayor. I'm sure she'll be interested in my ideas for promoting the town."

"Please go," Charlene said acidly.

Marla, nose in the air, strode from the restaurant.

"I'll show her," Charlene muttered.

"Have you got a minute?" Gordon asked me. "In private?"

Stomach curdling, I led him into my pokey office. "Gordon, if this is about—"

He pulled me against him and kissed me, long and hard, and when we broke apart, I braced my hand on my desk to stay standing.

"Oh," I said.

"Listen, I don't know what goes on in your head. But this idea that I don't see you clearly is nuts."

"But—"

"No, it's crazy. I checked out this honeymoon-period business. If you think for a second I didn't have your number from the moment we met, then you don't think much of me as a cop."

"Of course I do, but—"

"Yes, I'm a law-and-order guy. That's my job. And keeping an eye on my parents has made me more conscious of lists and schedules and all the other things that come with helping out two people who are having a harder time taking care of themselves. These are the things I do. But they're not all of who I am. You and Charlene . . ." He shook his head. "You're controlled chaos. Honestly, I don't know how you manage this pie shop so well *and* find time to dangle from statues of Spanish monks. But the fact that you can do it all gives me hope. I *want* there to be more to my life than work and elder care. That's not some romantic delusion. It's you, helping bring something into my world that I didn't even realize I was looking for or needed."

My heart expanded. "Really?" I laid my hand on his chest. The fabric of his navy suit jacket was between us, but I could feel his heart beating.

"Really."

I grimaced. "Then *I'm* sorry."

"For what?"

"Because it looks like I was the one with the delusions," I said. "I've been so worried about repeating my past mistake with Mark that I guess I didn't trust myself to see things clearly. And then I blamed you for being guilty of exactly the same thing."

He grinned. "I forgive you."

"But—"

"Controlled chaos, remember?" He pulled me close and kissed me again, warming me in all sorts of places.

"I need to get back to crowd control," he finally said when we moved apart.

"Yeah. And me. The kitchen." My brain was spinning too fast for complete sentences. I'd like to think this is why I didn't tell Gordon about the latest info Charlene and I had uncovered and intuited. But the reality was, I wasn't sure how to tell him about the human resources files without getting Ray and Henrietta into trouble. Or if they actually meant anything.

"Oh," I said. "Wait."

He paused, one hand on the office door, and raised a brow.

"I was taking another look at Starke's poem, which is

probably Aidan's story, since Starke wasn't at the college when Theresa Keller died."

He released the doorknob and folded his arms. "Go on," he said cautiously.

"I was doing a close reading—"

"A what?"

"It's when you analyze a work of literature by picking apart every word and line. And I think it's saying that some-one—Theresa, I think—was killed in the college parking lot, and then her car and body dumped over the cliff. That would explain the lack of skid marks, wouldn't it?"

"How do you get she was killed at the college?"

I explained about the poem, and what Abril, Charlene, and I had deduced.

He nodded. "Okay. What else?"

Wasn't it enough? "Um, that's all. But Starke wasn't working at the college when Theresa died. Aidan, however, was. So, when he accused Starke of stealing at the poetry reading, that's probably what he meant. Professor Starke had stolen his story."

He didn't say anything.

"You think it's ridiculous," I said, disappointed.

He sighed. "It's speculation. I can't base an arrest on this. And even if it *is* true, it doesn't tell us who killed Michael Starke and Aidan McClary."

I opened my mouth and closed it just as quickly. In my gut, I *did* know. But I couldn't say that, because Gordon needed evidence, not instincts.

"But thanks for letting me know," he said.

"You're welcome," I said.

"But why kill Theresa Keller?" he asked. "That's what we're saying, right? That the same person who killed Theresa killed the two professors to cover it up?"

I bit my lip. "Yeah, I heard a . . . rumor that she might

have been involved with one of her students too. Like Starke was."

Gordon's emerald eyes narrowed. "Where did you hear this?"

"Around?"

"Who's *Around*?"

"Look," I said, speaking rapidly, "I can't tell you. But if you get a warrant to take a look at the college personnel files, I'll bet you'll find something interesting in Theresa's."

"Val—"

"Trust me, you don't want to know how I got this information."

"Okay. I do trust you." His phone buzzed in his jacket's inside pocket. He pulled it out and checked the screen. "I've got to go." He pressed his lips to my forehead and walked out.

Smiling, I stared at the slowly closing office door. It hadn't been the sexiest goodbye kiss, but we were okay.

I leaned against the metal desk. I needed evidence. *Fine.* I had lots of puzzle pieces. It was time to assemble them.

Taking a yellow pad from a desk drawer, I drew three columns with the names of the murder victims at the top of each. I listed the suspects down one side. If I could logic this out, maybe I could prove my theory.

The office door swooshed open, and Petronella stuck her head in. "I saw Gordon leave. Is everything okay?"

"Sure, why wouldn't it be?"

She rolled her eyes. "Because you're in here, and things are crazy out there."

I dropped my pen, and my cheeks heated. Once again, I'd abandoned my team. "Sorry. I'm coming." I hurried into the restaurant and spent the next four hours racing around like a madwoman.

At some point, Charlene vanished, like she usually did in the afternoons.

No riots broke out inside or outside Pie Town, and I started to relax. We were selling pie and making news and managing to feed everyone. Maybe this would turn out okay?

"Val?" Doran said from behind me.

I jumped, and the plate swayed in my hands. Blowing out a slow breath, I steadied the dish and glanced over my shoulder. "Let me deliver this to the table." I walked the pecan pie slice to a two-top, retrieved the plastic number tent, and returned to Doran. "Hey."

"Hey." My brother jammed his fists in the pockets of his black leather jacket and looked out at me from beneath his shock of black hair. "So. I guess I overreacted."

"No. I mean—"

He laughed shortly. "I did. But . . . there's something I haven't told you."

"Oh?" I took a step backward and bumped against the Dutch door.

"There's just been a lot happening really fast. Discovering I had a sister. That business with dad. Moving here . . ."

"I know. And part of that's my fault. I was so excited to learn I wasn't alone, that maybe I was pushing this relationship too hard."

"Look, he said, "can we talk in private?"

"Sure. But I've got to be quick." I led him into my office. "What's going on?"

"It's nothing bad. I mean, I hope you won't think it's bad."

"What?"

"The thing I didn't tell you."

"Is . . . ?"

"My mom wants to come to San Nicholas and meet you."

"Oh." His mom? My heart thumped unevenly. His mother and I weren't related. Why would she want to meet me?

"Yeah. I know. Crazy, right? I've told her not to, but you

know—" He shook his head. "No, you don't know my mom. Look, I thought if I left, maybe she'd back off. But she's determined to meet her . . . stepdaughter."

"Step . . . ?" I blinked. I was a stepdaughter? But I already had a mother. She'd passed on, but . . . I scrubbed one hand across my face, realized what I was doing, and rubbed it on my apron. "Oh."

"I know. Look. She means well. I'll see what I can do, but the bottom line is, I can't control her." He smiled. "I'm not sure I'd want to try."

"No. It's okay." I shook my head. A stepmom. I could deal with a new relative. "Wait. So, the reason you wanted to leave San Nicholas was to avoid your mom?"

"No, it was because things felt like they were getting too complicated. And it *is* expensive here."

I blew out a breath. Wasn't that the truth. "Tell me about it." I hated what I had to charge for pie.

"But I could always raise my rates."

"Yeah! I mean, I'd love it if you stayed. And I promise not to be so in-your-face about us."

He laughed hollowly. "Oh, don't worry. Once you meet my mom, well, you'll see."

I felt myself blanch. I'll *see*? What did that mean?

I guess I'd see.

"Oh, and about Abril," I said. "Look, I think she might really be interested in you."

He grinned. "I know. We went out last night."

"You what?" Lightly, I punched him in the arm of his leather jacket. "That's fantastic! But if you hurt her, I'm dumping you as a brother. Seriously."

His dusky skin turned a shade darker. "I won't. Don't worry."

I glanced down at my desk and frowned at the blank yellow pad.

"What's wrong?" he asked.

"My notepad. I'd made some notes on the top page, but the sheet is gone."

"Was it important?"

"Well, no. I mean, I didn't get to finish . . ." My stomach rolled. I grabbed a pencil from the desk. Angling it nearly parallel to the paper, I brushed the lead across the page. Words in familiar handwriting emerged.

"Cool," Doran said. "That old detective trick."

"Not cool," I croaked. "Charlene finished my chart. She figured it out."

She'd gone to confront a killer.

CHAPTER 31

Grabbing my phone from my apron pocket, I called Charlene.

Voicemail.

I paced in front of my desk. "Charlene, where are you? I'm worried. Call me."

The wall clock above the supply shelf ticked away the seconds while I called Gordon. Again, I got stuck with voicemail.

"Gordon, it's Val. I think Charlene's gone to confront the killer." Hastily, I explained and hung up, dropping the phone on my desk.

"What can I do?" Doran asked.

"Gordon's somewhere in that crowd of demonstrators on Main Street. Find him and tell him what's happened. Give him this." I handed him the yellow pad. "He may need it."

"What are you going to do?"

I grabbed my keys and purse off the metal bookcase. "Find Charlene." She'd let Marla get under her skin about the pie tins. I really wanted to think she wouldn't do any-

thing crazy—at least, not without me. But this was Charlene.

Doran nodded and bolted out the door.

I followed him into the restaurant. "Petronella, it's an
emergency. You're going to have to manage without me."

The regulars at the counter leaned forward, peering
around the register.

Petronella's near-black brows curved downward. "Sure,
boss. Is everything okay?"

"It's Charlene," I said.

The regulars nodded wisely.

Hustling through the kitchen, I leapt into my van in the
alley. I roared to the end of the alley and screeched to a halt
when a group of UFOnauts waving picket signs marched in
front of me.

Moving more slowly, I took the back streets to the edge
of town and promptly landed in a traffic jam on Highway
One.

"Come on, come on." I pounded the wheel and inched
forward. But there was only one way out of San Nicholas
and to the college, and I was on it.

Teeth grinding, I made it to the traffic light for the
Ninety-Two, and I turned east. Cars crawled along the winding, forested road, past pumpkin farms and wineries. Finally, we gained another lane. I roared forward, my pink,
sixties-era van lurching past more sedate Teslas and Ca-
maros.

On the other side of the hill, I got stuck again in a winding section and a twenty-five-mile-per-hour speed limit.

Finally, the road straightened, and I was flying past the
reservoirs and onto a genuine freeway. I was only five miles
from the college, but I hauled ass, screeching into the college's parking lot.

My stomach bottomed. Charlene's yellow Jeep sat in the

visitors' lot near the English department. "Dammit, Charlene!"

Springing from the van, I slammed the door shut and sprinted toward the modern building's glass doors.

A student on a bike whizzed past. I skidded to keep from slamming into him, and stumbled onto the lawn beside the bell tower.

"Nice pie!" the bicyclist shouted. He grinned over his shoulder.

"What? Watch where you're going!" I looked down, realized I was still wearing my Pie Town apron, didn't care.

I raced inside the building. Dodging students in the wide corridor, I found the office I was looking for. I rattled the doorknob.

Locked.

If Charlene wasn't here, where was she?

I stopped a girl carrying an armful of books. "Have you seen an elderly woman in a purple tunic and striped leggings?"

"Oh, yeah. I saw her headed outside, to the parking—"

I ran down the hallway and pushed through the glass doors. *Charlene, where are you?* I jogged into the lot and turned in circles in the shadow of the bell tower.

A horn blared. I jumped out of the way of a red Honda Fit.

A flash of purple tunic vanished into the bell tower on the opposite lawn.

"Charlene!" I raced to the sidewalk and across the lawn.

The door to the bell tower slowly drifted closed. I grabbed its handle before it could shut, and I raced into a cool, concrete stairwell.

Footsteps sounded above me.

I bit back a shout. Charlene had huffed and puffed her way onto Tally Wally's roof. She wouldn't be climbing a bell tower willingly.

I sent a text to Gordon. FOLLOWING CHARLENE UP BELL TOWER. SHE'S NOT ALONE.

Dropping my phone into my apron pocket, I tiptoed up the stairs.

"You won't get away with this," she gasped above me. Her footsteps slowed.

"You think people won't believe you fell attempting your stupid pie-tin stunt?" a man's voice asked. "Move!"

I gripped the railing and felt the blood drain from my face. Pie tins? Fall? She'd brought a pie-tin UFO to confront a murder suspect?

"Everyone," she panted, "knows . . . I use Val . . . for the heavy . . . lifting."

"Do they? I rather doubt that."

I tiptoed higher.

"But Frederick!" She wheezed. "He's innocent."

"I'm not a monster. I wouldn't kill your cat. Er, you're sure he's alive?"

"He's got narcolepsy!"

"Cat's can get narcolepsy? That doesn't seem likely."

"And he's deaf."

"I've heard that about white cats," he said. "I wonder what the connection is between deafness and white fur?"

"Let's go downstairs and . . . check the Internet," she said. "I'm sure . . . we can find the answer."

He chuckled. "I do regret killing you. You're excellent at your job, and the random knowledge in your head is worthy of a modern college course. Unfortunately, most modern courses are useless garbage. The Sociology of *Harry Potter*. The Philosophy of *Buffy the Vampire Slayer*. On Being Bored. Those are all courses they tried to weasel into the English department."

"No *Stargate*? Now that's a show worthy of analysis."

"Never heard of it," he said.

"I need to stop. My heart."

My head jerked upward. Was this a delaying tactic, or was her heart pain real? My hand moved to my phone. I tried to quiet my breathing.

"You're having a heart attack?" he asked. "Even better. Falls from this height can be so messy. I imagine the college would have to hire a special cleaning crew."

"I knew there was something wrong . . . with you from the very beginning," Charlene said.

"Nice view, isn't it?" he asked. "I like to come up here at night."

"You would."

My fingers brushed across my phone's screen. I pocketed it and hurried to the next landing. Charlene and her captor must be at the top of the bell tower now. I was one level beneath.

Whatever the killer was up to—throwing Charlene from the bell tower?—it was going to happen soon.

Crouching, I crept up the stairs.

And came face-to-face with the wrong end of a gun.

"Ah," Dean Prophet said. "Val Harris. I thought you might be joining us."

CHAPTER 32

Charlene's pie-tin UFO clattered to the cement floor, and my heart seemed to stop.

"Hey, Dean Prophet." I waved limply. It was hard to play casual when there was a gun in my face.

Rectangles of light streamed through the bell tower's narrow concrete windows, open to the air. Sunshine glinted off the bells, high in the center of the room and protected by a plexiglass shield that went to the floor. Beneath the bells sat an unmanned keyboard.

Charlene leaned, wheezing, against the stair railing.

I took a step toward her.

"No," the dean said, raising the gun higher. "Stay where you are, please." Beneath his jacket, his V-neck sweater strained against his gut. And to think I'd once thought him jolly.

"What's going on?" My insides curdled.

He scratched his neatly trimmed beard. "Honestly? You can't figure it out?"

"Okay," I said, stalling. "You're trying to kill Charlene, because she figured out you killed Starke and Aidan. You also killed Theresa all those years ago."

"And now you, of course." He adjusted his glasses.

"And now me," I said weakly. "But you don't have to."

"No," he said, "it does sort of go against my theme."

Charlene raised a finger, as if to interject, then pressed her hand to her chest.

"Your theme?" I edged toward Charlene. Gordon must have gotten my text. He'd be here soon, and he'd have called the campus cops as well. All I needed was time. "You mean covering up Theresa Keller's murder?"

He scowled. "All of them, every single one, were ruining this college. Theresa and Michael fooling around with students— You have no idea what I went through covering up their peccadillos. And Michael was a tenured hack I couldn't get rid of."

"After only four years?" I asked.

"It takes three to get tenure. It was a relief to be able to dump Aidan too."

"And by dump, you mean . . . ?"

"Kill."

"You killed all those people because you couldn't fire them?" I asked, incredulous.

He laughed. "Of course not! I'm kidding. The expression on your face. It's priceless." He wiped his forehead with the sleeve of his tweed jacket. "I'm not a madman. You were right the first time. I was covering up Theresa's murder."

I forced down the panic welling in my throat. Joking with his future murder victim? He *was* insane.

"And you're telling us this now, because . . ."

"Because you'll be dead in minutes, so I might as well. They say confession is good for the soul. Not sure who I'll confess your murders to." The shoulders of his tweed blazer lifted and dropped. "Oh well. I'll just have to live with the guilt."

"I understand why you killed Michael and Aidan," I said. A breeze flowed through the windows, drying the sweat beading my brow. "When you heard Starke's poem, you thought he'd seen you in the parking lot the night Theresa died. You killed her there, then dumped her car with her body in it over the cliff."

Charlene gasped. "Tell him about the wrong spot."

"Your car wasn't in its usual reserved spot," I said. "You parked it beside Theresa's, didn't you?"

"Yes, it was that detail that made me certain Michael knew what he was talking about. Of course the fool didn't know. I should have paid more attention to Aidan's complaints about plagiarism. But he was always whining about something. *Dorothy won't marry me. I need a green card. My class schedule is too full.* Good God, it's a wonder someone didn't kill him sooner."

"You did a good job of making Theresa's death look like an accident." I strained my ears for sirens. "But Starke's death was obviously murder. Why did you change your MO?"

"Crime of opportunity," he said. "I saw Piotr slash Michael's tires, and then Michael came out carrying that stupid saber. He was furious when he saw what had been done to his car. I offered to hold his saber while he called for a tow truck. He died quickly. I'm not a cruel man."

"You call trying to electrocute Aidan kind?" I asked. *Gordon, where are you?*

"Kindness had nothing to do with it. Weren't you listening? He was incredibly irritating. I thought it would look like an accident."

"You'd been to his house before, for one of his faculty get-togethers, hadn't you?"

"Drinkfest is more like it. He did love playing the passionate Irish writer."

"That's when you noticed the electric cable wrapped around the tree."

"Noticed? You should have heard Aidan go on about that

stupid moving van. He was furious. Ah, Charlene. I see you're recovering. Please move toward Val."

She shuffled to me, and I wrapped one arm around her shoulders. *Stall, stall, stall.*

"Some movers delivering a sofa backed their truck into the power gizmo on top of his house," he continued. "For some reason I never could entirely understand, he couldn't get anyone to fix it. The sofa company's insurance wouldn't pay for the damage either, apparently. Aidan was never a good negotiator. No wonder Dorothy wouldn't marry him. He couldn't seal the deal. At any rate, I didn't care for all the police attention Michael's death was getting. So, I thought I'd return to making the deaths look like an accident."

"And when that didn't work," I said, "you followed him home after the pie-making class and killed him. I'm surprised he let you inside."

He quirked a brow. "I'm the dean. Why wouldn't he? Now, please walk toward that wall. No, not that one, the one over there."

Charlene and I backed toward the narrow windows. I gritted my teeth. If Gordon was listening in on his confession from somewhere below, he was cutting it close.

I swallowed. "There's one thing I don't understand. If you were joking about killing Theresa over her affair with a student, then why did you kill her?"

"Her death *was* because of the affair." His face darkened. "I loved Theresa."

"And so you killed her?" I squeaked.

"She was willing to throw her career away on that student! He was a football player!"

A breeze drifted through the windows and tossed Charlene's white curls. "Jealousy." She squeezed me around the waist. "One of the three motives for murder."

"I wasn't jealous," he snapped.

"You just admitted you were," I said.

"She wasn't living up to her full potential."

"Theresa Keller can't live up to anything now," Charlene said. "She's dead."

"And it's none of your damn business what her potential was," I said.

"That's true too," Charlene agreed. "You had no right."

His gun wavered. "How do you—?" He shook his head. "You're both delaying the inevitable. Val, I think you'll jump first. I was going to make Charlene's death look like an accident—the sad result of another of her pie-tin UFO stunts. But you being here changes things."

"No, it doesn't," Charlene says. "Val helps me with all the difficult shots."

"Charlene!"

"I'm stalling," she muttered.

That was stalling? Because it felt more like helping.

"Hm," he said, sunlight glinting off his round glasses. "Now your fall will look like suicide, and then Charlene fell trying to stop you."

"No," Charlene said. "Your pie-tin UFO idea was better."

"I suppose it works either way," he said. "Unless you'd prefer to go ahead with that heart attack."

"No," I said, "it doesn't work. Suicide doesn't make sense. I have a very happy pie shop. One of my customers is even making me an app!"

"Please." He rolled his eyes. "Everyone knows you were dumped at the altar."

"I wasn't at the altar!" I turned to Charlene. "See? This is what happens when you spread your inaccurisms."

"It's true," Charlene said. "She was *months* away from the wedding."

"Thank you," I said.

"Though she *was* dumped."

"Charlene!" *Come on! Trying to not be defenestrated, here.*

"Val." He waggled the gun. "In the window, if you please."

"No," I said, heart thumping against my rib cage. "You'll have to shoot me, and that will leave evidence."

"I suppose it will," he said, "since it's Piotr's gun. He keeps it in his desk drawer loaded with silver bullets, which I assure you, are just as good as lead."

"He'll frame Professor Jezek," Charlene said. "He's thought of everything."

"How do you think I remained dean of this madhouse for as long as I have? I plan ahead."

He pulled back the gun's hammer. "Now—"

"Okay, okay!" I backed against the cool concrete and climbed into the window, dislodging an irate seagull. It flapped, squawking, and sailed high into the air.

"Wait," Charlene said. "What about Frederick?"

"I told you I wouldn't kill your cat," he said. "Just put him down."

"But he needs to say goodbye to Val."

She lifted his limp paw, dangling from her shoulder, and waved it at me. "Goodbye, Val."

"Goodbye, Frederick," I said mournfully.

Charlene set him on the concrete floor.

I looked over my shoulder. The ground accordioning away from me. Dizzy, I lurched sideways and clung to one of the concrete projections. It's not that I'm afraid of heights. But I'm terrified of being thrown from the top of a twelve-story bell tower and landing on solid concrete. I closed my eyes. "I'd rather be shot."

"And let an innocent man take the blame?" he asked. "Come now, this isn't you. You're one of those truth-and-justice crusaders. All you need to do is lean back and let go."

"Professor Jezek *won't* be blamed," I said. "You made a mistake planning so far ahead. We knew it was you and not Jezek who killed all those people, and so will the police."

The gun wavered. "How?"

"If you tell him," Charlene said, "he'll just go back and fix his mistake, and then the cops will think Jezek's our murderer."

"You're right," I said. "We can't tell him."

He scowled. "You're lying."

"And yet," I said, "we figured out you were the killer."

"Enough!" He aimed the gun at my center.

Charlene clutched her chest and doubled over. "Oh!" She collapsed to the floor.

"Charlene!" I jumped from my perch to reach her.

A tremendous gong sounded, rocking the tower.

The gun went off.

Frederick leapt to his paws. The cat yowled and streaked down the stairs.

Doran tumbled over Frederick. He sprawled, facedown, on the concrete floor.

I shrieked, heart in my throat. "Doran!" But the word was lost in the cacophony of the bells.

Charlene snagged my ankle. I pitched forward. My shoulder rammed into Dean Prophet roughly at crotch level. The two of us went down in a jumble of flailing limbs.

When we untangled ourselves, Doran had the gun, Charlene was readjusting Frederick over her shoulder, and Gordon and a phalanx of campus cops were pouring into the campanile. The bells finally, blessedly, fell silent.

Gordon's mouth moved, and no words came out.

"What?" I asked, glancing anxiously at Charlene. She patted Frederick, checking for damage. The white cat tucked his head beneath her ears and shut his eyes.

Gordon's lips moved again.

I pointed to my ears. They were still ringing from the bells. "I can't hear you!"

In answer, Gordon pulled me into his arms and kissed me.

CHAPTER 33

Doran and I helped Charlene down the bell tower steps. We passed more uniformed police running in the opposite direction, their steps echoing off the cement walls.

"I thought you'd been shot," I choked out.

"Oh," Charlene said, "I was fine."

"Not you," I said. "Doran. What were you thinking?"

"What were *you* thinking?" my brother growled.

"Charlene was in trouble. I had to help her."

"Yeah, well." He shrugged, his leather jacket making crinkling noises.

"I can't believe Gordon let you up there," I said.

"I didn't," Gordon said from above us. There wasn't a crease in his blue suit, and he hadn't even broken a sweat running up and down those stairs. "When I turned my back, he ran into the tower. Then I had to go after him."

"What tipped you off that Dean Prophet was the killer?" Doran asked.

I glanced up at Gordon, and he smiled. "Oh, go on. You know you're dying to show off." Besides, he couldn't officially know about this until he'd gotten a warrant.

I opened my mouth.

"The personnel files." Charlene halted and sucked in deep lungfuls of air. "Only the dean would have had the power to get the student's name off that complaint about Theresa Keller. Everyone involved was over eighteen, so no minor was being protected."

"That's it?" Doran asked.

"Not entirely," I said. "It was like one of those logic puzzles. Dorothy had an alibi for the attack on Charlene's house, so she couldn't have been the killer, unless she had an accomplice. Dorothy and Brittany couldn't have killed Theresa Keller. Neither of them were around at the time. That left Professor Jezek and Dean Prophet."

"But that assumed the murder had anything to do with Theresa Keller's death," Doran said. "What if you were wrong?"

"Obviously," Charlene said, "we weren't."

Frederick lifted his head from her shoulder and meowed.

The disheveled, bath-robed man floated through a bowling alley, his image flickering on the rear wall of my tiny home. My friends sat on lawn chairs and ate popcorn, its buttery scent faint against that of the eucalyptus grove behind us. A cloud drifted over the moon, and the movie on my outside wall brightened.

Gordon pulled me closer on our blanket. "So, your brother is staying and all's well that ends well," he murmured in my ear.

I looked around.

Ray and Henrietta, cuddling on a nearby blanket beside the projector.

Tally Wally and Graham in lawn chairs, making wisecracks and throwing popcorn at the side of my house.

My friend from the comic shop, Joy, sitting impassively on a lawn chair and watching the makeshift screen.

Doran and Abril on a blanket, their hands loosely clasped.

My heart swelled. I was thrilled my brother was staying, but I hadn't had to worry about being alone. My family was here, in San Nicholas.

"What are you thinking?" Gordon asked in a low voice.

"I'm glad you didn't arrest me." I grinned.

"A fellow Baker Street Baker? Never. We got that warrant for the college's personnel files, by the way. It wasn't hard after catching Prophet in the act of trying to push you off the clock tower. He confessed to everything."

"Good." And Gordon was only an *associate* Baker Street Baker, but there was no sense rubbing it in.

"But I think Prophet's trying for an insanity plea."

I went rigid. "He knew exactly what he was doing." But he was kind of nuts.

"I said *trying*."

I relaxed. Gordon would gather the evidence he needed.

His hand made exploratory circles on my waist, and I sighed in the darkness, my body melting beneath his touch. Life was perfect. I wriggled closer.

Bones creaking, Charlene lowered herself onto the blanket beside us. "Did I hear *insanity plea?*"

"He was covering up for a crime of passion," I whispered. "He won't get away with it." But would he? In the bell tower, there'd been a moment when I was sure he was crazy. So why would an insanity plea bother me?

"You never know what a jury will think," Charlene said. "This *is* California."

A silhouette of a flying saucer lowered itself over the screen, and she laughed, nudging my side.

Joy, Tally Wally, and Graham booed.

"This isn't *Mystery Science Theater*," Joy shouted.

Graham hooted. "Down in front!"

I shook my head. "How did you . . . ?"

She drew her hand from inside her knit jacket and showed me the thick twine wrapped around her index finger. "Tee-hee! It's all done with wires."

"I thought you'd retired the pie-tin UFOs?" I asked.

"Don't worry," she said. "Tonight is my UFO's swan song. Can you believe Prophet was daft enough to think I'd dangle from the top of a clock tower for a shot? Maybe he is insane."

"Yeah," I said dryly, thinking of my misadventure on the Father Serra statue. "Insane."

Slowly, the UFO lifted and vanished over the roof of my tiny house.

Tally Wally and Graham cheered.

A woman's silhouette crossed in front of the screen. More boos and popcorn flew.

Marla brushed popcorn from her platinum hair and sat beside Gordon. "So this is where everyone is."

"And you weren't invited," Charlene snapped.

"Of course," Marla said in a ringing voice, "if we'd done this at my house, we could have used my private theater."

The crowd fell silent.

"You have a home theater?" Ray asked.

"I like watching movies outdoors," Henrietta said stoutly. "The weather's beautiful, and the stars . . ."

A family of raccoons waddled in front of the makeshift screen, and the crowd groaned.

"What are you doing here?" Charlene hissed at Marla.

"I'm having a little soiree at my home next month," Marla said. "I wanted to talk to Val about having some of those lovely pies in a jar for dessert."

"You could have come to Pie Town for that," Charlene said.

Marla leaned back on one elbow and rested a hand on Gordon's chest. "But I wanted to finalize this now, so I came here. Of course, I had no idea the rest of you would be here too."

Uh-huh. I wasn't sure how it had happened, but somehow Marla had become part of our little gang. She must have felt left out when we hadn't invited her to movie night. "Sure, Marla, but let's talk about it later. Why don't you stay and enjoy the movie?" I plucked Marla's hand from my boyfriend's chest.

She grinned, unabashed.

"Or," Charlene said, "Marla can go to——"

"Charlene," I said warningly.

"Fine. I'm getting more popcorn." Charlene clambered to her feet and walked around the side of my tiny house.

Marla smiled and rose. "She's just annoyed the media has lost interest in her UFO promotion. I'd better go help. She's getting so frail." The elderly woman swaggered after Charlene.

Gordon gave me a look. "Do you need to go after them?"

"They're both adults and are too old for a babysitter. Besides, if anything goes south, my bet's on Charlene."

He pulled me closer. "Mine's on you."

Recipes

Salted-Caramel Apple Pie

Ingredients

1 pkg (i.e., 2 crusts) refrigerated pre-made piecrust
(because Charlene's not giving up her secret recipe, and
pre-made crusts—when fresh—are pretty good)

¼ C all-purpose flour

¼ C sugar

½ tsp ground cinnamon

2½ lbs baking apples (e.g., Fuji or Granny Smith), peeled,
cored, and sliced quarter-inch thick (you should end up
with approximately 7 cups)

1 recipe salted-caramel sauce (see below)

Sea salt (optional)

1 egg, lightly beaten

1 T whipping cream

1 T coarse sugar

Directions

Preheat oven to 375°F.

Unroll one piecrust into a 9-inch pie plate. On a lightly
floured surface unroll the remaining crust.

For the filling, combine the flour, sugar, and cinnamon in
a small bowl. Place the sliced apples in a large bowl and
sprinkle the flour mixture over the apples, tossing to coat.
Spoon about one-third of the mixture in the piecrust-lined
pie plate. Drizzle roughly 2 T of the salted-caramel sauce
over the apples. Repeat with the remaining thirds and salted-
caramel sauce two more times. Sprinkle with a pinch or two

of sea salt if desired. Set the remaining salted-caramel sauce aside.

Combine the egg and whipping cream in another small bowl. Lightly brush the edge of piecrust with the egg mixture. Cover the pie with the second crust and pinch the two crusts together. Lightly brush the top of the pie with the remaining egg mixture. Sprinkle with coarse sugar.

To protect the crust's edge from overbrowning, cover the edges with aluminum foil or pie shields.

Place the pie on the oven's middle rack. Since there's a good chance the filling will overflow a bit, to protect your oven (and your sanity), line a baking sheet with foil and place it on the rack beneath the pie to catch any drips.

Bake the pie for 30 minutes and remove the foil or pie shield from the crust. Bake for another 20 to 35 minutes or until the top crust is golden.

Remove the pie from the oven and cool on a wire rack. Serve with the remaining salted-caramel sauce. (Note: If the caramel sauce hardens before serving, reheat on high for 30–60 seconds in a microwave-safe bowl covered with wax paper.)

Salted-Caramel Sauce

Ingredients
1 14-oz pkg vanilla caramels, unwrapped
½ C whipping cream
1 tsp sea salt

Directions
Heat and stir unwrapped caramels, whipping cream, and sea salt in a medium saucepan over medium-low heat until mixture is melted and smooth. Remove from heat.

Chocolate Cream Pie

Val can't use an Oreo crust in Pie Town, because Charlene would revolt. But when she makes a chocolate cream pie for herself, at home, she goes full chocolate crust. Here's her private chocolate crust recipe.

Crust
25 Oreos
5 T melted butter

Pulse Oreos in a food processor until you can't see any of the white filling. Drizzle the melted butter over the Oreo crumbs and mix.

Pour the crumbs into a pie tin and press into a crust shape with your fingers. (Note: You can use any flavor Oreos for a piecrust if you want to go wild. But for this pie, I recommended the "regular" chocolate flavor.)

Filling
½ C unsweetened chocolate chips, plus more for topping
1 14-oz can sweetened condensed milk
2 C heavy whipping cream
¼ C powdered sugar
1 tsp vanilla extract
Chocolate sprinkles (optional)

Instructions
Place chocolate chips in a medium-sized microwave-safe bowl. Heat on half power in the microwave in 30-second increments (so it doesn't burn). Stir between each heating increment, until the chocolate chips are melted and smooth.

Add sweetened condensed milk to the chocolate and stir. Set the chocolate mixture aside.

Beat the heavy whipping cream, slowly adding the powdered sugar and vanilla, until stiff peaks form.

Fold half the whipped-cream mixture into the chocolate
mixture. Pour/scoop into the prepared piecrust. Top the pie
with the remaining whipped cream. Garnish with chocolate
sprinkles if desired.

Chill the pie for at least 2 hours before serving. Store the
pie in the refrigerator, keeping the pie loosely covered.

Asparagus-and-Mushroom Quiche

Ingredients

1 lb asparagus, bottoms of the stems trimmed, and cut into
   1-inch pieces
6 oz sliced button mushrooms
¾ C onion, coarsely chopped
1 refrigerated pre-made piecrust
4 oz Emmentaler or Gruyère cheese, shredded
4 eggs
¾ C half-and-half
1 T yellow mustard
1 tsp fresh or dried thyme
½ tsp salt
¼ tsp fresh or dried parsley
⅛ tsp nutmeg
⅛ tsp ground black pepper

Directions

Preheat oven to 425°F.

Boil the asparagus, mushrooms, and onion for four minutes. Drain the vegetables.

While the vegetables are boiling, unroll the piecrust and press it into a 9-inch pie or cake pan.

Place the asparagus, mushrooms, and onion on top of the unbaked crust. Top with shredded cheese.

Mix the remaining ingredients in a large bowl and pour the mixture over the cheese and vegetables.

Bake for 30 minutes, or until firm. Cool briefly before eating.

Choco-Peanut-Butter Pie

Crust

25 Oreos (or peanut butter–flavored Oreos, if you can find them)

5 T melted butter

Filling

1 3.9-oz pkg chocolate-flavored instant pudding

2 C cold milk, divided in half

4 oz (½ of an 8-oz pkg) cream cheese, softened

1 3.4-oz pkg vanilla-flavored instant pudding

¼ C plus 3 T creamy peanut butter, plus 1 T for serving

2 C thawed whipped cream, divided in half

1 heaping T semisweet chocolate chips (for drizzling over the top of the pie)

Instructions

Preheat oven to 350°F.

Pulse 25 Oreos in a food processor until you can't see any of the white filling. Drizzle melted butter over the Oreo crumbs and mix.

Pour the crumbs into a pie tin and press into a crust shape with your fingers.

Bake the crust for 5–7 minutes, until it is set. Remove the piecrust from the oven and set aside to cool completely. (You can turn off the oven now.)

Beat the chocolate pudding mix and 1 C milk for two minutes until thickened. Spread the mixture onto the bottom of the cooled crust with a spatula or wide spoon. In a large bowl, blend the remaining 1 cup milk and cream cheese, beating constantly with an electric mixer until smooth and creamy. Add the dry vanilla pudding mix and beat for two more minutes.

Not including the 1 T of the peanut butter for serving, add

the peanut butter to the vanilla pudding mixture. Beat the
entire mixture until the peanut butter is well blended. Add 1
C whipped cream and gently fold it into the vanilla–peanut
butter mix. Spread the entire mixture over the chocolate
pudding layer to within one inch of the piecrust's edge. Top
the pie with the remaining 1 C whipped cream, bringing the
cream to the edge of the piecrust to create a mounded shape.

Refrigerate the pie for three hours.

You're almost ready to eat! But since Father's Day is special, this pie needs a little decorating. . . .

Just before serving, microwave the remaining 1 T peanut
butter in a microwaveable bowl on high for 15 seconds or
until it's melted when stirred. Melt the chocolate chips as directed on the pkg. Drizzle the melted peanut butter and next
the melted chocolate over the pie.

Love the Pie Town mysteries?

Keep reading for a peek at
GOURD TO DEATH
for the continuing adventures
of Val and the Baker Street Bakers.
Coming soon from
Kirsten Weiss
and
Kensington Books

CHAPTER 1

All it takes is one bad impulse.

In my defense, I'd had a late night of sexy aliens and pitched battles. So my impulse control was low this morning.

But . . .

Going along to get along to get-it-over-with was still a bad impulse. I was ditching work on what could be the busiest day of the year. My staff needed me. Pie Town needed me.

The thuds of hammers and clangs of metal on metal drifted through the pre-dawn fog. It shrouded Main Street, hiding the workers setting up festival stalls.

Yawning, I jammed my hands into the pockets of my winter-weight *Pie or Die* hoodie and hesitated guiltily in the doorway of my pie shop. The scent of baking pumpkin escaped Pie Town's open door and wafted into the chill October air.

"I can take only ten minutes," I said through another jaw-cracking yawn. Pie Town was still a startup, and I loved it like a helicopter mom. But I couldn't ruin Charlene's fun. "Then I need to get back to the prep work."

My elderly piecrust specialist, Charlene McCree, pulled the ends of her snowy hair from her jacket collar. "You work twelve-hour days, Val. No one's going to hold it against you if you take a peek. You won't get much chance when the festival's in full swing. Relax."

In a blur of purple knit jacket, she surged past me and onto the brick sidewalk. We'd both been up until midnight watching a *Stargate* marathon, and it was now five a.m. Charlene claimed old people didn't need much sleep. I felt like deep-fried death.

"Last year," she said, "the winning pumpkin was over two-thousand pounds. This year's would have been bigger if those arms dealers hadn't chiseled in on the action."

Hiding a smile, I let Pie Town's glass door swing shut behind us. Charlene might be the best piecrust maker on the NorCal coast, but I'd learned the hard way not to encourage her. "You know San Adrian isn't infested with gun runners."

But Saint Adrian was the patron saint of weapons dealers. The town's true crime, however, was starting a pumpkin festival to rival San Nicholas's. Farmers now had to choose between San Adrian and us. Our tiny beach town was feeling the pinch.

"You don't understand pumpkin festivals," she said darkly.

I yawned again and flipped up my hood, orange and black for Halloween.

Ray, a gamer who usually staked out one of Pie Town's corner tables, waved from beneath a festival booth's green awning. "Hey, Val! Hi, Charlene."

We ambled to his booth, one of dozens lining the middle of the street.

"Nice socks," he said.

Charlene pointed the toe of one of her high-tops, modeling the striped purple and black socks. They nipped at the hems of her matching purple leggings. "Thanks. I got 'em on sale."

I eyed the comic art hanging against the green canvas walls. "You drew these?" I asked, impressed.

Ray's round face flushed. His freckles darkened. "Well—"

His girlfriend, Henrietta, popped up from behind a stack of boxes. "They're all his. Isn't he amazing?" She tugged down her shapeless army-green sweatshirt. It matched the color of the knit cap flattening her sandy hair. "I told him he should work as an artist for a gaming company, but he's set on being an engineer."

Charlene squinted at a cartoon woman in a chain-mail bikini. "Looks uncomfortable. If I was going into battle, I'd want a lot more covered than those two—"

"It all looks great," I interrupted. Age had dulled Charlene's verbal restraint. If my friend had ever had any.

"And don't worry," Ray said. "I'll be sure to send customers into Pie Town."

Charlene laughed hollowly. "I don't think that will be a problem. This is my fiftieth pumpkin festival. They're wolves, I tell you. Wolves!"

Henrietta's eyes twinkled. "Werewolves?"

"Don't encourage her." I groaned, knowing it was too late. Charlene was convinced a local pastor was a werewolf. She also believed Bigfoot roamed the woods, ghost jaguars stalked the streets, and UFOs buzzed the California coast.

"I was speaking metaphorically," Charlene said, surprising me. "I meant the festivalgoers act like wolves. Though if I were you, I'd keep an eye on Pastor Hiller around the full moon. Not that he can help himself, poor man. Once you've been bitten, it's all over."

And there it was. "It was great seeing you two," I said. "We're going to check out those giant pumpkins, and then I'm going back to work." We'd left my staff slaving in the kitchen while Charlene and I scoped out the massive gourds. I wasn't sure how much pie we'd sell today, during the pre-festival, but I didn't want to take any risks.

"Speak for yourself," Charlene said. "I've already completed my piecrust quota. See ya, Ray. Bye, Henrietta."

We ambled two booths down, and I stopped in front of another green awning. A sign hanging from the top read, HEIDI's HEALTH AND FITNESS. Directly beneath it: SUGAR KILLS.

I sighed. "Seriously? At a pumpkin festival?" The gym had moved in next to Pie Town earlier this year. Its owner and I had a loathe-hate relationship.

Heidi turned to me, and her blond brows drew downward. "Sugar kills every day of the year."

"So does life," Charlene said.

Heidi tossed her ponytail. "Your life might be longer and more fulfilling if it included a better diet and exercise."

"I'm fit as a fiddle." Charlene thumped her chest and coughed alarmingly. "I eat what I want, and I stop when I'm full. And I have a drink every night for my heart. It's the French way."

Heidi's lip curled. "We're offering blood pressure and other fitness testing. You should stop by." She eyed me critically. "Especially you."

My eyes narrowed. I was *not* overweight.

She smoothed the front of her sleek and sporty Heidi's Health and Fitness microfiber jacket. "You're going to have some competition at the pie-making contest."

"I'm not competing, I'm a judge." Not that judging didn't have its own pressures. My boyfriend, Gordon Carmichael, had entered the pie contest. He was a good cook, and it was a blind tasting, but still. And then there was old Mrs. Thistle-blossom. She won every year, and I was super curious about her pumpkin pie. What was her secret? I'd never met the woman, but I'd heard she was over a hundred.

"I don't think it's fair for a professional baker to be in the contest," Heidi said.

I pulled my mouth into a tight smile. "Which is why I'm not in it. I'm a judge."

"Well, *I* am entering a sugar-free pumpkin pie," Heidi said. "It's low-fat and low-calorie."

What was the point? But I decided to be the better woman and refrained from comment.

Charlene had no such compunction. "And low-taste?" She squinted at my hips. "Though some of us *could* stand to lose a little weight."

"There's nothing wrong with my weight," I said. "And don't tell me anything more, Heidi. This is a blind tasting."

"Most of the calories are in the crust anyway," Heidi said, "so it will be crust-free."

"What!" Charlene flared. "Then it will definitely be taste-free."

"But now," I ground out, "I can't judge your pie, because it won't be a blind tasting." And I was going to have to report this to the head judge. San Nicholas took its pie contest deadly serious.

"Your style of pies are on their way out," Heidi said. "Tastes are changing. Most Californians find all that sweet food gross."

"Enjoy the festival," I caroled and walked on, hoping Charlene would follow. My pies on the way out. *As if!* Had she even met a Silicon Valley engineer?

In the stall beside Heidi's, a handsome, harried-looking man unpacked boxes of reading glasses. White earbud cords dangled from his ears and faded to invisibility against his white lab coat.

Charlene nodded to the man in the optometry stall. "Morning, Tristan."

He looked up and tugged an earbud from his skull. "Oh. Hi!"

"What are you listening to?" Charlene asked.

He blushed. "*Oklahoma!*" he said in a sultry Southern drawl. I might be a one-man gal, but I could listen to him talk all day.

Charlene chuckled benignly. "You and your show tunes."

"Have you seen Kara—I mean, Dr. Levant?" he asked.

We shook our heads.

"Why?" Charlene asked.

"She was going to help me set up for the pre-festival." He motioned around the half-built stall. "I guess she got hung up at the haunted house."

"What's she doing there?" Charlene asked.

"Her husband, Elon, is volunteering there today."

"If we see her," I said, "we'll let her know you're looking for her."

Charlene and I continued on.

"I hear Heidi broke up with that fellow who left you at the altar," she said in a casual tone.

"Mark didn't leave me—Wait, really?" I *had* been dumped, though not at the altar. We'd been months away from the wedding. But Mark had done me a favor. Now I had a new and improved boyfriend, Detective Gordon Carmichael of the SNPD. My chest tingled at the thought.

I glanced over my shoulder. The booths and Pie Town had vanished into the mist, and I shivered. "We need to hurry," I said. "I really should get back soon."

"Those pies will bake without you. Your first pumpkin festival is a special event. There's something magical about a giant pumpkin. Maybe it's because they're not supposed to be that big. But when you see them, anything seems possible. You can believe a pumpkin might actually turn into a coach."

I grimaced. "Or the Pie Town staff might riot."

"Never."

Charlene was right. The people who worked at Pie Town

were easygoing and professional. That was exactly why I didn't want to take advantage.

"I don't know what you're worried about," she continued. "With the street closed off to cars for the decorating today, business is going to be slow."

I jammed my hands into the pockets of my hoodie. "I hope not." The festival didn't officially begin until tomorrow. But for years, Friday had been its unofficial start. It gave stores and vendors an early jump on sales while the street was closed to traffic.

The stalls petered out. We strolled down the deserted road, our footsteps echoing. The dark shapes of low, nineteenth-century brick buildings wavered in the fog.

I squinted into the dense mist. "How far is it?" The fog this morning was deliciously thick and spooky, like something out of a Sam Spade novel.

"Why? Are you tired? Maybe Heidi was right about you needing more exercise."

I groaned. "Not you too."

"Hold on." Charlene vanished into the mist.

I waited, inhaling the crisp, October air. It smelled faintly of salt, and I smiled. Though I'd come to San Nicholas for all the wrong reasons, I couldn't imagine living anywhere else.

Charlene returned with a newspaper and inhaled gustily. "The ink is still warm." She rustled the paper. "The festival's on the front page. Pie Town might get a mention."

We walked on. Strands of damp hay lay scattered on the pavement.

"We must be getting close," I said.

Blob-like shapes rose before us. A gust of wind parted the fog, strands spiraling like phantoms across the street. Farm trucks with monster pumpkins in their beds blocked our way.

"Whoa," I said, stunned.

Pale and misshapen, the pumpkins lay on their flattest sides. They were big enough for me to crawl inside.

These could make a lot of pumpkin pies, if they were sweet enough. "What varieties are those?"

Charlene made a face. "They're cultivated from mammoth pumpkins. I don't think you'd want to eat them."

I nodded. My personal favorite for pumpkin pies were Jarrahdales, but blue Hubbards were good too, and Cinderellas . . . The latter not only tasted delicious, but they looked like something out of a fairy tale.

I studied the forklift that would be used for the weighing.

"Uh-oh." Charlene pointed at a monster pumpkin lying on the road in front of the forklift. A crack shaped like a lightning bolt shot down its side. Orange pumpkin guts oozed from the ruined shell. "They say it's not a party unless something gets broken, but someone's just lost the contest."

I frowned, edging closer. "Do you think the owner knows? How did it fall onto the ground?" These monsters couldn't exactly roll.

Charlene hissed, fists clenching. "Sabotage. It must have been one those rats from San Adrian. Or maybe another pumpkin farmer. I told you people turn into wolves. You think this pumpkin festival is all fun and games. But it's serious business. And—"

I gasped, stopping short, and grasped the sleeve of her soft jacket. "Charlene." Hand shaking, I pointed to the broken pumpkin.

Two white tennis shoes stuck from beneath the monstrous gourd.